FALSE TARGET

AN ADAM DRAKE NOVEL

SCOTT MATTHEWS

For my wife, Diana, and the family she's blessed me with.

"All warfare is based on deception."

SUN TZU

ONE

The white and blue Gulfstream G280 touched down on runway 09/27 at the San Diego International Airport at 11:15 AM Wednesday morning. Under a light blue sky, it taxied to the Signature Flight Support terminal.

When the G280 rolled to a stop and the stairs were lowered, Adam Drake walked across the tarmac to the terminal's passenger lounge. A National Car Rental employee was waiting outside with the keys to a Chrysler 300 for the short drive to the Sheraton San Diego Hotel and Marina. Drake was meeting with two men who were going to take the fight to the Mexican cartels and reclaim their country from the terror and violence it was suffering.

Pete Ramirez and Danny Vasquez had flown in the night before from Cabo San Lucas and registered to attend the Pacific Coast Sportfishing Tackle, Boat, Travel, and Outdoors Show in Costa Mesa. Their real purpose in traveling to San Diego was to meet Drake and find out what level of support the United States was prepared to give them.

Drake gave the car keys to the parking valet and entered the Sheraton's Marina Tower lobby wearing a gray suit and black tie and carrying a silver aluminum briefcase in his left hand. Passing under the exposed curved wooden beam ceiling, he walked directly to the bank of elevators and stood alone, waiting for the next available elevator to take him to the eighth floor.

Pete Ramirez opened the door and greeted him with a grin and a raised bottle of Modelo Negra beer. "Hola, amigo. How was your flight?"

"A little bumpy over northern California, Rammer, but otherwise fine," Drake said. Ramirez had been a breacher with the nickname "Rammer" when they served together in Delta Force.

Danny Vasquez came in from the balcony to greet Drake. "Hello, Major."

"Hi, Danny. How's your sister?"

Juanita Vasquez had been kidnapped by the head of a Chinese triad last year and rescued by Drake and Ramirez from his luxury superyacht sailing to San Diego.

"She's finishing high school and planning on enlisting in the army to become a U.S. citizen," her brother said.

"Tell Juanita hello for me," Drake said and walked across the room toward the blue sofa near the window. "We have a lot to talk about, so let's get started. I want to be back in the air after a lunch ordered from room service. Our meeting needs to be as "off the books" as we can make it."

He sat on the sofa, opened the briefcase and laid a file folder on the top of a glass coffee table in front of him. Ramirez and Vasquez joined him and sat in the blue chairs on each end of the table.

He handed them a business card. "This is the president and owner of a small private bank nearby. He's a friend. You have an appointment with him this afternoon at two o'clock, where you'll finalize a ten-million-dollar line of credit for Blue Pacific Fishing and Diving, LLC, the new business we asked you to set up.

"The documents he has will have the details of your LLC's plan to expand your sportfishing fleet, Pete, including the money for three new Hatteras GT59 convertible yachts. It also includes the money you'll need, Danny, to open three new dive shops in Cabo San Lucas, Mazatlán, and Puerta Vallarta. How long it takes you to acquire the GT59s and open the dive shops is up to you."

Drake handed each of them a second business card. "This is the name of an arms dealer who will get the arms and materiel safely across the border for you when you're ready to do business with him. We'll monitor the transaction, so you can trust him to deliver. My involvement or the governments can never be mentioned to him, or to anyone else, for that matter.

"You'll operate on your own, with the intel we'll get for you with the cartel targets that will hurt them the most.

"Use Signal Private Messenger to contact me," Drake said. "I'll be your only contact, for the foreseeable future. I will also be available to meet with you if it becomes necessary.

"This credit line will be paid down, according to the arrangement with the bank, but you won't be responsible for making the payments. We'll maintain the credit line at ten million dollars, for as long as you need it, to get the job done, and our role as your silent partner remains a secret. If that becomes a problem, we'll find another way to work together.

"Any questions?" Drake asked.

"How soon after we meet with the banker will the credit line be available?" Ramirez asked.

"As soon as the papers are signed," Drake answered. "Why?"

"You asked us to register and attend the Pacific Coast Sportfishing Show as a cover for our trip to San Diego. If there are things at the show we need, ordering them now would confirm the legitimacy of our new business."

"I agree," Drake said. "Use your best judgment. I'll get you a breakdown for the arms and materiel you plan on buying, so you can decide how much of the initial ten million you want to use now."

Vasquez raised his hand. "How much can we tell our men?"

"I know you trust your guys, but I'd like you to tell them you came up with a plan on your own to borrow the money to expand your business and use some of it for fighting the cartels, or something along those lines." Drake said. "They might guess there's more to it than that, but they can't be made to expose what we're doing if they don't know the details."

Ramirez looked down at his hands folded in his lap for a long moment before asking, "I know you said you'd try to find a way to help us when you were in Cabo last year, but you can't be doing this all on your own. How many others know about this?"

Drake smiled. "Officially, no one. Unofficially, Mike Casey, my wife, myself and one other."

"Is he the one who helped you get the U.S. Coast Guard to help rescue Danny's sister?" Ramirez asked.

Drake smiled again and picked up the file from the coffee table to put it back in his briefcase. As he spun the two combination locks on the briefcase, he asked, "You guys ready to order room service?"

TWO

The Gulfstream G280 was still climbing to a cruising altitude of 41,000 feet when Drake took out his iPhone and use the Wi-Fi Calling mode to call his wife in Seattle.

"Hi, Liz. I'm headed home. How are you feeling?"

"Tired. Fat. Hungry," she said. "Same as I felt this morning when you left."

"Want me to bring something home for dinner?"

"You're reading my mind again," Liz laughed. "Since you asked, I've been dreaming about Angelo's Fettuccini Alfredo with Chicken. Would you mind stopping to pick it up? I can order it online."

"Angelo's it is," Drake said. "I'll call you when I land. What did the doctor say today?"

"Keep doing what I'm doing. The baby's fine. I'm fine. He also said to make sure my husband is taking good care of me."

"He said that did he? What would your husband need to do to make sure he's taking good care of you?"

"Hmm, I'm sure there's something," Liz said. "I'll show you when you get home."

"I need to know, so I can hold you to it."

Liz chuckled. "I'm counting on it."

"Good-bye, Mrs. Drake."

He sat back and looked out the windows at the blanket of white clouds below. Liz was nearing the end of her second trimester of pregnancy and seemed to be enjoying every minute of it. Her cheeks were perpetually pink, and she had a glow that made him smile. He loved her before she became pregnant and couldn't imagine loving her any more, but he did.

While his phone was still in hand, he called his best friend, Mike Casey, the CEO of Puget Sound Security, and his partner.

"How did the meeting go?" Casey asked when he answered.

"I left them making a list of things they planned on getting at the sportfishing show, smiling like kids at Christmas. I think they're a little blown away with the line of credit."

"They should be. Did they give you any idea who they plan on going after first?"

"Rammer said the Chinese cartel, Los Zheng, has regrouped after we hit them last year and fighting the other cartels for control of Baja California," Drake said. "They'll start there."

"This all should have happened a long time ago."

"I'm glad he's willing to do it now."

"Are you coming back to headquarters after you land?" Casey asked.

"I wasn't planning to. We'll touch down around 4:30 PM. I promised Liz I'd pick up an order of fettuccine at Angelo's for her. Do you need me to stop by?"

"Chaplain Walker called. He wanted to know if he could meet with us tonight."

"Is he in town?"

"He will be tonight. He's driving in from Colorado Springs."

"I can't tonight," Drake said. "What about breakfast or lunch? Where's he staying?"

"He wasn't sure. He's having a few upgrades installed on his new Airstream travel trailer at the dealer in Milton. He'll either stay in

Tacoma or drive on to Seattle tonight, if he finishes with the dealer early enough.'

"You had dinner with him when he was here the last time. Did he tell you why he's back in the Northwest?"

"He didn't say. I'll call him and see if he wants to meet us tomorrow and let you know."

"Thanks, Mike."

Colonel Thomas Walker, Army Chaplain, retired, was a legend in the Special Forces community. Drake knew his story from having heard it one Sunday morning sitting outside the chaplain's tent, with several other soldiers. Walker was a legend not only because he was a great counselor, a wise advisor, and a soldier's best friend, but because he went with his men on all their missions.

Walker's grandfather was a B-26 Marauder pilot in WWII, flying the bomber in the Pacific Theater against the Japanese. His father was a retired Air Force two-star Major General and pilot, who flew F-4 Phantoms in the Vietnam War. Walker's two brothers were both Colonels in the Air Force, one was a JAG officer and the other was a pilot with the NATO Allied Air Command in Germany.

Growing up in Colorado Springs, Colorado, home of the Air Force Academy and a large military community, Tom Walker was the youngest of the three brothers and wanted nothing to do with his family's chosen profession.

He did everything in his power to make sure that option wasn't available to him, partying his way through high school and arriving at the University of Colorado in Boulder, Colorado, to continue his rebellious ways. He wanted to be a lawyer and prepare to take the bar exam and have a minor degree in philosophy to sharpen his analytical reasoning ability.

It was in one of his philosophy classes where he was challenged to examine his religious beliefs and consider how they influenced his worldview. Then a sophomore, he set out to prove the historical Jesus was not the Son of God, the basis of the Christian faith.

Chaplain Walker told the soldiers he became a Christian when he failed to prove his thesis. He transferred to a theological seminary, earned a Master of Divinity degree, and joined the army's Chaplain Candidate Program, realizing he wanted to serve his country as his grandfather, father, and brothers were doing.

If Chaplain Walker wanted to meet with them and needed something, Drake would listen and help him in any way that he could.

THREE

A white van waited with its engine idling early in the evening in the parking lot of the Stadium High School in Tacoma, Washington. The van was dwarfed by the size of the main school building it was parked next to that resembled a French chateau. Built in 1891 for the North Pacific Railroad and the Tacoma Land Company to serve as a luxury hotel. After a fire in 1898, it had been repurposed as a high school in 1904 by the Tacoma School District and had been called at one time "the best high school in the west."

Inside the van were four members of a street gang called the Hilltop Gangsters. They were watching an old Volkswagen Jetta belonging to a high school senior named Madison Sanchez. They were waiting for her to walk to the car after her basketball practice.

"There she is," Antonio "Adonis" Michaels, the leader of the Hilltop Gangsters said.

Madison Sanchez was wearing a Mariners jacket, a black Monster Energy hat, jeans and white Converse shoes.

"That's one sweet-looking lady," said Dreads, riding shotgun beside Adonis.

"Remember what Viper said, no one touches her," Adonis said.

"Her buyer's a man even Viper's afraid of. Razor, Bats, get her in fast when I stop beside her."

The van started rolling toward their target and stopped when she was at the trunk of the Jetta. The sliding door of the van flew open, and two gang members jumped out wearing black balaclavas, and dragged her inside.

They forced her down on the floor and drove away before the sliding door of the van was pulled all the way shut.

One gangster held her kicking feet down while another pulled her thrashing arms behind her back and zipped-tied her wrists.

"Girl," Adonis said over his shoulder, "No use fighting, you're ours now."

"Where are you taking me? Why are you doing this?" she yelled.

The gangster called Razor kneeled by her head slipped off his black hoodie and lifted her head to slip it underneath her face. "Don't want no scratches or marks on that pretty face of yours."

"Ricky is that you?" she hissed. "I recognize that awful cologne."

"He wears that cuz he's looking to get lucky," the gangster holding her feet down said, laughing. "Maybe he will tonight."

"Shut up, Bats," Adonis said. "Now she knows his name."

"Don't matter," Bats said, "She ain't telling nobody."

"No more talking," Adonis said. "Not another word until we deliver her."

"Deliver me where?" Madison Sanchez asked.

None of the Hilltop Gangsters spoke again until the van drove into an old warehouse near the Port of Tacoma and the building's sliding double doors were pulled shut by the men waiting there.

"Keep her quiet until I get back," Adonis said, getting out of the van and walking across the warehouse to men standing at the doors.

"Did anyone follow you?" a short Chinese man wearing cowboy boots and a camo hat asked.

Ruben Fang, the leader of Los Zheng drug cartel, was known as the "Viper". His cartel was fighting the Jalisco New Generation Cartel (CJNG) for control of the Northwest drug market. CJNG had a reputation as being the most dangerous and violent cartel in the world, a reputation Viper was determined his cartel would soon deserve.

In addition to supplying illegal drugs to the North American market, Los Zheng was also a major player in human trafficking and the sex industry.

"No," Adonis said. "There was no one around. I had two of my men on motorcycles follow us to make sure."

"Good," Viper said. "Your extra product is over by the wall for taking care of this for me. When it's dark, we'll put her in the shipping container outside we use to move girls to their buyers. Does she look okay?"

"Not a scratch on her, just like you ordered."

"She'd better be, for your sake," Viper said, "Her buyer is a powerful and very dangerous man."

"Why this girl?" There are younger girls around who will bring a better price."

"She's a loose end. She can't stay around here."

"How is she a loose end?" Adonis asked. "I don't understand."

"If you want to keep your head on your shoulders, you won't try to understand. Leave her in the van. Come back later for your product."

Fang watched the gang members leave. The Hilltop Gangsters had performed well, moving his product in North Tacoma, and doing little things when he asked them to. Snatching the girl was the first time he involved them in anything other than distribution, but their involvement in the death of the girl's boyfriend required using them to snatch the girl.

When the boyfriend's father started asking around for information about the dealer who supplied the Adderall that killed his son, Fang knew it was only a matter of time before he'd be forced to make sure Adonis and the Hilltop Gangsters weren't around to lead law enforcement back to him as well for the boyfriend's death.

FOUR

When Drake returned from his run the next morning with his German Shepherd, Lancer, his wife was on an exercise mat in the bedroom of their condo, doing her Pilates prenatal exercise routine.

"How was your run?" she asked as she continued doing side leg lifts.

"Wet but not too cold," he said and tossed his wet trail cap at her, frisbee style.

"Just for that, I'm showering first. Unless you want to join me?"

"Now that's an offer I can't refuse," he said and started to take off his running jacket when his phone chirped in his concealed carry fanny pack.

"Morning, Mike."

"Colonel Walker would like to take us to lunch. I have a meeting at eleven thirty. Is one o'clock okay for you?"

"Fine for me."

"Would Liz like to join us? He said he'd like to meet her."

"I'll let you know what she says when we get to headquarters."

Drake slipped out of his running gear, secured the Glock 19 from his fanny pack in the Liberty Centurion gun safe on his side of their walk-in closet, and joined Liz in their double shower.

An hour later, dressed for a day at the office, Drake drove to the PSS headquarters south of Kirkland, Washington, with Liz in his company car, a gunmetal gray 718 Porsche Cayman GTS 4.0.

"Have you decided about lunch?" he asked.

"Better take a rain check until I know how much work is stacked up on my desk."

"Want me to bring something back for you, if you don't go?"

"Depends on where you go."

"Fair enough."

Drake stopped at the security gate at the PSS headquarters compound and punched in the security code for the day. Someday soon, they were going to have to find another place to headquarter the company. The underground parking was full and half of the open area inside the walled compound was now crowded with employee vehicles.

He drove down the ramp and pulled into reserved spot marked simply "2". Casey's new champagne Suburban was parked in "1" to the left, and on the other side space "3" was empty. It was where Liz parked her white Cadillac CT5-V Blackwing when she drove it to work.

Casey promised her that she would have her own company car if she came to work at PSS, if she left the Department of Homeland Security where she worked as the Director's executive assistant.

When they returned from their honeymoon in Australia last year, she persuaded them to replace her older CTS with the newer CT5-V Blackwing, arguing that Cadillac was going all-electric any day now and she needed the Blackwing before they stopped making them. Despite Cadillac's goal of not going all-electric until 2030, Casey had given in to keep her happy. As the company's vice president for governmental relations, she'd proven herself to be invaluable in securing business around the Pacific Rim for them.

Drake followed her up the stairs to the third floor and opened her office door, which was next to his own, and continued on down the hall to Casey's office. "I'll find out where we're meeting Colonel Walker. Do you have a preference if you decide to go?"

"No, everything sounds good right now."

Casey's office was the corner office at the end of the hall and his door was open. Drake knocked on the door anyway.

"Did Colonel Walker say where he wants to go for lunch?"

"The Santa Fe Mexican Grill and Cantina downtown," Casey said. "He loves Tex Mex and his friend recommended it."

"I'll let Liz know. She hasn't decided if she'll join us yet."

"How is she doing?"

"She loves being pregnant. She's exercising, walking with Lancer, and can't wait to be a mother."

"You're lucky. Megan had a rough go of it with both of our kids."

"Anything hot I need to look at before lunch?"

Casey picked up a file and handed it to him. "Here's a new contract proposal for us to provide cyber security for that satellite surveillance company in Canada we used when you were looking for Xueping's island. Review it. They want a response as soon as possible."

"On it," Drake said.

Drake took the file and walked down the hall, stopping at Liz's door. "Lunch is one o'clock at the Santa Fe Mexican Grill and Cantina. Joining us?"

"Yes, because I'm hungry. Thanks."

He spent the rest of the morning reviewing the new contract proposal and working through correspondence on his desk. By 12:30 PM, he was ready for lunch and seeing their former chaplain, Colonel Walker, again.

Drake was the first one at the restaurant to notice Colonel Walker when he entered the cantina, wearing a black leather bomber jacket, jeans and a pair of tan mid-high tactical assault boots. Standing six feet four inches tall and weighing a little over two hundred pounds, Walker's long legs carried him quickly across the room to their tall bar table.

"Colonel, this is my wife, Liz," Drake said when he stood and shook hands with him.

"Mrs. Drake, it's a pleasure to meet you," he said and shook her hand.

"Likewise, Colonel. Adam tells me you just retired from the army."

"I did. It was time," he said, pulling back a tall stool to sit with them. "Hello, Mike."

"Colonel," Casey said, shaking his hand. "Get your Airstream squared away?"

"Not yet. They're installing solar panels and a better security system," he said and picked up a menu. "Lunch is on me. What's good here?"

"The carne asada fajitas," Casey said. "Megan had the Sante Fe salad with grilled chicken when we were here. Both meals were excellent."

"We haven't eaten here, colonel," Drake said. "Sorry."

"Well, let's start with guacamole and chips, if that's okay with everyone, while we make up our minds," Colonel Walker said and waved to a server.

"Colonel Walker, Adam said you have family in Colorado Springs. Is that where you were before driving here?" Liz asked.

"It was. My father and mother live there."

"Your father is a retired general in the Air Force," Casey said. "How did you wind up in the Army?"

"That's a story for another day, Mike. Right now, I'm here to find out if you can help me with something."

FIVE

Colonel Walker waited until the guacamole and chips arrived and the server had taken their orders before he explained why he was in Seattle.

"I was here earlier this year," he began, "One of my soldiers, Nathan Arnold, was dealing with the death of his son, Chris, who overdosed on fentanyl. Nathan was looking for the dealer and wanted to kill him if he could find him. He knew he needed help controlling his anger and rage and called me.

"I've told the men in my units that if they ever want to talk about something to call me, that I'd do anything I could to help them. Nathan got past his rage after his son's funeral and returned to Fort Bragg when his bereavement leave was up. He didn't find the dealer but hasn't given up hope that someone would, and the person will do time for killing his son.

"Then Nathan got a text from the father of his son's girlfriend the other day. She was kidnapped in her high school's parking lot. Tacoma police found the stolen van the next day, but it had been torched. They didn't find anything to identify the kidnappers.

"When Nathan was here for the funeral, he met the girlfriend's father," Walker continued, "He was hoping the father might have some idea where Chris got the Adderall that killed him. At that time, the father didn't have any idea. Since then, however, he's learned his daughter was using Adderall with Chris to help them study for exams. Both were on the school's basketball teams.

"The girlfriend's father called Nathan the other day. His daughter had been kidnapped and he asked if he had any information that would help him find his daughter.

"Nathan thinks the kidnapping is related to his son's death somehow and asked me to investigate the possibility. I don't know anyone in law enforcement around here. I thought you guys might point me in the right direction," Walker finished, seeing their server bringing their orders to the table.

Drake waited until the server left before asking, "Colonel, I don't know anyone in Tacoma law enforcement. Maybe Mike does. But we do have a private investigator on retainer who does our sleuthing for us. We could put you in touch with him. He lives in Portland, Oregon, and was as former detective in the Multnomah Sheriff's office. Paul Benning is his name and I'm sure he knows someone in Tacoma."

Liz nodded and added, "I used to be with the FBI, and we know the Deputy Director of the FBI, Kate Perkins. If the FBI is working with Tacoma law enforcement on the kidnapping, she might know something. I'll be happy to call her and find out."

"Thanks, Liz. I would like to talk with Paul Benning, Adam, if you'll arrange it," Walker said.

Casey set his tortilla down on his plate and asked, "Colonel, why does Arnold think the kidnapping and his son's death are related?"

"I asked Nathan that," Walker said. "When he was here, the Tacoma PD told him the dealer could do serious time for supplying the fentanyl that caused his son's death. The girlfriend can identify the dealer and Nathan thinks they may have taken the girlfriend to eliminate her as a potential witness."

'Why wouldn't the kidnappers just kill her, if that's what they were afraid of?" Casey asked.

"Maybe because they can sell her as a sex slave," Liz offered. "Seattle and Tacoma are two of the leading cities in the country for sex trafficking and the cartels are in the business."

"If that's the case, she could be anywhere by now," Drake said.

"Let's start with what we know, as little as it is, and I'll work from there," Colonel Walker said.

Walker's three guests silently thought of ways they could help Colonel Walker while they finished eating and listened to the country music coming from speakers around the cantina.

Casey finished eating first and ask the colonel where he was staying until he got his travel trailer back.

"I haven't looked for a place yet," Walker said. "Any suggestions?"

"Just one," Casey said with a smile. "We have a suite at the Woodmark Hotel and Spa on Lake Washington. We keep it for out-of-town clients. You're welcome to stay there."

"Thanks, I might take you up on that," Walker said.

"Is Colorado Springs your home, when you're not traveling?" Liz asked.

"Not really," Walker said. "My mom and dad live there, and I grew up there, but now I'm traveling around to check in with my soldiers who call me for help. Special Operations forces have a higher suicide rate than the other armed forces."

"So, you're not really retired," Liz said.

Walker smiled. "I resigned my commission, Liz, but I haven't stopped being a chaplain."

SIX

Jefferson Jackson, owner of the Northwest Security and Protection Services company in Tacoma, Washington, pulled his custom 2009 Black Hummer H2 around to the back of T-City, a custom t-shirt shop, and parked with the Hummer's engine idling.

He was waiting for Ruben Fang, known as "Viper", to join him. Fang was the local leader of Los Zheng, the Chinese drug cartel.

When the back door of the shop opened, Jackson watched Fang walk with his customary swagger to the Hummer in the amber light from the parking lot's flood lights. Fang was wearing his a digital pattern camo hat with a neon green snake's head on the front, black t-shirt and jeans, and python skin cowboy boots. Jackson knew the camo hat was meant to remind people that his nickname "Viper" signified that he was as deadly as the deadliest snake in the world, the saw-scaled viper he kept as a pet.

Fang opened the door of the Hummer and stepped up on the running board to get in and handed Jackson a 3x5 photo.

"I need you to find this man," Fang said.

"Who is he?"

"A new arrival from Culiacán. He's the Sinaloa cartel's replacement for the man I killed last month."

"I thought you got rid of the Sinaloa cell in Tacoma."

"We did, but they won't give up that easily."

"Where do I start looking?"

"He was seen in Puyallup, ten miles from here. They probably think I won't find out he's here," Salazar said.

"I'll let you know when I find him. What do you want me to do about him?"

"Nothing, I'll take care of it. We'll post a video so they know he's missing and what happened to him."

"Have it your way."

"I always do. You know that."

Fang took a slip of paper out of the pocket of his jeans and handed it to

Jackson. "This was deposited in your offshore account today."

Jackson looked at the five-figure number and smiled. "I see last month was good for you."

Fang nodded and opened the door of the Hummer. "Our clientele is growing. Let's make sure it continues."

Jackson watched him walk to the back door of the shop and go in before he put the Hummer in gear and backed up. He never turned his back on the man, even when he was driving away.

The offshore account in Belize didn't belong to him, although Fang would never know that. The account was opened in his name, but the money belonged to the secret militia society he belonged to, known as the 412s. The number represented the date the Confederate soldiers opened fire on Fort Sumpter and started the civil war; April 12, 1861.

The 412 wasn't like the other armed militias in the country. Its members all had military experience with training from the best army in the world and didn't need to train in secret locations to stay under the radar of the FBI and law enforcement.

Members of a 412 local militia only knew each other by the

number they were given, after a full and careful vetting before they were invited to join.

Each member maintained a personal armory of weapons and practiced with them on their own time at locations of their choice, but never together.

When a 412 member was contacted, it was by an encrypted text message on a number only the local militia leader knew.

When funds were needed for an operation, they were distributed from the offshore account by Jackson, who managed the account.

There wasn't a 412 manifesto or a stated mission, other than each member's pledge to defend the U.S. Constitution.

As far as Jackson was concerned, the time was now. But he was only one of the twelve members of the 412's governing Council, and the Council would decide when the country they loved had to be protected and its values preserved.

On the drive across town to his office that night, Jackson decided the man he would send to Puyallup was 2275, a former Marine gunnery sergeant and detective in the Tacoma Police Department. 2275 had access to the TPD's database and the OECP International Cartel Database. If Fang's man wasn't in either of the two databases, he would know how to identify the local participants in the CJNG cartel and start his reconnaissance from there.

Jackson stopped in front of a ten-foot-tall security fence gate, punched in the numbers on the keypad, and waited for the gate to open. The security fence with concertina barb wire on top surrounded the Northwest Security and Protection Services compound in southern Tacoma. The fence was probably overkill, but Jackson liked the image it projected of the company.

He parked in his reserved space near the front door and took out his Nokia XR2, a rugged military grade smartphone, from the center console to contact member 2275.

Locate the individual in the photo, believed to be a new Sinaloa arrival. Start in Puyallup area. Expand search as necessary. No action required.

Contact me asap. 12

His night crew of ten men were at their desks, monitoring security cameras and responding to client concerns when an alarm was tripped, or a security camera malfunctioned. They were all former military but not all of them were members of the 412.

In fact, of the ten men, only three of them were 412 members. The man who had been his sidekick in the Rangers, Jody Russel, was his righthand man and helped him manage the office.

Russell was a big Black man who'd never thought of himself a victim of racism and couldn't tolerate whiners blaming racism for their miserable lives. Russell grew up poor in South Los Angeles, knew the streets and the gangs who terrorized them. The army had been his way out.

"I thought you were going home," Russell got up from his desk when Jackson came in and stretched.

"After dark is when things happen," Jackson said. "Anything going on?"

"Nothing involving our clients. Police are dealing with a couple of drive-by shootings and there's a jumper on the Narrows Bridge."

"Join me in my office. We need to talk."

Jackson led the way and motioned for Russell to close the door of his office. He took out a bottle of tequila and two shot glasses out from the bottom desk drawer of his desk and filled both glasses.

"Viper wants us to find the new replacement for the Sinaloa guy they beheaded last month," Jackson said, emptying his glass. "Helping him with rival street gangs is one thing. Going after someone in the Sinaloa cartel is another. I don't like it."

"Neither do I. There's got to be a way to draw a line on what we're willing to do for him."

"If there is, I'm not seeing it."

SEVEN

The sun was trying to break through the gray clouds between storms Friday morning as Drake was driving south from Seattle on I-5 to meet Paul Benning in Tacoma, Washington.

Benning had finished vetting a new hire for a PSS client and offered to meet Drake in Tacoma to deliver his file on the woman in person. After they met for coffee, Benning had also arranged for them to meet a friend in the Pierce County Sheriff Department to ask about any information the department had about Chris Auburn's kidnapped girlfriend.

Paul Benning was Drake's friend and the husband of his former legal assistant, office manager and mother hen, Margo Benning. Benning had been the senior detective in the Multnomah County Sheriff's Department in Portland, before retiring and going to work for PSS to handle investigations and special projects.

Drake let the female voice from the GPS navigation system in his Porsche Cayman direct him off the I-5 freeway to a coffee and pastry café on Tacoma Avenue South near the Pierce County Sheriff Department's offices.

Benning's red Ford F-150 pickup was parked out front, and Drake saw his friend waving to him from a seat inside by a window.

When he entered the café, there was a plate of assorted donuts setting on the table in front of his friend.

"Does Margo let you eat these now?" Drake asked and sat down across the table.

Benning grinned, with a touch of chocolate on his upper lip, and shook his head. "Pastries and donuts are definitely not on my diet in Portland, but this is Tacoma."

Drake reached across and shook hands with Benning. "You look good."

"I feel good. She has me on a very restricted diet again, in Portland."

"How is Margo?"

"Presently she's redecorating your old office for the third time since we leased it from you," Benning said. "You need to come down and see it."

"It's already on the calendar. I heard Liz talking with Margo the other day."

"How is Liz doing?"

"She's healthy, happy, and still working. She seems to have more energy than she did before she became pregnant."

"Go get a cup of coffee to go along with one of these pastries," Benning said. "When you come back, you can tell me about your chaplain, and this kidnapped girl."

Drake got up and ordered a cup of house coffee, black with no cream or sugar, and returned.

"Mike and I knew Colonel Walker when he was our chaplain in Afghanistan. He's one of the few chaplains who wore a green beret, after getting through the Q course and selection. He went out on all our missions with us. You'll like him.

"He retired after thirty years and travels around in a Ram pickup and Airstream trailer, checking on his soldiers who are having a rough go of it. One of them, a Tier-1 operator named

Nathan Auburn, lost his son recently, who overdosed on Adderall laced with fentanyl. The boy's girlfriend was kidnapped last week and Auburn thinks his son's death and his girlfriend's kidnapping are connected somehow. Colonel Walker has agreed to help him and see if it is."

"The girlfriend was kidnapped in Tacoma?"

"In the parking lot of her high school after basketball practice. The van she was taken in was stolen and torched. The Tacoma police didn't get any forensics when they found it."

"Why does Auburn think the kidnapping and his son's overdose might be connected?" Benning asked.

"The son and his girlfriend were both using Adderall they got from a dealer to study for exams before Christmas."

"Are Adderall and the dealer the only things that connect them to the son and his girlfriend?"

"As far as I know," Drake said. "Colonel Walker might know something else he didn't tell us about, so you'll need to talk to Colonel Walker and find out."

"How do you want me to handle this? Is Colonel Walker my client, or are you?"

"I am."

"Is there anything else I should know?" Benning asked.

"Liz is available to talk to Kate Perkins at FBI, if they're working the kidnapping with Tacoma."

"All right, I'll get started. What's the girlfriend's name?"

"Madison Sanchez."

"And the soldier's son?"

"Chris Auburn."

Benning finished the half-eaten donut on his plate and asked, "You sure you don't want one of these?"

"I made a frittata for breakfast. I'm good, thanks."

"All right, I'll take the rest of them and find someone at the Sheriff's Department to give them to," Benning grinned. "It'd be a shame for them to go to waste."

"Donuts for cops," Drake said. "That's a cliché that might offend someone in the Sheriff's Department."

Benning turned his head on his way to the café's counter and said, "You know, you're right. I wouldn't want to offend someone. I'll find some hungry and needy person to give them to."

Drake shook his head and laughed. The donuts were destined to disappear along the way somehow, just like Madison Sanchez had from her high school parking lot.

The visit to the Sheriff's Department later that morning was a waste of time. Benning's friend was working in the gang unit and told them the Tacoma Police Department didn't share anything with the Sheriff's Department, unless they absolutely had to.

The only information they learned from the detective that might prove to be helpful was the name of street gang that probably sold the Adderall to Chris Auburn's girlfriend, the Hilltop Gangsters. The gang controlled the area around the girl's high school.

EIGHT

A day later, Paul Benning was driving north on I-5 to meet Colonel Walker at the Airstream dealership in Minda, Washington. Walker was picking up his upgraded travel trailer and had arranged a meeting with a Tacoma Police Department detective in the Special Investigations Unit (SIU).

Walker was hooking up his Airstream to his Ram pickup when Benning drove around to the back of the dealership's service department.

The retired Army chaplain didn't look like any chaplain, priest, or preacher Benning had ever met. Colonel Walker was tall, six feet four or five, with broad shoulders and a close-cropped haircut, when he straightened up and turned to see Benning's red F-150 approaching him.

For someone who had been in the army for thirty years and going on missions with Special Forces soldiers in some of the ruggedest terrains in the world, he had survived the wear and tear well.

Benning opened the door of his pickup and waved before getting out, seeing the wariness in Walker's eyes.

"Colonel Walker, I'm Paul Benning," he said, as he walked over.

"Paul," Walker said and held out his hand. "Call me Bill."

"Like your Ram?" Benning asked, nodding toward Walker's black pickup.

"I do. Always wanted a hemi. Thought I'd better get one before they outlaw internal combustion engines."

"I hear you," Benning said. "Can I help?"

"No, I have her all hooked up."

"Why don't we go somewhere and talk, before we meet with the detective?"

"We can meet inside," Walker said, hooking a thumb over his shoulder toward his Airstream. "I have a thermos of coffee in my pickup. Let me pull a little farther away from the service center."

Walker got in his Ram and pulled the Airstream forward fifty yards, out of the way of other the customers needing servicing.

Benning drove his pickup alongside Walker's and followed him inside the Airstream.

"I've never been inside an Airstream," Benning admitted. "This is nice."

"All the comforts of the home I never got around to buying. Have a seat and I'll get cups for our coffee."

Benning sat down at the leather dinette and looked around. To the front of the trailer was a sleeping area, with a queen size bed. Along the wall across from the dinette was a stove, double sink, microwave, and refrigerator. At the rear of the trailer, he could see a bathroom through an open door.

"Have you had this long?' Benning asked.

"I bought it just before I got out," he said with his back to Benning. "This is our maiden voyage. I figured it was the most practical way to get around to see my guys, without imposing on them for a place to stay."

Walker came back to the dinette with two black coffee mugs with the Special Forces emblem and logo "De Oppresso Liber" on the side and poured coffee from a thermos for each of them.

"Drake says you're a private detective now. How long have you been doing that?"

"This is my third year," Benning said. "When Drake closed his law practice his office and condo became available. My wife pushed me to retire from the Sheriff's Department. It was a good decision. I like what I'm doing."

"What does on "retainer" with PSS involve, if you don't mind me asking?"

Benning smiled. "A little of everything. Last year, I helped them solve the murder of a congressman's son and we uncovered a Chinese espionage plot. The year before that, Drake and PSS helped me find the kidnapped daughter of a research biologist who was being blackmailed by terrorists who were demanding a live sample of the H7N9 flu virus he was working on as ransom."

"Casey and Drake haven't gotten around to telling me what they do at PSS, but I'm getting the idea. They're still fighting the bad guys."

"Whenever they encounter them," Benning added.

"How do you know the detective we're meeting?"

"I worked a homicide case with her."

"Will she help me?" Walker asked.

"She owes me a favor. She would, even if she didn't. Rosa Benitez has twenty

years' experience working as a detective. She's angry because she doesn't get

the resources she needs to do her job, but she's a good detective.

"But don't let her appearance deceive you when you meet her," Benning cautioned. "She reminds me of Rosa Klebb, the SPECTRE agent in *From Russia with Love*, the old James Bond movie. She's the kind of detective criminals pray is never assigned to their cases. She can be mean and intimidating, but she has a good heart. And she never stops working a case, even when she's told to close it."

"Did she say anything about Madison Sanchez's kidnapping?"

"It isn't her case, but she said she'd find out what she can before we get there."

"Thanks for agreeing to help me, Paul," Walker said. "Nathan Auburn is pretty torn up about his son and I need to do everything I can to make sure he stays focused. I've seen too many men lose it going through a divorce, or grieving the loss of a loved one, and get sent home."

"I'm happy to help, Colonel. Which reminds me, Adam Drake is an attorney who hired me to investigate the death of Chris Auburn. Anything I discover or have discovered will be work product and, therefore, privileged. You're accompanying me as Nathan Auburn's spiritual advisor. Anything he's communicated to you about his son or his son's death is also privileged. You don't have to answer any questions Rosa might ask you."

"I understand," Colonel Walker said. "I'll let you do the talking unless you ask me to contribute something."

Benning looked at his watch and said, "We'd better get going if we want to be on time for our appointment. She expects everyone to be on "Lombardi Time" like she always is."

NINE

The Tacoma Police Department headquarters was a modern three-story building on South Pine Steet. After a short wait in the lobby, Benning and Walker were escorted to the Special Investigations Unit (SIU) where Detective Rosa Benitez had her office.

Detective Benitez remained seated at her desk when they were ushered into her office and motioned them to the chairs in front of her desk.

"Hello, Rosa," Benning said before sitting. "We met several years ago when I was a detective with the Multnomah County Sheriff's Department."

Detective Benitez nodded. "I remember. You must be Colonel Walker."

"I am," Walker said and reached his hand across her desk.

Detective Benitez didn't smile as she shook his hand. "I understand you were a chaplain in the Army."

"That's correct," Walker said. "Thirty years with Special Forces squadrons, for the most part."

"I understand you're here asking if the Special Investigations Unit has any information about the death of Chris Auburn. You told our secretary he died from a fentanyl overdose. Why are you asking about this young man's death?"

"Colonel Walker is a friend of his father," Benning explained. "Nathan Auburn hired an attorney, who hired me to investigate Chris Auburn's death."

"Then why is Colonel Walker here?" she asked.

Walker looked at Benning, who nodded.

"I advised Nathan Auburn to hire an attorney," Walker said. "After his son's funeral, Nathan's bereavement leave was over, and he had to get back to Fort Bragg. I told him I knew an attorney who might be able to help him."

"Why does Mr. Auburn need an attorney? Is he looking for someone to sue?"

"He wants to see the person responsible for his son's death put behind bars," Benning said.

"You mean the person who sold him the Adderall?" Detective Benitez said. "How do you know he didn't get Adderall on the internet? Surely you've considered that possibility."

"Of course, we did."

"Well, unless there's something you're not telling me, it sounds like Mr. Auburn is wasting his money hiring an attorney."

"Chris Auburn's girlfriend was also using Adderall," Benning said. "She studied with Chris before their exams. She was kidnapped a couple of days ago and Chris's father thinks her kidnapping might be related to his son's death."

"Are you talking about Madison Sanchez?" Detective Benitez asked.

"Yes," Benning said.

"Why does Chris Auburn's father think her kidnapping and his son's death are related?"

"Because she can identify the dealer who sold them the Adderall," Colonel Walker said.

"That's a long shot, Colonel. If every dealer who sells someone fentanyl turns around and kidnaps anyone who can identify them when a customer overdoses, we'd have hundreds of kidnapping cases in SIU."

"Rosa, we know it's a longshot," Benning said. "Is there anything you can tell us that will help my investigation? If this is a dead end, I'd like to tell Chris Auburn's dad that it is."

Detective Benitez looked up at the ceiling and sighed. "There is an open file on her kidnapping case. SIU is working with the FBI CARD team. I'll go get it and we'll see."

When she left her office, Walker said, "What's a CARD team?"

"The FBI's Child Abduction Rapid Deployment team," Benning said. "They work a lot of cases here and in Seattle. The last I heard, five or six hundred underage girls and boys are forced into the sex trade each year around here"

"I had no idea it was that bad."

Detective Benitez returned with a file and sat down at her desk. "I'm on the South Sound Gang Task Force, a partnership with the FBI, ATF, the Washington State Patrol, and the Lakewood and Tacoma Police Departments. So, I know about sex trafficking the gangs are involved in. The detective who's on our Child Exploitation Task Force isn't here right now. He might know the latest about this case."

She opened the file and flipped through several pages. "We found the van we believe she was abducted in. A teacher saw it drive away and gave us a description of a white Port of Tacoma van. It was abandoned and torched. No forensics and nothing else I see that we've turned up. I'm sorry, gentlemen. I'm afraid that's all we know at this point."

"Detective, you said that you're on the gang task force. If Chris Auburn and Madison Sanchez got their Adderall from someone, do you have any idea who that might have been?" Colonel Walker asked.

"Colonel, I wish I could be more helpful, but it could have been anyone."

"Is there anyone you know about who sells drugs to kids at

Stadium High School, where Chris and Madison were both seniors?" Benning asked.

"If it was anyone, it was the Hilltop Gangsters. The area north of the city on the hill where the high school is that gang's turf."

"Can you give me the name of a couple of the gang's members?" Colonel Walker asked.

"Why, Colonel?"

"I'd like to talk with them."

"For what purpose? They're not going to tell you anything. And we'll have another homicide case to deal with. The only thing that keeps us from getting shot every time we want to talk with that gang is the badge we wear."

Colonel Walker smiled and said, "I appreciate your concern, Detective Benitez, but I've talked with more dangerous people than these kids. I'll be fine."

"If you're determined to do this, let me suggest a safer way to get the information you're after," the detective said. "The neighborhood around the high school Madison Sanchez attended is one of the best neighborhoods in Tacoma. A private security company, Northwest Security and Protection Services, provides security for most of the neighborhoods there and used to have a night guard at the high school. Ask for Jeff Jackson, the owner of the security company. He keeps an eye on the gang activity in the Stadium District to protect his clients."

"Thanks, that's a great idea," Benning said and got up to leave.

"If you learn something I should know about, gentlemen, be sure to you call me," Detective Benitez said.

"Professional courtesy runs both ways, Rosa. If the SIU or the CARD Team turn up anything on the kidnapping that you can share, be sure to call me," Benning said.

"Of course," the detective said with a tight smile.

"I get the feeling she didn't really mean that," Colonel Walker said when they were out in the hallway outside her office.

"She didn't, but it doesn't matter. I know someone at the FBI."

TEN

When Paul Benning entered the name of the security company office in his Ford F-150's GPS navigation system, they saw the location of Northwest Security and Protection Services was five minutes away in south Tacoma.

When they got there, they saw that the security company's office building was a gray precast concrete building located inside a security-fenced three-acre compound. A black Hummer H2 was parked in front of the building, with a dozen vehicles parked along the west-side of the compound.

Benning stopped his truck in front of the security gate and looked for a buzzer button on the keypad. There wasn't one.

"Mr. Jackson must not want unexpected visitors," Benning said.

"I have the number for the company," Colonel Walker said and held up his phone. "Let's see if they'll make an exception."

He punched in the number and waited for someone to answer.

"Yes?" someone finally said.

"I'm here to see Mr. Jackson. My name is Colonel Thomas Walker."

"Do you have an appointment?"

"No."

"Does he know you?"

"He might," Walker said. "I have no way of knowing."

"Mr. Jackson is busy. Make an appointment and come back another time, Colonel."

"Detective Benitez said Mr. Jackson might be able to help me. He may know something about a member of the Hilltop Gangsters I'm looking for."

After a pause someone said, "I'll see if he has time to see you."

When the security gate rolled back, Benning pulled forward and crossed the compound to park beside the black Hummer H2 in front of the office building.

Before they got out of Benning's F-150, a large black man wearing camo pants and a tan t-shirt came out of the building and down the steps.

"You recognize the logo on his t-shirt?" Walker asked.

"75th Ranger Regiment patch," Benning said. "I was military intelligence before I was a detective."

Walker got out and approached the Ranger, who was holding his hand up for him to stop.

"Are you or your friend carrying?" he asked, nodding toward Benning who had followed him out of the truck.

"I'm not," Walker said.

"There's a Glock 19 in my truck, but I'm not armed," Benning said.

"You a cop?" he asked Benning.

"I was once. Now I'm a private investigator."

The man turned and went up the steps to open the door, "Follow me."

They walked past six men inside, watching them over the tops of their cubicles as they walked past to an office with a window at the back of the office.

Jeff Jackson was sitting at his desk waving at them to come in.

"Have a seat, gentlemen," Jackson said. "Jody says Detective Benitez sent you."

Walker smiled and said, "Not exactly. She said you were someone who might know something about a fentanyl dealer I'm looking for."

"Why did she say I might know something about this dealer?" Jackson asked.

"She said you keep an eye on gang activity in the Stadium District where you have clients," Benning clarified.

Jackson looked from Benning to Walker and back to Benning before motioning to Jody, who was standing by the open door, to close it.

"Why are you looking for a street gang dealer, Colonel?"

"The son of a friend of mine overdosed on fentanyl and died. My friend wants to see that the dealer pays for what he did."

Jackson shook his head and chuckled. "Good luck with that. Do you even know if the fentanyl came from a dealer? You can by the stuff on the internet."

"My friend thinks it's likely."

"Why, Colonel?"

"His son and his son's girlfriend were using Adderall to study for their semester exams. She was kidnapped recently, and my friend thinks her kidnapping and his son's death are related."

"Related how?"

"If the dealer learned my friend was looking for him while he was here a couple of weeks ago, he'd know the girlfriend could identify him or her. Kidnapping the girl would prevent that from happening."

"Are the police and FBI looking for this girlfriend?" Jackson asked.

"Yes," Walker said.

"Then you don't need my help. If the son's death and the kidnapping are related, the FBI's investigation will find out. If they're not related, I still can't help you. I know about the Hilltop Gangsters, but I can't tell you who individual members are. The one member I did know was the gang's leader, "Little Joker", and he was killed last month."

"Where does this gang hang out?" Benning asked.

"Why? Are you going to just walk up and ask if they sold the Adderall that killed this boy? You think they would tell you before they shot you?"

"I'm an optimist," Walker said, standing and reaching across the desk to shake Jackson's hand. "Thank you for agreeing to talk with us."

"Colonel, if I do hear something, how would I reach you?" Jackson asked.

"I'll be in the area for a while," Walker said and handed him a card with his name and email address on it. "I rented a campsite at Dash Point State Park and my travel trailer has internet reception. You can message me there."

The man Jackson called "Jody" opened the door and led them back through the office and out to Benning's truck. "JJ's right, colonel," he said. "They're not going to tell you anything. They will kill you, if you come calling."

"What battalion were you in?" Walker asked, looking at the man's t-shirt.

"Second Battalion, why?"

"Then you've heard of the Combat Applications Group at Fort Bragg. I was its chaplain until I retired at the end of the year. Street gangs are like the terrorists I've dealt with, except not as smart. I'll be fine."

Ranger Jody stood outside the office door until the security gate closed behind the red Ford F-150 as it drove away, before he returned to Jackson's office.

"He's not going to back off," Jody said. "You need to let Viper know there's someone looking for one of his street kids."

"Who, that private eye?"

"No, Colonel Walker. Do you know who he is?"

"A retired Army colonel."

"He's the Delta Force chaplain who went out with them on all their missions. He made it through Q-course and wears the beret. The guy's a legend."

"Yeah, I'll have to tell Viper, but you know what he's going to do. What he always does; eliminate a little threat before it becomes a bigger one," Jackson said. "I'll tell Viper about the chaplain when I see him, but let's find out for ourselves what this guy is really doing in Tacoma. Have Tim do an internet search on Walker. I'll call Detective Benitez and see what she knows about him and the private investigator."

"Roger that," Jody said. "You think the Hilltop Gangsters kidnapped this girlfriend?"

"If they did, Viper would know."

"Are you going to ask him?"

"Maybe later," Jackson said. "Right now, I want to know if this kidnapping and kid's death Walker's asking about are going to cause us problems."

ELEVEN

Paul Benning watched the security gate close in his rearview mirror as they left the compound before asking Colonel Walker, "What do you think?"

"I think we need to know more about Mr. Jackson. He knows more than he's telling us. If the Hilltop Gangsters is the street gang operating on his turf, he's going to know who the leader is and where the gang hangs out.

"I got a look at the screens those men were monitoring. They're watching video from surveillance cameras. If this street gang gets anywhere near the home of a client, they'd be able to identify them if they wanted to."

"He's hiring vets, from the looks of the men in the office," Walker said. "I respect that, but he's hiding something."

"Why didn't you give Jackson your phone number?"

"I don't want anyone tracking me."

"Still adjusting to being out of the army?"

"Maybe."

"What now? Any ideas?"

"None right now."

"I need to see Drake in Seattle and let him know what we've been doing," Benning said. "I'll find out what Liz learned when she called the FBI when I get there. What are your plans?"

"I'd like to check in at the state park and get my trailer set up this afternoon. I'll see if Adam has time to see me tomorrow. Maybe he has an idea about where we go from here."

"I'll let him know you want to see him," Benning said. "I'm curious, by the way, why are you camping out instead of staying at the swanky hotel Adam offered you?"

Walker laughed. "What I'm doing is called "glamping", Paul. That's enough swankiness for me. I bought the RV to have a place to stay when I travel around to see my guys. I've been deployed overseas most of my time in the army. Having the trailer gives me a chance to explore the America I haven't had time to see."

Benning followed his GPS navigation map to I-5 for the short drive back to Milton, Washington, and Walker's Airstream dealership, asking along the way, "How far do you want to go investigating Jackson, Tom?"

"What do you mean? How much do I want it to cost me?"

Benning shook his head, "No, I mean how deep do you want us to dig?"

"I don't understand."

"I can't put my finger on it," Benning admitted, "But I think there's more to Jackson and his security company than we're seeing. Jackson's sidekick had a look in his eye when I said I'd been a cop. I saw it in the eyes of the other men watching us when we walked past their cubicles. There's something going on there they don't want the cops or us to know about."

"Will investigating Jackson and his company help us find who sold Chris Auburn fentanyl-laced Adderall, or find his girlfriend?"

"I don't know, it might. Even if it doesn't, I think it needs to be done."

"It's your call, Paul. You're the detective."

Benning pulled his Ford F-150 alongside Walker's Ram TRX in

the Airstream dealer's lot and shook hands with his passenger before Walker got out. "Let me know what you and Adam decide to do. I'll block out as much time in my schedule as you need."

"Thanks, Paul. I'll let you know as soon as we decide something."

Walker let his truck warm up and entered the address for Dash Point State Park and left the dealership towing his upgraded Airstream Caravel travel trailer.

The 461-acre state park was located on the edge of Puget Sound between Tacoma, Washington, and Seattle, Washington. It had a beach and a 4.4-mile looping trail that, according to the literature, would take the average hiker one hour and forty-six minutes to walk. Walker was interested in finding out how much faster he could walk it.

He'd chosen the park because it offered him the privacy and seclusion he wanted as he adapted to his new life. He'd gotten used to the adrenaline rush of combat he experienced going out on missions and needed time to recalibrate his senses.

The local AM radio station hosts he skipped through were explaining their opinions on the latest political news out of the state capital in Olympia, Washington, so he switched to an FM station playing rock and roll oldies from the seventies, the music he grew up with. He was surprised he remembered the words to so many of the songs.

It was late afternoon when he stopped at the park ranger's station to register and pick up a map to his utility campsite. It was one of the few the park offered with a maximum site length of forty feet. He followed the map to a forested area and stopped on a bend in the graveled road fifty feet away from the campsite to figure out how to back his trailer in.

Tall fir trees bordered the site, with a space for his trailer on one side and space for his truck on the other side. In between the two spaces there was a fire pit and a picnic table. There was even a small stack of firewood at the back of the site the previous occupier had left.

Walker got out and walked around the site and saw that it would be easy to back in and get the trailer positioned.

In thirty minutes, he had his new home on wheels parked, leveled, and his truck backed into the space on the other side of the campsite.

He selected pieces of firewood and began working to get a fire going and begin enjoying the peace and quiet of his surroundings. Tomorrow he'd see how far out of shape he was, after missing the daily exercise he was used to getting with his squadron back at Fort Bragg before he retired.

TWELVE

Colonel Walker was sleeping soundly in the early morning hours of Sunday with the windows of his Airstream Caravel canted open for fresh air when he heard a whirring buzzing sound outside. He wasn't sure what it was, but his hearing was sensitized by nights in Afghanistan listening for incoming mortar rounds.

Slipping out of bed and rushing outside, he saw the dark shape of a large quadcopter descending above his travel trailer and the drone's payload suspended below it had a blinking red light.

Walker spun around and dove to the other side of the fire pit. The blast wave from the exploding payload picked him up and slammed him headfirst into the door of his truck.

His first sensation when he regained consciousness was a ringing in his ears and a throbbing pain in his head and neck. When he lifted his head and tried to sit up, a hand in his chest gently pushed him back.

"Just relax, sir. We won't know how badly you're hurt until we get you to the hospital," an EMT standing over him said.

Walker tried to ask what happened when his vision dimmed and he closed his eyes.

When he regained consciousness again, he strained to hear the voices nearby and understand what they were saying. The sounds were muffled, but the beeping sound behind his head was familiar. He was in a hospital room somewhere.

When he opened his eyes, he saw a doctor reading something on a clipboard at the foot of his bed. A nurse was talking with him.

The doctor saw that his eyes were open and walked around the bed and stood beside it. Leaning down, he asked, "Mr. Walker, my name is Doctor Patel. How are you feeling?"

"What happened?" Walker mumbled.

"Apparently a propane tank in your travel trailer exploded. Fortunately, you were outside when it did."

"Anything broken?"

"Unfortunately, yes," Dr. Patel said. "Your skull is fractured, and you have two fractured cervical vertebras. You've suffered a concussion and there's a lot of bruising. Is there anyone you'd like us to call to let them know you're here?"

"Where is here?"

"Tacoma General Hospital."

"There's a business card in my wallet. Please call my friend, Adam Drake, in Seattle," Walker said.

Dr. Patel turned to the nurse and whispered something before turning back and saying, "The only thing that arrived with you, I'm afraid, are the boxer shorts you're wearing."

Walker forced a smile. "Better than nothing, I guess. Adam Drake works for Puget Sound Security in Seattle. They can get word to him."

"Certainly," Dr. Patel said. "Is there anything else?"

"How long will I be here?"

"At least a couple of days. We'll want an orthopedist to have a look at your neck before you leave. You'll probably have to wear that cervical collar for a while, but the doctor can decide that when he sees you. For now you just need to rest. We'll call your friend and I'll check in on you tomorrow."

Walker watched the doctor and nurse leave the room and closed his eyes. There was no reason for the propane tank to explode. The Airstream was new and had never been used.

He could remember arriving at the park on the shore of Puget Sound, parking the Caravel and having a look around before dinner; he'd had a nice rib eye steak grilled on his portable Weber Q and a salad.

After reading a couple chapters in a new book about the history of the Indian Wars in America, he'd gone to bed around ten o'clock. That was the last thing he could remember.

He opened his eyes later when he heard someone talking and saw Adam Drake and Mike Casey standing at the foot of his bed.

"You didn't need to come," he said. "I just wanted you to know why I wouldn't be able to see you tomorrow."

"How are you feeling, colonel?" Drake asked.

"Nothing serious, headache and sore neck is all."

"What's the cervical collar for, then?" Casey asked.

Colonel Walker smiled and shook his head. "Your sniper-eyes never did miss much, did they Mike? Doctor says I fractured a couple vertebras in my neck."

"What happened?" Drake asked.

"They're telling me a propane tank in my trailer exploded. I'm not buying it."

"It wasn't your propane tank," Casey said. "We talked with the EMTs who brought you here. They said the fire department investigators found traces of C4 and the tip of a small propeller made of carbon fiber. They think it was from a small drone."

"I don't understand?" Walker said.

"Someone tried to take you out, colonel," Drake said.

"Why? Who? I don't have enemies; except the ones in the Middle East we've been fighting. There's no reason for any of them to come after me. Besides, no one knew where I was staying except Paul Benning."

"Paul wouldn't have told anyone," Casey said. "Anyone else you can think of who might have known?"

"Someone at the park, I guess. I registered there for the campsite a week ago. We did stop to see the owner of a security company in Tacoma," Walker said. "I gave him my email address when I asked him to let me know if he heard anything that would help me find the drug dealer. I don't remember if I mentioned I'd be at the park or not. But he wouldn't have a reason to want me dead."

"Maybe he doesn't, maybe he does," Drake said. "What's his name?"

"Jeff Jackson, Northwest Security and Protection Services in Tacoma."

"We'll take a look at Jackson and his company to make sure, colonel," Casey said. "Is there anything you would like us to do while you're here?"

"Find out if my truck's okay. It sounds like I may have lost everything else."

THIRTEEN

Drake and Casey stopped at Dash Point State Park on their way back to Seattle to check on Colonel Walker's truck.

They found the park ranger checking out campsites to make sure the ones that were supposed to be vacant were and clean, ready for new occupants. The ranger told them the police crime scene investigators were still at the campsite and the truck was damaged, but salvageable. The travel trailer, however, he said looked like it was a complete loss.

"I'm trying to hurry and get them to finish their work," the ranger said. "The explosion has the other campers nervous, with reporters all over the park questioning everyone. People come here to relax and get away from city life, not to be reminded of what they left behind."

They followed the park map the ranger gave them and found a sheriff's cruiser blocking the road to the campsite fifty yards away. A small crowd of people were standing around the cruiser, watching the crime scene techs working on the other side of the yellow crime scene tape down the road.

"I'll see if I can find someone who will talk with us," Drake said and walked around the crowd and headed down the road toward the crime scene.

As soon as he passed the front of the sheriff's cruiser, the sheriff's deputy standing at the edge of the crime scene tape raised his left hand and started toward Drake, dropping his right hand to the grip of his holstered pistol.

"Get back with the others, mister," the sheriff's deputy called out.

Drake stopped and waited for the man to come closer.

"I'm Colonel Walker's attorney. He asked me to check on his truck."

"Didn't take him long to find an attorney."

"Be nice, Deputy Simmons," Drake said, looking at his name badge. "I was helping him on another matter when this happened. Will his truck be in the custody of the Sheriff's Department or the Police Department?"

"Pierce County Sheriff's Department."

"Thank you. What happened here?"

"Can't say. It's an ongoing investigation."

"I understand. I was a senior prosecutor in the Multnomah County District Attorney's office. Unofficially, what do you think happened?"

"Looks like someone didn't like your friend," Deputy Simmons said, turning to look at the remains of Colonel Walker's Airstream trailer. "I heard them say it was C4."

"Who's in charge of the investigation?"

"Detective Riley. He left."

"Thank you, Deputy Simmons. "You've been very helpful," Drake said and walked back to Mike Casey standing behind the sheriff's cruiser.

'Learn anything?" Casey asked.

"Not much. He heard a CSI say it was C4, but we knew that. He's just here for crowd control. The Sheriff's Department will have the truck."

"Ready to head back?" Casey asked.

"Yes, let's go. I'll ask Paul to come up and find out what they've learned. He's a former Sheriff Department detective, they'll talk to him. "

On the short walk back to Casey's Suburban, Drake said, "There are two groups using C4 these days, other than the military; terrorists and the cartels. I can't see either one of them going after Colonel Walker."

"Neither can I, unless it has something to do with his friend at Fort Bragg. We don't know about him."

Drake nodded, "Or Colonel Walker. Maybe one of his soldiers is involved in something he doesn't the colonel to know about."

"That certainly expands the range of possibilities. He's not going to want us to investigate all of them."

"So, we'll work with what we know now and see where it leads us."

As they were leaving the state park to return to Seattle, Casey asked, "Want to get something to eat? We passed a fish taco food truck at the exit coming off I-5."

"If you're hungry, why not."

Casey started humming a song Drake didn't recognize when his phone buzzed. "How are you doing Colonel?" he asked.

"Doing fine. A detective was here asking questions and said my trailer's a write-off. Is your company's suite at that hotel is still available?"

"Absolutely," Drake said. "When do you think they'll let you out of the hospital?"

"The orthopedist says I can leave in a day or so, depending on how I'm feeling. I'm ready to leave now, but probably tomorrow. I'll be wearing the neck brace for a while."

"I'm going to ask Paul to visit the Sheriff's detective in Tacoma handling your case tomorrow," Drake said. "He can give you a ride to the hotel."

"I'll need a ride, but not to the hotel just yet. I want to go back and ask the owner of that security company a few questions."

"Why?"

"I remembered I saw a couple of kids drive by my campsite last evening. They looked like gang bangers riding in a loud black Honda Civic. Jackson might know who they are."

"Colonel, I'd like you to wait before going back there until we know more about Jackson," Drake said. "He knew where you were camping."

"I know, but I'm good at reading people. I'll know if he's lying when I ask him if he told anyone where I was staying. Paul will be with me. We'll be fine."

"All right, I'll let Paul know what you're planning. If we turn up anything that will make your visit ill-advised, I'll let you know."

"Did you get a look at my truck."

"It needs some work, but you'll drive it again someday."

"That's great. I love the rumble of that hemi."

FOURTEEN

Ruben Fang stood in front of a glass reptile terrarium in his office watching the beautiful coiling reaction his pet saw-scaled viper had when he tapped the front glass panel. The snake coiled itself in its characteristic flowing S-shape, rubbing sections of its serrated peaked scales over each other to produce a sizzling warning sound.

The green snake was small, no more than eighteen inches long, with a pear-shaped head and vertical slits for eyes. Its venom was the deadliest of all the snakes in the world, and its lightning-fast strike whenever he fed it a baby chick, or a white lab rat, still amazed him.

The way the viper aggressively attacked anything that threatened it was the way he moved against his own enemies; fast and deadly. The way he wanted to strike the Sinaloa cartel replacement Jackson located in the nearby city of Puyallup, Washington.

Before he did, he knew he needed to get approval from the cartel's new leader, Chen Huang, who took over when Frank Xueping, the cartel's previous leader who mysteriosly disappeared the year before.

Xueping had been the head of the Chinese triad chosen to flood America with fentanyl to kill off as many of its young men of fighting age as possible. The plan was still operational and would continue, as long as America had an appetite for the poison, but the rumor was Huang was in Mexico to do more than just direct the cartel's enterprises.

In addition to manufacturing and distributing counterfeit opioids and building up the cartel's sex trafficking profits, Huang had a cadre of men with him who were former People's Liberation Army soldiers from China. Huang himself was said to be a former Naval Sea Dragon commando.

He wasn't privy to Huang's intentions or plan, but he knew enough to make sure he cleared things with the man before he did anything that might bring unwanted attention to the cartel. Like killing the Sinaloa cartel rival in a most gruesome and brutal manner, as he planned on doing.

Fang unlocked the top right drawer of his desk and took out the new Kwanmi Ultra smartphone he'd been given to use for his calls to Huang. The phone was equipped with China Telecom's special SIM card and had an app that allowed quantum encrypted phone calls to be made.

"What is it, Fang?" Huang asked.

"We found the Sinaloa man, sir. What do you want me to do?"

"Not what you did the last time and what I suspect you'd like to do again."

"What then?"

"Where is he?"

"He's in an old farmhouse outside a small town ten miles from here."

"Does this farmhouse have neighbors close by?"

"The farmhouse is located in the middle of a large field in a rural area," Fang said. "I can't tell from the pictures I have how close a neighbor might be."

"Does he move around a lot?"

"My source says he stays at the farmhouse and people come see him there."

"Your source? It's not from one of your own men?"

"No sir. I had the man I use to deal with rival street gangs find the Sinaloan."

"Do you trust him?"

"I own him."

Fang waited for Huang to continue.

"You may own him, but I don't want him to know anything about how I'm going to take care of the Sinaloan. If he's going to serve our purpose later, I don't want him anywhere near that farmhouse. Tell him you've decided to leave the rival alone, for now. Instead of you doing it, I'll send a team to remove the man in a way that no one will have a reason to suspect your involvement."

"I don't understand. Why send any of your men here? I can take care of this man without anyone knowing it was me?"

"What I want is for you to do what you're told! The men I'm sending need the experience of operating on foreign soil. Dealing with the Sinaloan is way to prepare them for later. Call the man you say you own and tell him you changed your mind. If he has anyone watching the Sinaloan, tell him to pull back and leave him alone. Do you understand?"

"Yes sir," Fang said and heard Huang end the call.

He didn't understand, but he was beginning to. Huang was a former commando, and his men were soldiers. If Huang's men needed experience operating on foreign soil, that soil wasn't in Mexico. It was in America, and it wasn't about selling drugs or making money from young girls they kidnapped for the sex trade.

But it did it have something to do with Jackson and his security company. When he met with Huang in Mexico, he was told Jackson was a member of a secret militia that had a plan to take out America's power grid to stop the government from continuing to encroach on their rights as American citizens.

He'd been ordered to make sure Jackson was happy with his

alliance with the cartel, even if the man became greedy and demanded more money. Huang said the money he deposited in an offshore account to support his secret militia was available to them when they needed it back.

If Jackson and his militia were going to serve a purpose later, it would be because Huang, and presumably China, planned on doing something that Jackson's secret militia would be blamed for.

Fang was Chinese and doing what he did because he liked the money and the power that being a cartel leader provided him. But getting involved in a Chinese false flag operation wasn't why he joined the cartel, and he didn't like what it might mean for him if it failed.

Spending time in an American jail was a price he was willing to pay for selling drugs and girls into prostitution. Being tried and executed for being an enemy combatant in America wasn't.

FIFTEEN

Drake found Liz at her desk when he got back to PSS headquarters.

"How's Colonel Walker?" she asked.

"Lucky he wasn't in his trailer when it blew up. He has a concussion from the blast and he's wearing a cervical collar. Otherwise, he's okay."

"Do they know what caused it?"

"C4, apparently. They found the tip of a drone propeller and think a drone delivered the explosive."

"That's pretty sophisticated," Liz said. "They have any idea who's responsible?"

"The Sheriff's Department is handling the investigation, but we didn't learn anything from the deputy at the crime scene. I'm going to have Paul find out what they have."

"Who do you think is responsible?"

"I don't know, but I'm going to find out," Drake said. "Is your doctor appointment this afternoon or tomorrow?"

"Tomorrow afternoon, four o'clock. But you don't have to come."

"Of course, I do. Get you anything before I get to work?"

"I'm fine, thanks."

Drake closed her door and smiled. He knew women continued working right up to the day they had their babies, but he was impressed with his wife, nevertheless, working on a Sunday. If you didn't look closely, you could miss seeing her baby bump and not even know she was pregnant.

Thank God men didn't have babies.

He closed the door of his office, hung up his jacket and took out a legal pad to make a list of the things he needed to do today.

First, call Paul Benning and ask him to drive to Tacoma and find out what the detective investigating the attack on Colonel Walker had learned. He wanted to know what Paul thought about the owner of the security company before Colonel Walker returned there to ask about a black Honda Civic.

Second, have Kevin McRoberts to find out what he could about the owner and his security company. Kevin had an uncanny and sometimes mysterious way of using the internet to tell him things even most other white hat hackers couldn't.

Third, it had been over a week since he'd heard from his friends in Mexico. He wanted to know how they were doing with the first round of funding. He also wanted to know what they knew about the Los Zheng cartel operating in Tacoma and the Northwest.

The year before, he'd help cut off the head of the cartel snake with the help of Pete Ramirez and Danny Vasquez in Baja California. Two of the cartel's leaders had been killed and the third was being interrogated by the FBI in a secret location before his arrest. He was being held as an agent of China for his involvement in the plot to flood America with fentanyl.

The Los Zheng cartel, however, was still selling drugs and killing Americans and he wanted to know who its new leader was.

And last, he wanted their real estate agent to find something different than what she'd been showing them. The condo Liz owned they called home was great, for the time being, but he wanted to find property where they could build a house.

A property that met all their needs and provided the privacy and security they needed. He'd made some powerful enemies in the last few years and didn't want to make it easy for any of them if they came after him or his wife and child.

None of the properties they'd been shown since they returned from their honeymoon on the Great Barrier Reef in Australia had come close to what he was looking for.

Drake put a check next to the first item on his list and called Paul Benning in Portland.

"Afternoon, Paul. Have you seen the news about what happened in Tacoma?"

"I don't watch the news," Benning said. "What happened in Tacoma?"

"Someone blew up Colonel Walker's trailer. He's in the hospital."

"No way! How badly is he hurt?"

"He was lucky. He was outside his trailer at the time. The blast was from a C4 explosive delivered by a drone. He has a concussion and he's wearing a cervical collar. He says they're letting him leave the hospital tomorrow."

"What can I do?"

"He'll need a ride to the Woodmark Hotel, where he's going to use the company's suite for a while. Before you take him there, he wants to go back to the security company in Tacoma. He remembers seeing a black Honda Civic cruising the park, the kind with loud exhaust gang bangers and street racers drive. He thinks the security company owner might know who the driver was."

"I don't think that's a good idea," Benning said. "I didn't like the looks of the men they have working there."

"Explain."

"I got the feeling they're hiding something. The guys working there look like they're all former military, which isn't unusual for private security companies. But they knew Colonel Walker was a former army officer and that I was a former Sheriff's detective by the time we left. The men stared at us like we were the enemy. There wasn't a reason for them to look at us that way."

"There could be another reason," Drake said. "Someone knew where Colonel Walker was staying, and he told the owner of the security company he was going camping at the state park with his trailer. Maybe someone who heard that passed it along who tried to take him out."

"I remember him saying that. We'll need to check out Jeff Jackson and his employees before I want to go back there."

"I'll have Kevin do that for us tomorrow. When you go to Tacoma to bring Colonel Walker to the hotel, stop and see if the Sheriff's Department detective investigating the explosion has learned anything about who might be responsible."

"On it," Benning said.

SIXTEEN

A cold front moved in from Alaska Monday morning and Drake was standing under hot water in the shower to warm up after a five-mile run in the rain. When he stepped out and reached for a towel, he smelled a sweet and yeasty aroma coming from the kitchen.

He wrapped the towel around his waist and walked down the stairs and found Liz standing and humming in front of her new countertop smart oven.

"Is this for my breakfast?" he asked.

"It could be," she said when she turned around and saw wet footprints across her white porcelain tile kitchen floor. "After you mop up after yourself."

"Sorry," he said and walked over to wrap his wet arms around her. "The smell made me do it. What are you baking?"

"Sticky buns. I wanted something sweet. You have time to dress and mop the floor before they're ready."

Drake kissed her and said, "Aye, aye captain."

Baking was a new hobby for Liz that began after a friend raved about some online baking podcast. Cooking was something he enjoyed, and he was delighted that Liz was adding something new to her culinary repertoire.

When he returned wearing a v-neck sweater over a button-down chambray shirt and tan slacks, Liz had wiped up the water on the floor and was sitting at the table in the breakfast nook. A plate with a sticky bun, a berry smoothie, and cup of coffee were set across the table from her. Lancer was on the floor at her feet.

"Have I told you that you're beautiful," he said as pulled out the chair to sit down.

"Me or my sticky buns?" she asked with a smile.

"You and your buns," he said with a wink.

"Would you like to have Colonel Walker over for dinner tonight?"

"Let's take him to dinner at the Woodmark. That way we won't have to rush home to cook something after your doctor appointment."

"All right," she said.

Drake took a bite of the sticky bun and gave it a thumbs up. "If you keep feeding my sweet tooth, I'll have to run an extra five miles in the morning."

"Don't worry, you're not having breakfast like this every morning."

"When we get to the office, will you call Kate Perkins?" Drake asked. "She has access to the FBI's Guardian Threat Tracking System. I'd like to know if there's anything in there about the owner of a small private security company in Tacoma, or any of its employees. Colonel Walker and Paul Benning stopped there the day before yesterday."

"Why?" Liz asked.

"Paul got the feeling when he was there that the owner, or his employees, were hiding something. Security companies hire a lot of vets and some of the domestic terrorists arrested in the last couple of years have been vets. If the company is vetting new hires for security work carefully, they're not going to have criminal records so it's not likely it's criminal activity they're hiding But it might be involvement in militia activity they don't want anyone to know about."

"What's the owner's name?"

"Jeff Jackson is the owner of Northwest Security and Protection Services in Tacoma."

"I'll call her as soon as I get to the office."

"Thanks," Drake said. "I'll put things away after I finish eating. Go ahead and get ready to go."

He watched her leave and looked down to see Lancer watching her leave as well.

Drake motioned for Lancer to go with Liz. "Go ahead. Make sure she's okay."

Lancer jumped up and ran up the stairs. He'd become very protective of Liz during her pregnancy, following her everywhere and stretching out on the floor at night on her side of the bed.

Before noon that day, Drake had the lowdown on Jeff Jackson and his company. While his security company and its employees were not mentioned in the FBI's classified Guardian system, Jeff "JJ" Jackson was.

Kate Perkins, the deputy director of the FBI, told Liz when she'd called her back from FBI headquarters in Washington, D.C., that Jackson was mentioned in the Guardian system as a "friend" of a man he served under as an army Ranger, Lt. Colonel William "Bull" Browning. Browning was rumored to be a militia organizer in South Carolina and in several other southern states.

Jackson was not known to have been involved in any domestic terrorism activities or threats, but he was on the FBI's radar as a possible domestic violent extremist (DVE).

While William "Bull" Browning might just be a Patriot militia organizer in the South, Drake knew the Pacific Northwest had a long history of harboring armed militia groups and nationalist movements.

When Antifa demonstrated violently in the cities Portland and Seattle in recent years, armed militia groups showed up at the rallies claiming they were there to protect the groups opposing Antifa who were tired of the rioting in their cities in 2020 and 2021. Membership in those groups had grown with the widespread efforts in many states and Congress to ban military-style rifles. Viewed as an attempt to take away a patriotic citizen's Second Amendment Constitutional right to bear arms, along with a longing to restore traditional values in the country, the Patriot militia movement had spread from coast to coast.

But it was back in 1974 in northern Idaho, Washington State's neighbor to the east, where the Pacific Northwest was the headquarters of the Aryan Nations, a North American neo-Nazi, white supremacist terrorist organization. Today, the Aryan Freedom Network kept the movement alive.

If Jeff Jackson was a member of a militia group or affiliated with William "Bull" Browning and didn't want anyone to know about it, Drake had no reason to discount the idea that was what he was trying to hide.

Which was why he asked Kevin McRoberts to dig as deep as he could to find out if Paul Benning's suspicion might be right.

SEVENTEEN

Ninety-one miles east of Tijuana, Mexico, if you traveled by air, is the town of Mexicali, the capital of the Mexican State of Baja California. An official from China's consulate in Tijuana by the name of Zhu Chao was waiting at a table in the China House Restaurant.

He was waiting to meet the head of the Los Zheng cartel. It was the first time, and likely the last time, they would meet, given the singular reason for the meeting. Chao had a flash drive with information the cartel leader needed.

At exactly two o'clock in the afternoon, two young and tall Chinese men wearing jeans, black windbreakers, and plain black baseball caps entered the restaurant and stood on each side of the front door. They stood silently, looking around like Secret Service agents searching a crowd to protect an American president.

After a minute that allowed everyone to notice conspicuous bulges beneath their windbreakers and make sure the restaurant was safe, the one on the left went back outside and escorted a muscular and older Chinese man with short-cropped hair inside.

Chen Huang walked directly to Zhu Chao's table and motioned

for him to get out of the chair facing the restaurant's front door. After they swapped seats and two more Chinese men dressed like the two at the front door came out from the kitchen area and stood behind Huang.

"What do you have for me?" Huang asked.

"A flash drive with the information you requested," Chao answered.

"How was it obtained?"

"His Nokia military grade phone he uses was made in Dongguan. It was built with a back door in it that allows us to monitor his messages. We were able to locate the other 412 militia cells in the country."

"How many are there?"

"Ten, including his in the Pacific Northwest."

"I thought there would be more."

"Our intelligence confirms they only want to attack ten power substations to take out the U.S. energy grid."

"How do we know it's only ten?"

"Because these 412 cells are located near the same power substations we identified that would take down the American power grid."

Huang tipped his head back and looked up for a moment before saying, "I have twenty men here. I will need the other eighty men."

"The PLA soldiers you selected will finish their training in two weeks and arrive, as the others have from South America. Their equipment is already on the way," Chao said.

"The date is still the same?"

"Yes, this summer, just before we invade Taiwan. Our social media campaign will have people prepared to protest their government for taking military action against us and starting a war. When the government isn't able prove China was responsible for taking down their power grid and the evidence they will find that the 412 militia was, America will not risk starting World War III."

Huang reached his open hand across the table and waited for Chao to give him the flash drive. "Have the shrimp and scallops before you leave," Huang said when the flash drive was in his hand.

Chao watched Huang leave, as he walked across the restaurant with two of his men behind him and out the front door with the two men at the door leading the way.

THE RESTAURANT MANAGER standing next to the kitchen door was also watching Huang leave. As soon as he and his bodyguards were out the door, he walked to the hostess station to see who the man had been meeting with. When he found the man's name with the reservation sitting at Table 17, he walked to his office and closed the door.

He opened the coat closet door and used a key on his keyring to open the locked cabinet where the security system recorder was located. Rewinding the video recordings back twenty minutes to make sure the cameras provided a good look at the faces of two Chinese men and the four bodyguards, he transferred the day's video to a new USB flash drive and locked the cabinet when the transfer was completed.

After a moment to consider what he should do with the flash drive, he called his son.

"Before you leave work, stop by the restaurant. I have something for you."

"I was going to get some things Mom wanted me to get and take them to her for dinner tonight. Can it wait until I do that for her?"

"No, you need to come by as soon as you can. I have something for your army buddy."

"Does it involve what he talked to me about?"

"Yes, the man with bodyguards who was here and a person he met, someone from the Chinese consulate in Tijuana."

"I'll be there in half an hour."

The manager's son was a former U.S. marine, and his army

buddy was trying to recruit him to join a resistance movement to fight the cartels. His mother was vehemently forbidding it, but the manager knew it was something their son was going to do.

Someone had to do something to stop the violence and corruption the cartels' drug money caused in their country. The government couldn't or wouldn't do it, and

for all the talking America did about working with Mexico to make things better, nothing changed.

And now, if China was somehow involved with the cartels, it was even more important for their son to stand with the resistance, the men and women who were being called Las Sombras, the shadows.

Mexicali was home to as many as twenty thousand Mexican Chinese, as Chinese immigrants had been instrumental in growing the city in the mid-1800s. There were three hundred Chinese restaurants now and seventy percent of the Chinese population worked in the local Chinese restaurant industry.

If China was assisting or cooperating with the cartels in any way, it was shameful and had to be exposed. He hoped the security camera footage on the flash drive he was giving his son would help Las Sombras find out what China was up to.

EIGHTEEN

Drake was on the second floor talking with the head of the PSS IT division when his phone notified him that he had a message on his Signal Private Messenger app.

When the screen opened, he saw Pete Ramirez was calling and stepped out of Kevin's office to take the call.

"You have a minute?" Ramirez asked.

"Yes, fire away."

"The father of a man we're trying to recruit gave us a security video recording of two Chinese men meeting in the Mexicali Chinese restaurant the father manages. One of the men had bodyguards and the other is an official from the Chinese consulate in Tijuana. We think the one with the bodyguards is Xueping's replacement as the head of the Los Zheng cartel."

"Do we know anything about the consulate official?"

"We know he arrived by air from Tijuana and handed a flash drive across the table to our guy," Ramirez said. "That's all we know."

"I might be able to get someone to help identify the consulate official. What about the new Los Zheng guy?"

"He arrived at the China House Restaurant in an armored

Mercedes with two black Suburbans and bodyguards. We haven't seen him before. He looks military to me, maybe late thirties or early forties."

"Any idea where he came from?" Drake asked.

"He could be from Mexicali. There's always been a large Chinese population here. But we haven't heard anything about a top Los Zheng guy needing bodyguards being around here. Mexicali is the capital of Baja California and Baja is where Los Zheng is fighting to control, but they're usually not around Mexicali."

"What are you planning to do?"

"We need that intel you said you could provide us," Ramirez said. "Who is the new Los Zheng leader, who is the consulate official? Is he military, Chinese intelligence or just a consulate messenger. We'll try to find a Los Zheng's base around Mexicali, if there is one, but I'd like to know how this Chinese connection might change things for us."

"Send me the video recording and I'll see what we can find out. Is there anything else you need help with?" Drake asked.

"Not right now. We've established cells and added recruits. We'll step up our "whack-a-mole" operation in the next couple of weeks. They're calling us Las Sombras, the shadows, because they don't know where the kill shots are coming from or who the shooters are. Guerrilla warfare at its finest."

"Buena suerte, Rammer. I'll be in touch."

"Your to-do list just got longer," Drake called Kevin McRoberts and told him. "I'm getting a video recording that we need to identify the people on it."

"Sure, no problem. How soon do you need it?"

"As soon as possible when it gets here."

"Is this related to the private security owner in Tacoma?"

"No, it's another matter," Drake said.

"When you said dig deep on Mr. Jackson and his company, does that include having a look inside his company's system?" Kevin asked.

"See how sophisticated his system is. I don't want him to know we're snooping, just yet. There's a possibility he's involved with a militia movement. That's what I want to find out."

Drake's phone buzzed again as soon as he ended his call to Kevin, and he saw it was a text from Ramirez with an attachment. He forwarded the attachment to Kevin and left his office to look for Mike Casey.

Casey was standing in the hall in front of Liz's office with a file in his hand.

"Let me know if they're okay with keeping the date we proposed," Casey said before turning toward him.

Drake nodded in the direction of Casey's office and asked, "Have a minute?"

Casey said yes, and Drake turned to walk with him to his office at the end of the hall.

"Was that about doing more penetration testing for New Zealand?" Drake asked.

"Yes, we offered to meet them in Hawaii, so Liz wouldn't have to fly so far. But they want to move the date back a month instead and still meet in Wellington. I think it's too close to her due date, so we're asking them to stick with the date and location we originally proposed."

"I don't want her flying anywhere, but she won't listen to me. She has an appointment with the obstetrician this afternoon and I'm going with her. I'll see what he says about her flying."

"Be careful with that," Casey cautioned. "Megan got mad every time I tried to keep her from doing things."

"I know, I've already been lectured about doing that."

"What did you want to talk about?"

"Let's wait until we're in your office."

When they got there, Drake closed the door and said, "Pete Ramirez sent me a video that shows a Chinese consulate official meeting with the man he thinks is the new head of Los Zheng in

Mexicali, Mexico. He wants our help identifying the men and finding out what China's involvement with the cartel might mean."

"Does he have any idea what the meeting was about?"

"No, but the video shows the consulate official handing over a flash drive."

Casey leaned back in his chair and whistled softly. "It's not only what China's involvement might mean for them, but for us too. The last time the U.S. was caught providing aid to a resistance movement in another country, all hell broke loose. If China's involved in something down there as well and discovers that we're interfering as well, it would be double hell."

"I know. I'll have to tell the president about this."

"He'll certainly want to know why a Chinese consulate guy was meeting with the cartel in Mexico, and he's going to want us to find out. We have to be very careful with this."

"I know, especially since we're the intelligence contractor he wants to be able to use and that doesn't wind up in the news, like the intelligence community in Washington keeps doing."

"How are we going to find out why a Chinese consulate official was meeting with the head of Los Zheng?"

"I haven't figured that out yet," Drake said.

NINETEEN

Paul Benning looked at his watch for the third time in the last fifteen minutes and got up to leave the Sheriff Department's lobby, when the clerk at the counter called his name.

"Mr. Benning, Detective Riley can see you now."

The clerk waited for him at the reinforced door with electronic locks door she held open and walked ahead of him down a hallway to Detective Riley's office.

Detective Riley was young, but Benning could see that he'd been in law enforcement long enough to have the weary look of someone who had seen too many things he wished he hadn't.

"You're Colonel Walker's friend?" Detective Riley asked.

"Yes," Benning said. "I'm also working with the colonel and his attorney on another matter I hope you might be able to help me with."

"In what capacity are you working with Walker and his attorney?"

"I'm a licensed private investigator. I'm also a former detective in the Multnomah County Sheriff's Department."

"Have a seat, then, and tell me why you're here."

"To find out if you have any idea who blew up his travel trailer?"

"I'm waiting for a report about forensic evidence from the crime scene."

"Did any of the campers or visitors at the state park see or hear anything?"

"They all heard something, but no one reports seeing anything?"

"Other than the explosion, did they hear anything unusual?"

"Like what?" Detective Riley asked.

"Like a loud car driving through the park, maybe a street racer or something?"

"Why, did Colonel Walker hear a loud car? If he did, he didn't say anything about it when I saw him in the hospital."

"He didn't remember it until he was talking with his attorney. He remembers a loud black Honda Civic driving by his trailer twice that night before the explosion."

"There's no mention of a loud black Honda Civic that I've heard about."

"By any chance, have you heard of any Tacoma street gang members driving a loud black Honda Civic?"

Detective Riley's eyes squinted a little when he asked, "Why do you think some gang banger might be involved in this?"

Benning hesitated long enough before answering that Detective Riley asked, "What is it you're not telling me?"

"Just a hunch, I guess. Colonel Walker is a retired Special Forces chaplain. He's here trying to find the fentanyl dealer that sold fake Adderall pills that killed a soldier's son he served with. The father was here in Tacoma asking questions about who sold Adderall to high school students at Stadium High School. Colonel Walker volunteered to travel here and keep looking for the dealer and was asking the same thing."

"And you think Walker's asking these questions is what led to someone dropping a bomb on his trailer?"

"It's a possibility."

"How does Walker's attorney fit into all of this?"

"Colonel Walker knew a friend of mine who was in Special Forces with him and is an attorney in Seattle. He asked my friend, the attorney, if he knew anyone in Tacoma that could help him," Benning said. "I live and work in Portland and I got the call."

"Who's the attorney that's your friend?"

"Adam Drake. He's house counsel for Puget Sound Security in Seattle."

"Is he the Drake the Chinese triad tried to gun down and then blow up his condo in Seattle a while back?"

"That's him."

"I'm getting the feeling there's more to this than you're telling me."

Benning shrugged and said, "Not much more. My wife was his legal assistant when he was a prosecutor in Portland and later his office manager when he opened his own office. I'm leasing his old office and living in his condo above it."

Detective Riley thought for a moment before saying, "Give me your card. If you agree to call me if you learn anything, I'll agree to call you if I hear anything about a loud black Honda Civic who some gang banger might be driving."

"Deal," Benning said and handed the detective his card.

Walking down the hall to the lobby, he thought about going back and mentioning the kidnapping and how that might be related to everything. He decided not to. He'd already said more than he intended to.

By the time he drove across town to the hospital to pick up Colonel Walker, it was almost two o'clock Monday afternoon. His ride was standing outside the main entrance with his arms folded across his chest.

When he walked to Benning's pickup and opened the passenger side door, he said, "I'm going to pay Jeff Jackson a call before I go to Seattle. If Drake's told you not to let me go there, I'll take a cab."

"Drake said he didn't think it was good idea, but he didn't tell me not to take you there. Get in."

Colonel Walker climbed in and said, "I also need to stop somewhere and buy some clothes. A janitor at the hospital loaned me a spare pair of jeans and work shirt he had in his locker. I'll have to return these."

"Sure thing. Where would you like to go?"

"There was a mall out by the freeway. We can stop there on the way to Seattle. For now, I'm okay dressed like this to go see Jackson."

"Adam said you want to ask him if he knows anyone driving a black Honda Civic," Benning said. "I stopped and saw the detective who's investigating the bomb that blew up your trailer. He said no one mentioned seeing or hearing a loud black Honda Civic at the state park."

"I know what I heard. Jackson may not know anyone driving a car like that, but if he does and lies about it, I'll know that he knows more than he's saying. That alone will give me something to work with. I don't have anything else, no leads, no truck, no trailer, and no clothes."

Walker laughed and said, "This retirement gig isn't working out like I planned."

TWENTY

Jackson's black Hummer H2 was parked in front of the Northwest Security and Protection Services building when they stopped at the security gate.

Colonel Walker called the company's office and waited for someone to answer.

"Mr. Jackson isn't seeing anyone today, Colonel Walker."

"He'll see me if he wants to keep his name out of an ongoing police investigation."

"What investigation would that be?"

"The one the Sheriff's Department in Tacoma is conducting."

"I'll ask Mr. Jackson if he has time to see you."

Paul Benning turned toward Walker and whispered. "That should get us in."

"We'll see," Walker whispered back.

Five minutes later the security gate rolled back and Benning drove forward to park next to the Hummer.

Jeff Jackson walked out alone this time and stood in front of Benning's F-150 with his hands on his hips.

"Make it quick, Colonel" Jackson said, as the doors of the truck opened and they both stepped out.

"You're familiar with street gangs in Tacoma," Walker said. "Do you know someone who drives a black Honda Civic with loud pipes?"

Jackson ignored the question and asked, "Why would I be mentioned in an investigation about someone trying to kill you?"

"That's why I'm here, to find out if you should be."

"Because I might know someone who drives a Honda Civic with loud pipes?"

"Among other things."

"What other things?"

"I'll make it quick, like you asked," Walker said. "Tell me if you know a gang member who drives a black Honda Civic with loud pipes. If you say you don't, we're out of here."

"Then I guess you're out of here," Jackson said, and walked back to the stairs and into his office.

Walker stayed where he was and waited.

When the security gate rolled back, Benning asked, "Are we staying or leaving?"

"I got what I came for," Walker said. "We're leaving."

Colonel Walker took his time tightening his seatbelt over his sore chest and ribs in the passenger seat of Benning's truck before saying, "I didn't say anything about someone trying to kill me."

JEFF JACKSON STOOD in front of the security cameras monitor and watched the red Ford F-150 pickup drive out through the security gate. Jody Russel, his number two, was standing by his side.

"What now?" Russel asked.

"I need to talk to Fang. I can't believe he's stupid enough to send someone after this guy."

"Maybe it wasn't Fang."

"It was Fang," Jackson said. "Detective Benitez called me about a punk we had her arrest. She also asked me if Colonel Walker had ever come to see me. When I asked why she was asking, she said she'd given Walker my name and thought I might want to know that someone had dropped a bomb from a drone on his travel trailer. Fang's cartel has been using drones to hit their rivals in Mexico."

"But why would Fang go after Walker? He doesn't need that kind of heat?"

"Unless he's involved in more than drugs and sex trafficking," Jackson said.

"What else are the cartels into? It they can't make money doing something, they don't do it."

"I don't know, but we need to find out."

"How?"

"I need to tell him Walker was here asking if I knew someone driving a black Honda Civic with loud pipes. My guess it's one of his Hilltop Gangsters he uses to distribute his drugs. When Walker was here the first time, I told Fang about it. He wanted to know where Walker was staying, and I told him. If I tell him I can't have anything he did to Walker coming back on us, he might tell me why he did it."

"If he doesn't, we could grab one of his kids and find out if they were involved."

"Let's see if Fang will tell us first."

"You're the boss."

Jackson went to his office and closed the door. The problem was he needed to meet with Fang and ask him face-to-face about Walker, and he wasn't sure if the risk of being seen with Fang was worth it.

But he also couldn't take the chance that Fang had done something that would expose their alliance, or worse, expose his being a member of 412.

He would have to take a chance and minimize the risk of being seen with Fang. It couldn't be at Fang's business, T-City, even if it was at night, and it couldn't be here at the office.

But he did know a place Fang liked to visit that was as private as any place in Tacoma or the surrounding area; the roving location of a cock-fighting pit that moved from one rural farm to the next every week.

Fang was old fashioned and wouldn't discuss business over the phone, but he did use end-to-end encrypted messaging using Telegram's Secret Chat mode.

Jackson opened the Telegram app on his iPhone, selected "Snake" in his contacts, tapped "More" and hit "Start Secret Chat".

We need to talk. Meet me at the pit tomorrow night.

He knew Fang always came to the cock fights with security and would make sure no law enforcement personnel were in attendance. He would do the same, of course, but he would know ahead of time that it was safe to attend. The host of the roving cockfights was the brother of one of his employees.

TWENTY-ONE

Drake spent a quiet hour after leaving Casey's office thinking about what to tell President Ballard about the meeting between the Chinese consulate official and the man believed to be the new leader of the Los Zheng cartel. More specifically, what he would tell the president they should do about it when he was asked.

They already knew that China's practice of Unrestricted Warfare involved supplying Mexican drug cartels with fentanyl to weaken America. The year before, after being kidnapped by a Chinese triad in Australia, he'd gone head-to-head with the triad and the cartel that resulted in putting the triad leader in a U.S. maximum-security prison.

China had wisely used the triad as a proxy in its war against America to be able to deny its involvement in the plot. Sending a Chinese official from its consulate in Tijuana signaled that China was willing to risk being found out that it was working with the cartel and wasn't worried about what the U.S. would do about it.

Meeting with the cartel's leader could also mean China was widening its secret war and was planning something new.

If that was the case, helping friends in Mexico in their fight against the cartels wasn't going to be enough to counter a potential new threat from China.

They would have to use all the weapons in their arsenal to find out what China was planning and then take the offensive before China's aggression triggered a war neither country wanted.

And when they took the offensive, it had to be done in a way that didn't expose the support they were providing Las Sombras.

Drake jotted down the short list of recommendations for the president and opened Contacts on his phone and scrolled down to "Ben" to have a private and secure conversation with President Benjamin Ballard.

"Adam, I'm going upstairs and drink some bourbon to forget about the meeting I just left. I hope you have good news for me."

"I wish I did, Mr. President."

"Give me a moment to take my tie off, pour a glass and I'm all yours."

Drake heard the president say something to a Secret Service agent, close the door of his study and drop ice in a glass.

"Okay, what's the news I don't want to hear?"

"I have video of a Chinese consulate official meeting with the man believed to be the new leader of Los Zheng."

"Where and when was this meeting?"

"Mexicali, Mexico, yesterday."

"Do we know what the meeting was about?"

"We don't have audio, but the video shows the consulate official handing over a flash drive."

"Does this come by way of your friends in Mexico?"

"The video was given to one of their members. Their only involvement has been to send the video to me."

Drake heard the president sigh and the sound of ice being swirled around in his glass.

"Are you healed up enough, after your last go-round with these guys, to find out for me what the hell they're up to in Mexico?"

"I am, Mr. President."

"How will you do it?"

"I thought I'd ask my Mexican friends to find out what they can about the Chinese consulate official from the Chinese consulate in Tijuana. Then, I'd like to use a private satellite surveillance company in San Francisco, Planet Labs, to find where the new leader of Los Zheng is hanging out. If Los Zheng is planning on doing something more than selling drugs, satellite imagery might help us figure out what it is. It will also give us the location of Zheng's new leader for my friends to hunt down."

"Be careful with footprints in Mexico," President Ballard said.

"I understand, sir."

Whatever he did with Las Sombras in Mexico to an agent of China with diplomatic immunity could create an international crisis. No matter what they proved the consulate official was doing with Los Zheng, it would be lost in the noise that China would create in the news.

Arranging for satellite surveillance of locations in Baja California wouldn't make anyone suspicious. Puget Sound Security and Information Services had American companies with plants in Mexico who were clients in Mexico and disclosing the purpose for the satellite surveillance wasn't required.

But identifying the Chinese consulate official would be, unless he could think of a way to do it without involving the president or anyone in the Department of Homeland Security or the FBI.

Kevin McRoberts could, he was confident, access the IT system the Chinese consulate in Tijuana maintained without being discovered. Identifying the consulate official's name would be easy, but finding out who he really was and why he was meeting with Los Zheng wouldn't be. The risk that Kevin would set off alerts if he hacked into the consulate system, therefore, wasn't worth taking.

But there was someone they knew that kept a close eye on China and its operatives who might be able to identify the consulate official. The PSSIS penetration contract they had with the New Zealand Defence Force involved probing the NZDF system for vulnerabilities and finding out enemies who were trying to gain access to New Zealand's secrets. China was enemy number one and New Zealand, and its neighbor Australia, kept a close eye on Chinese diplomats and officials in their countries and shared information with their allies.

Casey and Mark Holland, the head of their Sound Security and Information Services division and former chief of the NYPD's Counterintelligence Bureau, made friends with New Zealand Defence Force's top brass last year when SSIS initiated its IT system penetration work there.

Holland would be the best person to ask the NZDF for help to identify the Chinese consulate official in Tijuana, but Holland wasn't privy to what they were doing in Mexico with Las Sombras. Casey was, though, and he would have to be the one to ask for New Zealand's help identifying Chinese officials they knew about operating abroad.

TWENTY-TWO

Drake and Liz were sitting at a table in Como's restaurant at the Woodmark Hotel, talking softly about their appointment with her obstetrician that afternoon, when Drake saw Colonel Walker with the hostess and waived to him.

Walker was dressed casually, wearing a cervical brace above a white fisherman sweater, tan khakis, and brown penny loafers, moving somewhat stiffly as he walked toward them.

Drake stood to shake hands as Colonel Walker asked, "I hope I'm not dressed too informally for a restaurant like this?"

"You're fine, Colonel. New clothes?"

"I left the hospital wearing a pair of jeans and a work shirt a janitor loaned me," he said. "We stopped at a mall in Tacoma to buy these. Liz, you look radiant tonight."

"Thank you, colonel. How are you feeling?" she asked, as she saw him sitting down carefully.

"A little sore, but I'll mend."

"Would you like something to drink?" Drake asked when he saw Colonel Walker looking at Liz's berry spritzer.

"That looks good, Liz. May I ask what it is?"

"It's a blackberry and strawberry nonalcoholic spritzer," she smiled. "Doctor's orders."

"Then I'll have a Jack Daniels," Colonel Walker said with a wink. "My doctor's orders as well."

"I'm sorry about your Airstream," Liz said.

"I am too, but it's insured."

Their server came to their table and asked, "Would you like something else from our bar?"

"Colonel Walker would like a Jack Daniel's and I'll have Maker's Mark."

"Certainly, sir. How would like your drinks served?"

"Neat, for me," Drake said. "Colonel?"

"Just a splash of water, thank you."

When the server left, Colonel Walker thanked Drake for his room and insisted on paying for it. "I may be here for a while and that suite looks expensive."

"We keep it for visiting clients, colonel, and it's very reasonable. It's yours for as long as you need it."

"Thank you, Adam."

Their server brought their Jack Daniel's and Maker's Mark and announced the night's specials and left, to give them time to look at their menus.

"I don't eat a lot of Italian food. What are you two having?" Colonel Walker asked after glancing at his menu.

"I usually let Liz order for me," Drake said. "Italian food's her favorite."

"Colonel, I usually order an antipasto, like the Capaccio for me and the Lopez Island clams for Adam. Then, an order of Tortelli with crab for me and the Risotto with crab for Adam. Last, I like the steelhead and Adam likes the New York Strip," Liz said.

"Let's make it simple. I'll have whatever you order for Adam," Colonel Walker said.

After Liz ordered for them and Drake added a bottle of Cabernet

Sauvignon to go with their steaks, Drake asked the colonel what he thought about Jeff Jackson after seeing him again.

"He knows more than he's saying, that's for sure. I never told him someone was trying to kill me, but he knew that's what someone intended with the explosion.

"There may be any number of people he knows in law enforcement who knew it was C4 and not propane that exploded," Drake said.

"Yes, but I still think he knows."

"What are you going to do now?" Liz asked.

"I'm going to try something else," Colonel Walker said. "Did you ever hear about the "Ash Street Shootout?"

"No, I haven't," Liz said.

"I have. It's modern-day Army Ranger history they're proud of," Drake said.

"In the fall of 1989, an Army Ranger from Fort Lewis bought a cheap house in the Hilltop area of Tacoma on Ash Street, as an investment," Colonel Walker explained. "Tacoma and the Hilltop area was like the Wild West, with gang shootings and drug dealers on every corner.

"The police weren't doing anything, so the Ranger started video recording the gang activity at a house across the street. He got into an argument with its gang members who told him to stop. When he refused, they started throwing rotten pears at his house and tried to shoot out his video camera in an upper room window, before than ran away.

"The Ranger called his off-duty Ranger buddies at Fort Lewis to come and help him defend his home. They showed up armed for a barbecue he'd invited them to.

"The Ranger then went over to the gang members' house, suggested they stop shooting at his house, stop selling drugs, and turn their lives around. They told him to mind his own business and he left.

"Later that night, the gang members started shooting across the street from their darkened house and the Rangers returned fire. Three hundred rounds of ammunition were fired in ten short minutes or so. No one was killed or injured, but a 911 call resulted in police cruisers swarming the area and the gang members fleeing, except two who were arrested.

"The army considered the shootout to be self-defense, and Tacoma's mayor was ready to impose a city-wide version of martial law, and the governor was ready to send in the National Guard. The shootout got national attention and gave birth to the Safe Street movement in Tacoma that turned things around in the city."

"I don't understand how that story is going to help you find out who blew up your trailer, colonel," Liz said.

"I got a little carried away telling that story, Liz. I'm sorry. I should have said I knew some of those Rangers, and I know a Special Forces chaplain at Fort Lewis McChord. The military keeps a close eye on drug activity and the sex trade that might entangle any of the base personnel. I'm going to see my chaplain friend and see if he knows anything that will help me find the dealer selling Adderall at the high school and the sex traffickers who may have kidnapped Madison Sanchez."

TWENTY-THREE

Jefferson Jackson flashed his lights three times before turning off the rural road onto a muddy rutted path. A man wearing an olive green military surplus rain parka holding an AR-15 at port arms stood blocking his way.

Jackson rolled down his window and held out a five-dollar bill folded in half. "Evening, Jones."

"Take it slow, the road's a mess."

"That's why I drove the Hummer," Jackson said.

"Enjoy the evening, sir."

The cockfight was held this week on a farm east of Puyallup, Washington, out near Bonney Lake. A dilapidated old barn at the rear of the property was all that was left of some family's abandoned dream of living off the land.

If they'd been willing to take the risk, Jackson thought, they could be making a fortune today. With the revenue earned from renting the land for the cockfights, and their cut of the other accompanying income sources from drug and arms sales that took place, they'd be living high on the hog.

It was all illegal, of course, but sometimes you had to break a few rules to live the life you wanted.

Two hundred yards down the muddy path, another man wearing Mossy Oak camo hunting clothing with a shotgun in his left hand motioned for Jackson to turn into a grassy field, where pickups and cars were parked in rows.

He had to walk another hundred yards to reach the barn. From the yells and cheering coming from inside, he knew the evening's entertainment was well under way.

In the center of the open space beneath a hayloft was a circular pit with a two-foot high gray PVC wall, surrounded by men cheering on two fighting gamecocks they were betting on to win.

Jackson saw Ruben Fang on the other side of the pit, standing in front of a plywood table on sawhorses that served as the bar for the evening. Fang was holding a shot glass in his left hand and a bottle of tequila in his right hand.

When Jackson joined him, Fang held out a new shot glass and the bottle. "It's not the Patrón you like, but it's not bad."

"Thanks."

"Why am I here?" Fang asked.

"Because you enjoy the fights and have a problem you should know about."

"What problem would that be?"

"Remember that army colonel I told you about? The one asking me if I knew someone in a street gang selling Adderall to kids at Stadium High School. He came back, asking if I knew anyone driving a black Honda Civic with loud pipes? Like the one Adonis drives."

"Did he say why he was looking for a black Honda Civic?"

"He thinks it has something to do with his trailer being blown up," Jackson said, watching to see how Fang reacted.

Fang smiled and refilled his shot glass. "Maybe he had a bad propane tank or something. Why are you telling me this?"

"Because I need to know why this Special Forces chaplain keeps coming around asking questions. If you tried to take him out, I need to know it. I think he thinks I'm involved and he isn't going away."

Fang moved closer and tapped Jackson's chest with his shot glass. "You are involved. You told me where he was camping. So, you take care of the chaplain. He doesn't know anything about me. If he comes after me, it will be because of you. Then I will come after you and you don't want that."

Jackson pushed Fang back and said, "If anyone comes after you, it will be the FBI. They're investigating the girl you kidnapped. She was the girlfriend of the kid who overdosed and brought the chaplain here asking questions.

Fang blinked twice and glared at Jackson. "Be careful, Jackson. You're the one who should be worried about the FBI."

"What's that supposed to mean?"

"I think you know what I mean."

Jackson smiled and set his shot glass on the sheet of plywood. "I said what I came to say, Fang. Clean up the mess you and Adonis made and maybe we'll both be okay."

He saw Fang look toward one of his bodyguards and shake his head. Walking around the fighting pit to leave, where one handler was holding his gamecock up in victory and the other handler was picking his dead bird up from the blood-stained sand, he saw two more of Fang's men near the barn's door.

Jackson stopped to speak with his employee's brother on the far side of the pit, who was hosting the night's event and was in charge of security. When he turned around to look back to see where Fang was, he saw that he was staring at him.

"Jimmy, Ruben Fang has two men back there with him, and two others over there across from you. When I leave, make sure none of them follow me to my car."

"Roger that, JJ. Want an escort to your car?"

"No, I'm good," Jackson said, pulling back his long brown canvas jacket he liked to wear with his brown Stetson Bozeman hat and his

Tecova boots. He was carrying a Heckler and Koch MP5A3 on a sling under his jacket.

A light rain was falling as he walked to the field and down a row of cars and trucks to his Hummer, worried about what Fang had said about why he should be worried about the FBI.

The money he took from Fang for making sure rival street gangs got tired of the extra attention they received when they were on the Hilltop Gangster's turf, and took their business somewhere else, wasn't something the FBI would know about. Even if they did, the FBI would leave it to local law enforcement to deal with. When it did, his sources with the Tacoma PD and Pierce County Sheriff's Department would let him know about it.

The only thing the FBI would be interested in was knowing about his involvement in the 412 militia, and there was no way Fang could know about that. He never met with the other members, and they only communicated with each other by using their Nokia XR20 military-grade phones that had encrypted text messaging.

There was no way Fang knew about the 412s, or that he was a member. If he did, they were all in trouble.

RUBEN FANG WAITED until Jackson disappeared into the dark night outside the barn before he called his enforcer waiting for him at T-City.

"Jihao, I need to move swiftly tonight," Fang said. "Have Adonis and his crew meet us at the warehouse at midnight. Don't explain why, just say "Do as you are told". Go into my office and bring my supply of special Adderall pills. We'll see how well they work."

"When they do, what do you want me to do with them afterwards?"

"Take the bodies to the park where they hang out. We'll let the other members of his crew who just do the street selling find them tomorrow. If they come in the black Honda Civic Adonis drives, leave it at the warehouse. I need it to disappear."

"Understood," Jihao said. "Are you meeting me at the warehouse?"

"I'm an hour from town, at the warehouse."

Fang left the barn with his four bodyguards in a box formation on the way to his used black Ford Expedition that he kept at T-City. He was thinking about who the Hilltop Gangsters might choose as their new leader, or whether it would be smarter to just replace the Hilltop Gangsters and find a new gang to handle distribution.

When his driver stopped an hour later in front of the two sliding doors of his warehouse at the Port of Tacoma, he honked twice for one of the doors to open.

When it rolled back Fang saw that Adonis had driven his black Honda Civic. The three Hilltop Gangsters who were with him when they dropped the C4 bomb on the Airstream trailer were leaning back on his car, talking with Adonis.

Jihao pulled the door closed when the Expedition was inside and walked to the passenger side door to open it for his boss.

Fang waited for his four bodyguards to get out and go stand behind the Hilltop Gangsters, before he got out and walked over to stand in front of them.

He crossed his arms over his chest with Jihao at his side and looked each gang member in the eye, one by one.

"I learned tonight that you violated my trust and did not keep the promise you made to me," Fang said. "I am very disappointed and very angry."

He watched as Adonis looked back at him, while Dreads, Razor and Bats looked around at each other nervously.

"How did we do that?" Adonis asked.

Fang smiled. "Did you think I wouldn't find out, Adonis? That you were meeting the growing demand for Adderall that developed during the pandemic by getting Adderall with methamphetamine from someone else? All to make more money than you were making from what I supplied you?"

"That ain't true!" Adonis said. "You're our only supplier!"

"Oh, it's true all right," Fang said. "One of your customers came to my place of business and complained about the product you sold him. Don't lie to me, Adonis."

"Boss, I swear to you. You're the only one we work for?"

"Do you like the stuff Sinaloa is giving you better than our product? Is that it?" Fang shouted."

"No, boss! I swear!" Adonis shouted.

"Maybe it's time for me to bend the rules and let you try the product I give you to sell. Then you can tell me if you like their product better than mine," Fang said. "Jihao, give them each one Adderall pill and let's see what they say."

Fang saw them relax when they thought all they had to do to escape punishment for their side hustle was swallow the pills, say they were sorry, and promise they wouldn't sell anyone's product than his ever again.

Adonis was smiling when Jihao handed him one of the Adderall pills they kept in a locked safe, and then quickly moved down the line giving each one a pill.

As soon as he swallowed his pill, Adonis's lips turned blue and gurgling sounds combined with frantic gasping for air started within seconds, before he crumpled and fell onto the cold cement floor.

The other three members of the Hilltop Gangsters swiftly joined Adonis on the floor, with foam spewing from their lips.

Jihao stepped back to Fang's side. "You want us to clean them up?"

"I want them found just like this to be added to the tragic list of Tacoma's drug overdose victims," Fang said. "Leave their bodies in that park, close to the house where they were living. Make sure no one sees you."

"What about his Honda?"

"Put it in the shipping container. We'll send it south with our next shipment of T-shirts and girls."

Fang took the keys from the bodyguard for his Expedition and left his men to move the bodies. He needed a good night's sleep before deciding what he was going to do about Jeff Jackson.

He'd told Jackson to take care of the chaplain himself, but he doubted that Jackson would follow through and do it. The man may have killed when he was in the army, but from the text messages Huang told him Jackson exchanged with his 412 buddies, Jackson was keeping his nose clean. 412 wanted to remain a secret militia and made sure none of its members were attracting the attention of law enforcement.

Jackson and his men did a good job running off rival street gangs for him, and he didn't mind the money he paid him for the service. But that wasn't the reason Jackson was important to him. It was his involvement with the 412s.

If this chaplain wasn't going away, as Jackson was convinced he wouldn't, it was something he'd probably have to take care of himself. And that meant he needed to know more about the chaplain.

TWENTY-FOUR

Colonel Walker took the exit off I-5 South Wednesday morning nine miles southwest of Tacoma, Washington, and entered Joint Base Lewis-McChord through the Madigan Gate to meet his chaplain friend for lunch.

After showing his Department of Defense ID card, Walker drove the green Avis Ford Edge he rented and followed his directions to 9179 Cramer Avenue, where the Odin Café in the 1st Special Forces Group Warrior Restaurant was located.

Major Brad Michaels, a chaplain for the 1st SFG(A) had not only agreed to meet with him but was buying his lunch.

Maj. Michaels was waiting at the door of the red brick building and saluted Colonel Walker when he approached. Colonel Walker returned the salute.

"Welcome to Joint Base Lewis-McChord, Colonel," Major Michaels aid.

"Good to see you again, Brad."

"How are you spending your time, now that you're retired?" Michaels asked, as he held the door open for Walker.

"That's what I'm here to talk about."

The Odin Café was consistently rated as one of the best, if not the best restaurant on the base. Walker saw why, as they made their selections for lunch.

Major Michaels led the way and ordered Balsamic Pot Roast, Italian Potato Salad and Tuscan Kale with Tomatoes. Colonel Walker felt obliged to try the Chef's Baked Salmon, Lemon Cilantro Pasta and Cauliflower Parmesan.

"I heard they spoiled you guys out here," Walker said when they were sitting across from each other at a long cafeteria-style white table with individual black chairs.

"They take good care of us, Colonel."

"How's the family?"

"Mary is teaching at the base elementary school to keep an eye on Billy, age 9, and Mia, age 7. Everyone is healthy and we like it here. Where are you living now?"

"I'm a rolling stone these days," Walker said. "I had a travel trailer, until it was blown up the other day. Someone dropped a charge of C4 on it from a small drone. I'm staying at a hotel in Bellevue now."

Michaels stopped a fork of potato salad halfway to his mouth and stared. "Your trailer was blown up here, stateside?"

"Yeah, I was camping at Dash Point State Park."

"I was going to ask why you're wearing a cervical brace. Is that why?"

"I was lucky. I heard the drone and stepped outside my trailer just before the explosion."

"Wow! You have enemies that followed you here?"

"I don't know who's responsible, but I will find out."

Both men concentrated on eating for several minutes, before Walker asked, "Brad, one of my soldier's sons overdosed in Tacoma after taking Adderall laced with fentanyl recently. I told him I'd try to identify the dealer and see that he's held accountable. He was losing control of his anger, wanted to kill someone, and was smart enough to call and ask for my help.

"I've been to the Tacoma Police Department and the Pierce County Sheriff's Department. I'm not getting anywhere. To add to that, the boy's girlfriend has been kidnapped.

"I know you and the other chaplains hear things counseling soldiers and their families and might know someone around here who's familiar with the high school drug scene. Also, someone working with victims of sex trafficking. I think it's a waste of time trying to get information from local law enforcement."

"Is helping your soldier the reason someone blew up your trailer?"

"Probably," Walker said. "Why?"

"I know a nonprofit organization that might be able help. They won't get directly involved to help you, because they'll worry you might put girls in danger they rescue at their facility. But they work with an outreach minister who helps them rescue girls."

"Do you know the minister?"

"No, I do not. The woman who started the nonprofit met with us to explain the work she was doing and mentioned the outreach minister. You will have to talk with her. I have her number on my phone."

"Thanks, I'd like to speak with her."

Major Michaels got up and said, "I'm going back for dessert. Would you like some carrot cake?"

"No, I'm fine. Thanks."

Walker watched his younger friend stop and shake hands and talk with two soldiers, before returning with a piece of carrot cake on a plate. The two soldiers he talked with followed him back and stood behind him when he sat back down.

"Colonel Walker, sir, it's a pleasure to see you again," the taller of the two soldiers said.

"Thank you, Master Sergeant."

"Are you living in the Northwest now, sir?" the other soldier asked.

"Just visiting, sergeant," Colonel Walker told SFC Connors.

"Enjoy your visit, sir," MSG Rodrigues said. "Just wanted to say hello."

Colonel Walker watched the men leave and said, "Master Sergeant Rodrigues was my instructor when I went back for a MACP refresher at Bragg."

"I knew you completed Q-Course and wear the beret, but why did you need a refresher course in hand-to-hand combat?" Major Michaels asked.

"I liked competing with the guys when I'm deployed. It helped me stay sharp and keep in shape. Now, glad I did," he said and pointed to his cervical brace. "You never know when a little extra training might come in handy."

TWENTY-FIVE

The executive director of the 501c3 nonprofit restoration home for young sex trafficking victims wouldn't identify the outreach street minister she knew, but she did agree to meet Colonel Walker at a café in Wilkeson, Washington, for coffee.

Forty-five minutes after leaving Fort Lewis and driving east on WA Route 167, he pulled into the small town at the foot of the Carbon Glacier entrance to Mount Rainier and stopped at the Nomad PNW café.

Katrina Diaz was sitting at the only occupied table in the café, smiling at him when he walked in. She was dressed casually in jeans, a red plaid shirt, and was wearing laced hiking boots.

Colonel Walker walked to her table and leaned down to shake her hand. "Ms. Diaz, thank you for agreeing to meet with me."

She held up her cup of coffee and said, "This is the best coffee in the state. You should try their oak milk latte with honey."

"I might get some to go when I leave, thanks," Walker said and sat across the small table from her.

"You're a retired army chaplain, Colonel. Why are you interested in finding someone who knows people involved in sex trafficking young women in Tacoma? I know who gave you my name, but I don't understand why Colonel Warner thinks I might be able to help you."

"A young woman was kidnapped in Tacoma. I think it might have something to do with the sex trade there."

"But why are you looking for this young woman?" she asked. "Is she someone you know?"

"No, I don't know her or her family. I know a father whose son overdosed on Adderall. The son's girlfriend is the one who was kidnapped."

"That doesn't explain why you are looking for this young woman?"

"Ms. Diaz, I'm not a threat to Madison Sanchez, that's her name. She and the son of my soldier were using street-dealer Adderall to help prepare for their exams. It's possible Madison was kidnapped because she can identify the dealer who sold them the Adderall. He knows we're looking for him."

"Is it possible Madison is running away from something," Katrina Diaz asked. "Some of the girls who wind up in the sex trade left home because of an abusive father or a messed-up family life. Sixty percent of sex trafficked young girls or boys are runaways and have been bounced around in the foster care system."

"Madison was an Advanced Placement student with good grades and a stable family life, as far as I know," Colonel Walker said. "I don't think she was running away from anything."

Katrina Diaz rested her elbow on the table and cradled her chin in her left hand. "What will you do with Madison if you find her? These girls need a lot of help to recover from a life no person would ever knowingly choose. They're sold for sex ten to fifteen times a day or more, beaten by their pimps, kept hooked on drugs and fed maybe once a day. When they're rescued, they're suffering from PTSD, depression, guilt, and they're often suicidal. Will Madison get the help she needs if you find her?"

"I promise you she will."

Ms. Diaz sat back and folded her hands in her lap. "The odds are you'll never find Madison, Colonel Walker. The traffickers move their assets around from market to market and overseas. Or they sell them as sex slaves on online auctions, to be thrown away when they're no longer young and desirable.

"But if it will help, I'll give you the name and number of the person who helps us rescue young girls in Tacoma and Seattle. His name is Bobby Turner. He's a twenty-something Latino whose sister was kidnapped, and sex trafficked.

Bobby isn't ordained but works as a volunteer with rescue organizations. He's supported by a few local churches and knows the Tacoma streets and the prostitutes who work there. I'll let him know who you are and why you want to talk with him."

Colonel Walker left the Nomad PNW café with a Mexican Mocha and a ham and cheese empanada for the drive back to Seattle. With any luck, he was one step closer to finding Madison Sanchez and the drug dealer he was looking for.

As an army chaplain, he was aware of the world-wide sex trade and the profits it generated for the sex traffickers, and more recently for the Mexican drug cartels. It was the fastest-growing criminal enterprise in the world.

Selling under-age girls for sex could make a pimp a hundred and fifty thousand to two hundred thousand dollars a year per child. Which helped to explain why five hundred to seven hundred children were forced into prostitution each year in Seattle, according to news reporting in King County, Washington, he'd read.

Deployed in the Middle East, Africa, and South America, he'd seen the worst of humanity exploiting children, and it had always made his blood boil. But still, getting acquainted with the scope of sex trafficking at home in America shocked him.

As a Christian man, he knew he was supposed to hate the sin but love the sinner. But when he came face to face with the men who kidnapped Madison Sanchez, he prayed he'd remember both the former and the latter of those teachings.

TWENTY-SIX

Bobby Turner was waiting in a booth for Colonel Walker when he entered the ParkWay Tavern in Tacoma early Wednesday evening. The tavern was a classic neighborhood gathering place, with an old neon sign out front and seating for maybe thirty people. It was in the Stadium District, not far from the Stadium High School where Madison Sanchez was kidnapped.

Turner waved when Walker looked his way and slid out of the booth to greet him.

"Colonel Walker?" he asked.

"One and the same," Walker replied. "Thanks for meeting with me."

"Katrina's a friend and I trust her. I hope you're okay meeting in a tavern."

Colonel Walker smiled and said, "I was in the army for thirty years. I've been in a few taverns."

Turner nodded toward his pint of beer on the table and asked, "Get you something? They have over thirty craft beers."

"Coors Light, I grew up in Colorado."

Walker watched the young man walk to the bar and return with a pint for him.

"That's where I'm from too, Denver," Turner said, when he sat down.

"How did you get to Tacoma?"

"Did Katrina tell you my story?"

"She told me about your sister and the work you're doing."

At the mention of his sister, Turner looked across the room with a faraway look in his eyes. "I came here looking for my sister. Seattle and Tacoma are centers for sex trafficking on the west coast."

"I'm sorry about your sister," Walker said. "When was she kidnapped?"

"She was twelve, five years ago. I'll find her someday."

"I'm buying, what's good here?" Walker asked to change the subject.

"I've only had the Jalapeño Cheeseburger and it was good."

Colonel Walker ran his finger down the menu on the table and raised it to get their server's attention.

When the server left with an order for two Jalapeño Cheeseburgers, with salt and vinegar Kettle Chips, Turner leaned back in the booth and asked, "How can I help you, Colonel?"

"Madison Sanchez was taken from the parking lot of Stadium High School ten days ago. Her boyfriend overdosed on fake Adderall laced with fentanyl. I told the boy's father I would help him find the dealer who sold them the drugs. Madison knows who the dealer is, and I think that's why she was kidnapped. If I find her, I can help my friend with closure about his son's death."

"So, you're not trying to find this dealer on behalf of Madison's family," Turner asked.

"Not directly. Her father was the one who contacted my friend and told him about her kidnapping. Her father thinks her kidnapping and her boyfriend's death might be related. My friend said he'd try to help find her. I'm trying to help them both."

"Why are you trying to help them?"

Walker sat back in the booth when their server arrived with their burgers, and waited until they were alone again before explaining.

"When you're an army chaplain, you get close to the men you're serving. The bond you create lasts beyond your time serving with them. I tell all my soldiers that if they need help with anything to call me. My friend, who is still enlisted, reached out to me and that's why I'm here in Tacoma."

Turner nodded his head and said, "Okay, tell me what you know about Madison Sanchez while I'm eating."

Walker grinned at the young man's apparent satisfaction at hearing him explain his motivation. "Madison Sanchez is seventeen and a student at Stadium High School. A witness saw her being tossed in a van in the school's parking lot after her basketball practice. She was an AP student with good grades, and from what I know, had a stable home life. Tacoma Police and the FBI are investigating, but they haven't discovered anything that identifies the kidnappers, or a motive for taking her."

Turner set his burger down and shook his head, "The motive for taking her isn't going to help find her. It could be to sex traffic her, or a gang's party, or so she can't identify the dealer you mentioned. It could be all the above. But you're on the right track, looking for the dealer. The cartels have increased their profits by taking over the sex trade. They let their street dealers bring them young girls."

"Do you have any idea who the street dealers are who might have taken Madison?"

"I have an idea that I can check out. It might take a little time."

"Do we have a little time?" Walker asked.

"Not much to find Madison. They move the girls around to other cities, other markets. Sometimes, even out of the country. If they moved her, she could be anywhere. But the people who took her will still be around. That's where I'll start."

"Is there anything I can do to help you?"

"Maybe," Turner said. "Do you have a computer?"

Walker had to think for a moment before he realized he didn't have his laptop anymore. It was in his travel trailer when it exploded.

"Not at the moment."

"If Madison is here, they might have a picture of her on one of their websites. If she's out of the area, there are too many websites to search them all. But you could look at auction websites where they sell girls online to see if she's on display there. Do you know if Madison was a virgin?"

"No, I don't." Walker said. "Why?"

"Young virgins are sold worldwide for top dollar on these websites. They feature them on these sites, dress them up and make them look pretty. If she's one of them, they'll take good care of her until she's sold. If she's lucky, she might be one they take good care of."

"I don't know if I'd call that being lucky."

"No, it would be lucky because it would give you more time to find her," Tucker said.

TWENTY-SEVEN

Chen Huang waited for the dust to settle before getting out of the military green Boeing MD-500 helicopter, with markings identical to the small attack helicopters the Mexican army flew. He used it to fly from his mountain cartel hideout to the abandoned sulfur mine forty-nine kilometers south of Mexicali they would use to stage an attack on America's power grid.

The Ministry of State Security (MSS), China's intelligence service, used one of China's biggest mining companies as cover to acquire the rights to the sulfur mine and hide it's real purpose in the China's expanding global mining activities.

Sulfur, he knew, was a mineral that most industrial processes required massive amounts of and was called "Devil's Gold." Mined it in sufficient tonnage could make the mining company a profit, but Huang knew the old mine would never become operational.

The man camp that had been constructed onsite to accommodate a thousand Chinese workers, would only house a hundred PLA soldiers at a time, as they waited to be smuggled across the border. If the United States was willing to let people illegally enter their country, China was willing to take advantage of the opportunity and get as many of its soldiers in the country as it could.

You could only shake your head in amazement, he thought, as he walked to his temporary office at the mine, *at how the country that saw itself as the leader of the world could be so foolish.*

Huang passed the portable building the mine's manager used for an office to greet Mexican officials when they visited the site, and continued onto a luxury motorhome, built for him by the world's largest bus converter, Marathon Coach in Oregon, to be used as an office when he was there to coordinate his non-cartel business for the MSS.

His aide-de-camp was standing at attention under the awning by the door of the motorhome to greet him.

"Get the Sergeant Major for me," Huang said, as his aide opened the motorhome's door for him. "Are his men ready to leave?"

"Yes, sir. They're moving out as soon as it's dark."

Huang nodded and stepped up into the coolness of his office on wheels. Wiping the sweat off his forehead, he walked to the refrigerator in the middle of the motorhome and selected a bottle of Perrier. Continuing a few feet, he sat in one of two black leather swivel armchairs to wait for the Sergeant Major.

Of the two hundred soldiers who were at the mine, only twenty would travel north to deal with the Sinaloa crew trying to establish itself in Los Zheng's territory. When his cartel men helped them get across the border, they would ride in a tour bus to Washington State, with forged H-2A Temporary Agricultural permits, MSS created for the training exercise. After finding and executing the cartel's rivals, they would return to Mexico for further training.

Twenty soldiers would remain at the mine to provide security and maintain the illusion that they were there to reopen the old sulfur mine, where they would not have to speak English and blend into communities in America like the rest of the soldiers to be deployed.

Huang heard two knocks on the motorhome's door and Sergeant Major came up the steps and breathed in the cool air with a smile on his face.

"Grab a bottle from the refrigerator," Huang said and pointed. "Join me."

Sergeant Major Kwan was a veteran PLA soldier who looked uncomfortable, wearing jeans and a blue denim shirt with sleeves rolled up in front of a former Naval officer.

When the Sergeant Major settled into the armchair across a small oval table from Huang's chair, Huang asked, "How are your men?"

"Ready for the mission, sir."

Huang raised his hand and waved it in the space between them. "I don't doubt that, Sergeant Major. I want to know how they are dealing with being in Mexico, the heat and dust of this place. How is their morale? Are they questioning why they've been here at this old mine for a month? They must be curious."

"They're trained for combat, sir. Providing security here is like standing guard duty when they were recruits. They're mostly bored. There's not much to do here."

"Your trip north will break the monotony. Do you understand what I want you to do when you reach your destination tomorrow?"

"Yes, sir. Find the hideout and eliminate your cartel's rivals in Puyallup."

"I want a little more than that, Sergeant Major," Huang said. "I am here, acting as the head of a drug cartel, and drug cartels are as violent as our triads. After you use the kamikaze drones as practice for your real mission, move in quickly and behead of all the men with a chainsaw. Leave the heads on poles and put their dismembered body parts in a big pile. The brutality is a message to the other cartels."

"I understand, sir."

"When you return, I'll take you and your men to Mexicali for a little R&R. The cartel has a brothel there with some beautiful young girls. I need to check to see how the new girls are doing before the auction."

"Thank you, sir. The men will enjoy that."

TWENTY-EIGHT

The weather in the Pacific Northwest in the month of March was typically cold, rainy, and windy. Thursday morning driving to PSS headquarters, Drake was pleased to see patches of blue sky. It didn't mean the rest of the day would be warmer than it was that morning on his run with Lancer, but a glimpse of sunshine made the warmer weather of spring seem a little closer.

It also meant he was closer to becoming a father. Liz was as happy, decorating their guest bedroom as a nursery and preparing herself for the day or night when they would rush to the hospital.

He was happy as well, but he knew he was also getting closer to having to decide what his role at PSS was going to be in the future. Liz wasn't forcing the issue, but he knew it was something she was thinking about whenever he mentioned anything about the Chinese consulate officer they were trying to identify, or what the man's meeting with the head of Los Zheng might mean.

Which he had just done when he knocked on her office door and told her he was joining Mike to make the call to the New Zealand Security Service Director-General to ask for help identifying the Chinese consulate officer. It was her quick pursing of her lips that signaled she was worried about what his involvement might mean in the future.

Drake started to turn back in the hallway to say something to her, but decided to wait until sometime later when he knew what he was going to tell her.

Mike Casey was thumbing through a file when Drake knocked twice on the doorframe and entered his office.

Casey looked at his watch and said, "They're twenty hours ahead of us in New Zealand. I arranged to speak with the Director-General in ten minutes, ten in the morning her time."

"Do you want me to say anything about how we got the video of the meeting between the consulate officer and Los Zheng?" Drake asked.

"I'm hoping she won't press me too hard on that. I don't want her to know we have any connection to or involvement with our friends in Mexico. She knows that Sound Security and Information Solutions is an intelligence contractor and part of the U.S. intelligence community. She knew Mark Holland before we were down there negotiating the penetration contract for our work with the NZDF, and she knows he joined us to help put the new company together. I'm sure there will be a quid pro quo in exchange for anything she gives us, but that's to be expected."

"I think she'll understand why we don't want to say where we got the video, but she will want to know who the two Chinese men are as much as we do," Drake said.

Casey looked at his watch again and asked, "Ready?"

"Ready."

Casey tapped in the number he had for the NZSIS on his smartphone, a Finnish-made Bittium Tough Mobile 2C with a Signal encrypted app, and put it on speaker-mode for Drake to be included in the conversation.

"Mike Casey," he said to the NZSIS receptionist. "I have an appointment to speak with the Director-General."

"Certainly, Mr. Casey. She's ready for your call."

"Good afternoon, Mr. Casey. How's your weather in Seattle?"

"Good morning, Director-General. It's cold and windy today. I suppose it's warm and sunny in Wellington."

"Yes, clear skies and warm for March. What can I do for you today?"

"I have video of a Chinese consulate officer I need to identify. I'm hoping you can help me do that."

"Is this consulate officer in the U.S.?"

"No, he's in Mexico, posted to the consulate in Tijuana as a defense attaché, we've learned," Casey said.

"The second bureau of China's Ministry of State Security likes to use defense attachés as cover for its spies," she said. "Do we know his name?"

"The video was taken from a restaurant's security camera. He used the name Peter Lei for his reservation."

"Is there anything else you know about him?"

"He can be seen passing a USB drive to another man," Casey said. "We believe the second man is the head of a Chinese drug cartel in Mexico."

"Does this have anything to do with the fentanyl drug operation you took down last year?" the Director-General asked.

Casey chuckled and asked, "Are there no secrets?"

"Not from intelligence services, if they're any good. The ASIS shared information with us after they lost their man, Lucas Barrett. Their investigation learned about the abduction of your man, Adam Drake, and your rescue of him in Brisbane before you flew him here to New Zealand. He seems to have a reputation for catching out the bad guys. How is he, by the way?"

"Adam is fine and about to become a father. He's here with me now. Would you like to say hello?"

"Hello, Mr. Drake," she said. "Have you recovered from your injuries?"

"I have. Thank you for asking," Drake said. "Are you at liberty to tell me what the Aussie intelligence service found out about Lucas Barrett?"

"Unfortunately, they never found anything, other than his car being abandoned at a marina. The consensus at ASIS is that Sam Xueping, the man you dealt with, snatched him and dumped his body at sea from his yacht. We've heard rumors that your government has him in custody. Have you heard anything that I could pass along to ASIS?"

"No, and I can't confirm that he's in U.S. custody, Madame Director-General," Drake said with a wink at Mike Casey. "If it's true that we have him, I'm sure we'll find out what happened to Lucas and that information will be shared."

"Well, then it's nice to hear you're doing well, Mr. Drake. Mr. Casey, as soon as you can get the video to me, I'll get someone on it. We come across Chinese spies down here all the time. We'll check with the ASIS if we can't identify your man."

"Thank you," Casey said. "You'll have it by the end of the day."

Casey tapped his phone to end the call and smiled at Drake. "So, you now have a reputation for "catching out the bad guys."

"I guess that's one way of describing what keeps happening," Drake said.

TWENTY-NINE

Before leaving for the day and taking Liz out for dinner, Drake took the stairs down to the second floor to see Kevin McRoberts, PSS's Director of Information Technology.

Kevin was talking with an IT employee at her workstation when he entered the large open workspace, so Drake went to Kevin's office to wait for him.

"Sorry, Mr. Drake," Kevin said when he rushed in. "I didn't know you were coming."

"I didn't know myself until a minute ago, Kevin. I thought I should stop by for an update on the projects we talked about."

Kevin dropped into his chair and asked, "Where do you want me to start?"

"Do we have anything yet from Planet Labs on the satellite surveillance I ordered?"

"The first imagery came in this morning, but I can't see anything that might be where the cartel guy in the video might be hanging out," Kevin said. "The northern part of Baja California is rugged east of Tijuana. The only thing I did see that's a little weird is an old sulfur mine that someone's trying to mine it again. There's a large man camp there. The mine is down Highway 5 south of Mexicali."

"What's weird about it?"

"There's a lot of mining going on in Baja, but it's mostly for copper and gold. The old sulfur mine was abandoned because it wasn't profitable."

"Who owns the mine?"

"A company called World Industrial Minerals, LTD."

"Find out who owns it," Drake said. "What about Jeff Jackson?"

"Ah, that is another story. JJ Jackson, as his friends call him, is an interesting guy. I didn't find any direct connection between him and the retired Ranger colonel, "Bull" Browning, but I poked around in his and his company's finances. He's not getting rich with his security company, but he personally spends a lot of money on guns and stuff. A lot of money. So do a number of his employees."

"He's a vet and most of his employees probably are as well. What's a lot of money?"

"Fifty to sixty thousand dollars."

"That is a lot, but he owns the company. He probably writes most of it off."

"He might, but his employees cannot. There are seven other employees who spent an equal amount of money last year for weapons and equipment. None of them make enough money to afford a personal arsenal that expensive. And here's the most interesting thing about it; they're all buying the same things. 300 Blackout AR-15s and Sig Sauer P320s from ghost weapon suppliers, so they can be privately assembled and be untraceable. FLIR PVS-7 night vision goggles that cost $9,250.00. Thousands of rounds of ammunition. Why would all of them buy the same exact equipment?"

"I have a good idea," Drake said. "Dig as deep as you can on each employee, including Jackson. I want to know everything about them; where they grew up, where they went to school, where they served in the army and which branch, their hobbies, families, everything. We might not have found a connection between these men and "Bull"

Browning, but we found a group of men arming themselves for war. Like some militia armorer had given them a list of things to buy, and money to buy them with, and said to be prepared when you're called. I want to know who these guys are and who is paying for these weapons."

"I'll find out, Mr. Drake."

Drake took the stairs to the third floor deep in thought. Colonel Walker was right about Jackson and his security company. They were hiding something. He wasn't surprised that Jackson and the vets he employed might be militia men, but Kevin hadn't found anything that explained how they could afford the expensive materiel they each had.

And then there was Colonel Walker's suspicion that Jackson knew the person or persons who bombed his Airstream trailer and, why they did it. If he was right about the car cruising the park the night they bombed his trailer being the type of a street racer punks and street gangs liked to drive, was Jackson connected to them in some way?

He knew community police forces organized in Mexico to protect their families from the smaller cartels, and took money from a larger cartel to keep anyone from setting up business on their turf. In a way, it was like what Jackson's security company did to protect neighborhoods by running off the street dealers.

It seemed unlikely that Jackson would be stupid enough to take money from a cartel to help it protect its turf from a rival. You couldn't hide that kind of selective private security services for very long from clients who were paying good money to keep just some of the drug dealers out of their neighborhoods.

But it would be one way for him to pay for the things that he and his employees were buying. And it might explain why Jackson knew someone intended to kill Colonel Walker.

Proving that Jackson was in bed with a cartel wouldn't be easy, but he was beginning to think it might make sense to try. Colonel

Walker didn't have the resources to do it by himself, as much as he might want to, but PSS did.

It was something he would have to think about. Right now, he needed to think about finding a nice restaurant where he could spend time with Liz and make sure he knew what she expected from him in the coming months. Thinking about identifying the Chinese consulate officer in Tijuana, and supporting his Los Sombra friends in Mexico, while trying to think about how he could help Colonel Walker was keeping him from focusing on his number one priority: his wife and their baby.

THIRTY

After getting a call from Bobby Turner, Colonel Walker waited at noon on Friday, in the same booth at the ParkWay Tavern they'd occupied previously. Turner had called to say he'd learned something about the Adderall dealer selling drugs to students at Stadium High School.

Turner took his Seahawks cap off when he arrived, shook it to get rid of the rain on it, and walked quickly over to Walker.

"It might be best if you leave now through the kitchen, colonel," he said, without sitting down. "Two members of a street gang followed me here."

"Are you in danger?" Walker asked.

"No, I don't think so. They know me, but they probably heard I was asking around about Madison Sanchez and her Adderall dealer at Stadium High. They'll want to know why."

"If they see me, they'll know why," Walker said.

"What do you mean?"

"Someone didn't like it when I was doing the same thing, asking about Madison. They've tried to make sure I'd never get the answers

I'm looking for. I suspect it was the street gang that sold the drugs to the kids at Stadium High."

"That would be the Hilltop Gangsters," Turner said. "It's their gang members who are outside."

"Sit down, Bobby. I'm not going anywhere. I'll get us some beer and you can tell me what you've learned before we have lunch. What was the craft beer you like?"

"The Skookum Porter, but Coors Light's fine. I don't have time to drink a growler."

Colonel Walker got out of the booth and walked to the window on the left side of the door. The two gang members were standing on the sidewalk across the street with their arms folded across their chests, staring at him. He waved and walked to the bar to order their beer.

While he was standing there, he saw Turner get up and head toward the men's room. When he returned, he came over and said, "There are two more of them out back."

"It's okay, Bobby," Walker said and handed him a can of Coors Light. "They won't come in after me. Let's sit down and talk."

When they were seated, Walker took his phone out and spent several minutes texting before asking, "Now, what did you find out about the drug dealer at the high school?"

"A girl I'm trying to get off the street told me the name of the current dealer at Stadium High. The former dealer went by the name of Adonis, but he overdosed two days ago, along with three other Hilltop Gangsters. The police found their bodies in a park near Stadium High."

"So, Adonis was the dealer who sold the Adderall to Madison Sanchez?"

"She said "Adonis" was the name everyone knew to call for Adderall."

"Did she know anything about Madison?"

"The only thing she knew was that she'd never seen Madison

around on the street or heard that she was working for any of the pimps she knew."

Walker tipped back his can of Coors Light and swallowed, before shaking his head. "I bought a new laptop and couldn't find anything online advertising Madison on any of the auction sites. She's just disappeared. Are the Hilltop Gangsters involved in sex trafficking here in Tacoma?"

"Not that I've heard," Turner said. "They're distributers for the Los Zheng cartel and they sex traffic young boys and girls."

"Do we know who runs the Los Zheng cartel's operation around here?" Walker asked.

"The rumor I've heard is the guy's nickname is "Viper", but that's all I know."

Walker looked at his watch and said, "Let's order something. They'll still be out there when we finish eating. We can deal with them then."

Turner raised his eyebrows and asked, "Deal with them how?"

"You'll see. What else is good here, other than a Jalapeño Cheeseburger?"

Turner hadn't tried anything else on the menu, so Walker ordered the Twisted Brit, a sliced roast beef and turkey sandwich with Tillamook Cheddar, lettuce, pickles, and maq sauce, whatever that was. Turner ordered another Jalapeño Cheeseburger.

As they waited for their food, Walker asked Turner about the girls he was trying to rescue. "How do they wind up working as prostitutes?"

"Most of them have been in and out of foster homes. They're runaways, who wind up latching onto the first guy they think really loves them and they wind up selling themselves to make him happy or have a place to stay. Some of them have left an abusive family situation where they've been abused by a father, a brother, or a mother who's ignoring what's going on.

"Occasionally, I'll find a girl from a good home, who's just rebellious and looking for some excitement and thinks the sex trade might be fun. It's not. It's an awful way to live, being sold multiple times a day, working long hours and being knocked around by her pimp."

"Why don't more of them let you help them get out?" Walker asked.

"They're afraid, ashamed of what they're doing, and traumatized. PTSD is often the first problem we deal with, when we get them out and help them learn the things they'll need to survive off the streets."

"I don't know how you do it, Bobby."

"I do it just like you do, I suppose," Turner said. "One person you're able to help makes up for a lot of ugly stuff you can't do anything about."

Colonel Walker heard the front door open and slid out of the booth with a smile on his face.

"Master Sergeant Rodrigues, it's good to see you and your friends," Colonel Walker said, reaching out to shake his hand, and then the hands of the other three Special Forces soldiers from Fort Lewis McChord standing behind him.

The soldiers Walker had invited for lunch were all wearing camo BDUs and blue Special Forces berets.

THIRTY-ONE

By the time Colonel Walker and his friends finished eating lunch, the two gang members were nowhere to be seen when they left the tavern. Walker promised his brothers-in-arms he'd come see them again before saying good-bye and walking down the street with Bobby Turner at his side.

"Are you worried about being followed and seen meeting me?" Walker asked.

"I let them know I don't work with the police, and they've left me alone," Turner said. "I'll be okay."

"Bobby, this is different. They know I'm looking for one of their gang members. That was enough to make them come after me before. The fact the dealer is dead may not make a difference. Why don't you take a short vacation somewhere until this gets sorted out?"

"Colonel, I appreciate your concern, but I can't leave the girls I'm trying to pull out. I'll be careful, I promise."

"Make sure you do," Walker said. "Keep my card and call me if you think you're in danger."

"Roger that, colonel," Turner said, saluting and walking off on down the street.

Walker opened the door of his rented Ford Edge and stood with his forearms resting on top of the door.

What now, he thought. *The dealer's dead, and my only lead is someone called "Viper" in the Los Zheng drug cartel that happens to sex traffic girls and boys here in Tacoma. I need to see Adam Drake and Mike Casey again.*

By the time he drove to PSS headquarters in Seattle through rush hour traffic on Friday afternoon, it was four o'clock. Drake had promised he'd wait for him at headquarters when he called but didn't know if Casey would be there; Casey's oldest daughter was playing her last soccer game of the season later that afternoon.

Drake was at his desk looking intently at something on the screen of his laptop when Walker rapped twice on the open door of his office.

"Colonel, come in and have a seat," Drake said and closed his laptop.

"If you need to finish with that, go ahead. I can wait."

"This will keep. Are you feeling better? You're not wearing your neck brace."

"I'm better, thanks."

"Making any progress?"

Walker shook his head and said, "Not really. I had lunch today with someone who rescues young girls from prostitution in Tacoma and knows the streets. He looked for Madison Sanchez, but no one had seen her or knew where she might be. He heard the dealer who sold Adderall to kids at her high school OD'd a couple of days ago. He was a member of the Hilltop Gangsters street gang, who distribute drugs for a guy they call the "Viper". He's the only lead I have, and I only have his nickname."

"I'll have Paul Benning get in touch with his friends in law enforcement and see if they know the guy," Drake said. "Have you been back to see Jeff Jackson, by any chance?"

"No, why?"

"We did a little digging and found out that Jackson and some of his employees are spending a lot of money on weapons, night vision goggles and ammunition. There's a good chance Jackson and his boys are militia men. Jackson was a Ranger who served under Colonel "Bull" Browning. Browning is rumored to be a militia organizer in the South. You might want to steer clear of Jackson and his security company."

"I felt he was hiding something. That's probably what it is."

"There might be more," Drake said. "Jackson and his men are spending more money than their tax returns say they're earning. Someone might be funding them."

Walker smiled and asked, "Are tax returns public records now?"

"They are if you know where to look," Drake answered with a matching smile.

"You said there was more."

'In Mexico, it's common for cartels to pay a civilian community policing group to run its rivals off. The small-town rural community benefits from the boost to their budget and from the protection of a bigger cartel.

"We're trying to find out if Jackson and his security company might be doing the same thing; allowing one street gang to operate in a neighborhood he protects, without being too disruptive, and making sure rival gangs gets so much attention they'll take their business somewhere else. Selective neighborhood protection services might be the way he's able to afford the weapons he and his men are buying."

"How will you prove that?" Walker asked.

"We might not be able to prove it, but police records may establish a pattern of never making a police report about one particular street gang in a neighborhood he's paid to protect."

Walker shook his head. "I can see Jackson as a member of an armed militia organization, but he didn't strike me as someone who would be in bed with the very people his clients pay him to protect them from."

"Militias view the government as the enemy," Drake said. "*The enemy of my enemy is my friend*, as the saying goes."

"If it's true, it would explain something."

"What?"

"How they knew I would be at Dash Point State Park with my Airstream. I gave Jackson my card and asked him to call me if he remembered anything that might help me find the Adderall dealer at the high school. I told him I would be at the park the night they bombed my trailer."

"It's a good thing you're staying at the Woodmark, then. Whoever they are, they won't have a way of knowing you're staying there," Drake said and looked at his watch. "Liz left early today and the Woodmark is on my way home. Why don't I follow you there. I'll buy you a drink and we can figure out where we go from here."

"I'll take you up on that," Walker said. "A stiff drink might help keep my head from exploding with all the things I need to think about."

THIRTY-TWO

Drake walked with Colonel Walker down to the first floor of the building and asked the receptionist there to tell Mike Casey he was leaving, before continuing down another level to underground parking. Colonel Walker was waiting for him out in guest parking in the front of the building for him to drive out through the security gate and drive with him to the Woodmark Hotel.

Dark rain clouds had moved into the area from the north that afternoon and a heavy downpouring of rain pelted the roof of his Porsche Cayman GTS 4.0 as he drove out onto the street and turned on his windshield wipers and headlights.

When the security gate rolled back, he pulled forward over the sidewalk and looked to his right to see if Colonel Walker was waiting for him. When he saw that he was, he looked back to his left for traffic and saw a lime green motorcycle idling at the curb twenty yards away with two men on it.

The motorcycle's head lamp wasn't on, and Drake couldn't tell if they were about to pull out onto the street or not. He waited a moment and was about to drive out onto the street when the motorcycle's headlamp came on and it edged slowly forward.

Drake looked to his right to see if the colonel saw the motorcycle coming, but his green Ford Edge was already out onto the street and driving away.

When he looked back to the left, the motorcycle was speeding forward and when it went by, he saw the second rider was holding an AK-P down along his right leg. Drake recognized the submachine gun pistol from its reddish-brown wood forward handgrip.

The motorcycle flashed by, and Drake fishtailed out onto the street after it. Colonel Walker's SUV was stationary at the traffic light half a block away, waiting for a break in the traffic to turn to his right.

The motorcycle was fast, but when it reached the intersection Colonel Walker had already turned right. The two men had to wait for the next break in the traffic to follow the colonel.

Drake accelerated as fast as he could on the slick city street and reached the intersection in time to follow the motorcycle out into traffic. When the first rider turned his helmet left to see if a car was coming in the second lane, he hesitated for a split second before chasing after Colonel Walker. That gave Drake a chance to pull alongside and crowd the motorcycle out into the second lane.

Both riders whipped their helmets around to see who was alongside them and the first rider raised his hand with his two fingers extended toward Drake, signaling the other rider to shoot.

Before the AK-P could turn and aim at him, Drake swerved hard left into the motorcycle and sent it sliding across the wet street on its side and crashing into the grassy median planted with shrubs.

He saw the second rider in his side mirror hitting headfirst into the median's curb, as the first rider disappeared through the planted shrubs.

Drake hesitated for a moment, then accelerated again to catch up with Colonel Walker. If they were bold enough to try and kill the colonel a second time, they would need to make sure they didn't fail again and have others waiting for him up ahead.

Walker's maroon Ford Edge was a block ahead driving through

an intersection on a green light. Drake had driven down Lakeview Drive often enough to know he would have to hurry, if he wanted to make it through the same intersection on a green light.

Drake called on the three hundred and ninety four horsepower of the Cayman GTS 4.0's and its ability to go from zero to sixty miles an hour in 4.3 seconds to make it through the intersection before the yellow light changed to red.

He followed behind Walker down Lakeview Drive and across Carillon Point Road to the Woodmark Hotel and Spa, parking next to Walker's Ford Edge in the self-parking lot.

When Colonel Walker got out of his car, he waited for Drake to join him and said, "You must need a drink more than I do. You were flying back there."

"Let's go to your room, order a bottle from room service, and I'll tell you why."

When they got to the suite the company reserved for out-of-town clients, Walker called room service for a bottle of Maker's Mark, turned on the suite's fireplace and waited for Drake to explain.

"You were followed," Drake said. "Two assassins on a motorcycle were waiting for you when we left headquarters. Someone wants you dead, colonel."

"What happened?"

"I saw that the second guy on the bike had an AK-P submachine gun when they took off after you. I caught up to them and they had an accident. We're okay for the time being, but we need to figure out how they found you."

Walker told Drake about his meeting with Bobby Turner and the two gang members standing across the street from the tavern. "I called in a favor from Fort Lewis McChord and four soldiers from the 1st Special Forces Group joined me for lunch. When we left, the two kids across the street were gone. I didn't see them again when I left, but they must have followed me to your office."

The doorbell chimed and Colonel Walker went to open the door for the Maker's Mark he ordered.

When he returned with the bottle and went to the wet bar to pour them each a drink, Drake said, "I think it's time to find out who "Viper" is, and I know who's going to help us find him."

THIRTY-THREE

It was still raining Saturday morning when Drake drove back to PSS headquarters in Liz's white Cadillac CT5-V Blackwing, instead of his Cayman GTS 4.0 he left parked in their condo's garage. It was damaged on its left door from bumping into the assassins' motorcycle that he didn't want to be questioned about right away.

Mark Holland, their director of Sound Security Information Systems, had learned that morning that the Kirkland Police Department's report on the dead motorcycle assassin identified him as a Chinese national in the country illegally.

Because of that, the FBI were investigating his death. Drake wasn't on the best terms with the Kirkland Police Department. His explanation about why a Chinese triad had tried to kill him twice the year before had failed to satisfy their curiosity, and the Deputy Director of the FBI had intervened on his behalf and told them to back off, He was now basically *personae non gratae* in his own city, as far as the FBI was concerned.

That was why Director Holland was meeting him, to discuss

when and how they were going to explain his involvement in the death of the Chinese national. Mike Casey was also going to be at headquarters, after Drake told him the night before what had happened and asked for a close protection team be assigned to Colonel Walker.

Holland and Casey were laughing in the conference room, standing over a pink box of Voodoo doughnuts and laughing at the weird selection Casey had brought with him to the meeting.

Holland turned around with a brown and gold Memphis Mafia doughnut in his hand that Drake recognized, because it was Mike's favorite, and said, "He just offered me ten bucks to trade with him, because I picked out his favorite before he got to it. Are these things really that good?"

Drake had to laugh. Holland was new. He would learn how serious his friend was about pastries, and especially Voodoo doughnuts.

"Try it," Drake said, "Before he tries to take it away from you."

Casey walked away from the sideboard with a plate of doughnuts and cup of coffee. "It's a good thing you were following Colonel Walker, instead of leading him back to the hotel."

"That makes two times they've missed," Drake said over his shoulder as he filled a mug of coffee. "He might not be so lucky next time. That's why I asked for the protection team."

"Have you figured out why they're trying to kill him?" Holland asked, sitting on Casey's left at the head of the long conference room table.

"Not exactly," Drake admitted and sat across from Holland. "I have a pretty good idea who the "who" is, but not the "why". If we can nail down the "who", we'll discover the "why".

"What's the plan for doing that?" Casey asked.

"I want Mark's surveillance team to slap a GPS tracker on Jeff Jackson's Hummer. See if he'll lead us to the head of the cartel I think he's working with."

"Based on what?" Holland asked.

"First, Colonel Walker went to Jeff Jackson's office the day someone dropped C4 on his trailer. Walker told him where he was staying and why he was in Tacoma.

"Second, the fentanyl dealer Walker's looking for was a member of a street gang that handles distribution for the Los Zheng cartel in Tacoma. The dead motorcycle assassin last night is a Chinese national and Los Zheng is a Chinese drug cartel from Mexico.

"Third, Colonel Walker thinks Jackson is hiding something, and I agree. It could be that Jackson and several of his employees are probably in a secret militia and don't want anyone to know about it.

"It's also possible that Jackson is protecting Los Zheng's street gang, the Hilltop Gangsters, in the neighborhoods Jackson's paid to protect, and he's being paid by the cartel for his services. I'm working on proving that.

"But it's no coincidence that Colonel Walker tells Jackson that he's camping with his trailer at the state park, and someone drops C4 on his Airstream trailer that very night. Walker says he didn't tell anyone else."

"That doesn't explain why the cartel or Jackson want Walker dead?" Holland said.

"Like I said, I don't know why," Drake said. "Colonel Walker's source told him the dealer who probably sold his friend's son the Adderall overdosed on fentanyl and died a couple of nights ago. His street gang or the cartel can't be worried that he'll be arrested and testify against them any longer, so there must be something else. I just don't know what it is."

"Tracking Jackson may or may not lead us to this "Viper", Casey said. "Could our friends down south help with that? Have a talk with someone in the Los Zheng cartel who might know him."

"It's worth a try," Drake said.

"Shall I go ahead and put a tracker team on Jackson?" Holland asked.

"Mike?" Drake asked.

"Go ahead. Either way, we need to know more about Jackson. It's bad enough that he might be in bed with a drug cartel. It's even worse if he's in bed with a drug cartel and some secret well-armed militia."

THIRTY-FOUR

Chinese Naval Sea Dragon Commander Guan Biao watched the farmhouse through a pair of BBG-011A night vision goggles to make sure all five of the Sinaloa cartel members remained inside before he gave the order to launch the assault.

To make sure as many of his men as possible had the training they needed for the attacks planned for the summer, he'd stationed four three-men teams in a distant perimeter of the farm on the shoulders of rural roads in the area. Each team was equipped with American-made small kamikaze drone called Switchblade 300s.

The unmanned aerial vehicle didn't fire a missile – it was a missile with an explosive warhead. Two feet long and small enough to carry in a backpack, it was launched from a tube and had a range of ten kilometers, or a little more than six miles.

Commander Biao had set the waypoint himself for the missiles' GPS satnav systems, that centered on the farmhouse. As soon as the four missiles destroyed the structure, he would send in a ground force to behead the cartel members and display their heads on poles around the smoldering ruins.

Biao was a soldier and thought that displaying the heads of the men they killed was unprofessional and unnecessary, but he understood how it was necessary to carryout the false flag operation that was planned.

The American militia that would be blamed for the attack on the country's power grid next summer by his own commandos, would ultimately be found to have received money from Los Zheng, but that was as close to proving China's involvement as the Americans would ever get. They would be too distracted by the invasion of Taiwan to ever complete their investigation.

He signaled each team to prepare for launching their drones on his count and gave the order to launch.

The drones flew at a speed of sixty-three miles an hour and dropped silently down on the farmhouse thirty seconds later. The warheads on the four kamikaze drones exploded together in a fireball, blowing out windows and doors and collapsing the moss-covered roof of the farmhouse.

As soon as the explosion rocked the night, six commandos wearing army-surplus camo gear and black balaclavas ran out from the tree line along the farm's southern border toward the smoldering remains of the farmhouse. Five of them carried meat cleavers in their right hands and four-foot fiberglass fenceposts in their other hands.

Commander Biao watched stoically as his five commandos came out of the flickering shadows of the ruins holding the severed heads and impaled them on a line of fenceposts, while one commando stood guard watching them.

In less than five minutes from the time the kamikaze drones were launched, the six commandos ran back across the grassy field and into the trees, where Biao was waiting for them. When they reached him, he joined the formation and together they jogged toward two rented vans idling on the other side of the forested area that bordered the farm.

THE 412-MEMBER 2275 Jeff Jackson asked to keep an eye on the farmhouse where the Sinaloa cartel members were staying, watched the grim massacre from a pullback off the rural road two hundred yards from the old farmhouse.

As soon as he heard the explosion and saw dark figures running toward the burning remains of the farmhouse, he reached for his Samsung Galaxy S23 Ultra and videoed the scene with his camera on Night Mode.

One by one, a figure ran out from what was left of the farmhouse carrying a severed head and jammed it down on a stake. When the last head was impaled, the killers formed up in a six-man diamond formation and ran for cover across the field.

2275 heard tires on a gravel road from the other side of the forested area bordering the farm and waited to be sure the sounds were moving away from him, before reaching for his Nokia XR20 smartphone on the seat beside him. When the video he'd taken was on its way to the man who told him to keep watching the farmhouse, he called him.

"Watch the video I just sent you, then tell me what you want me to do," he said.

Two minutes went by before he was asked, "Are they still in the area?"

"Not on the farm. I heard cars driving off on the other side of the forested area."

"Get out of there, before the fire department arrives," Jackson said.

"I'm leaving now. Do we know who they are?"

"No, but I think I know who sent them."

"They've had military training and have worked as a team before."

"Agreed. After this has been investigated, get a copy of the reports for me."

"I'll try. What are you going to do with the video?" 2275 asked.

"Nothing right now. I need to know who sent them first."

"How will you do that?"

"Talk with a source. I'll let you know what I find out."

"Are we involved in this somehow? Why did you have me find the farm and keep an eye on it? Did you know this was going to happen?"

"We're not involved. I just had a hunch," Jackson said.

"For the record, I don't like whatever it is you're doing."

"You don't have to, 2275. 412 knows and he approves. Just do what you're asked to do, until it's our time to do what we pledged to do."

THIRTY-FIVE

At five o'clock Monday morning, Wayne Beardon was drinking the last of a Starbuck's Caffe Americano when Jeff Jackson came out of the Grit City Fitness and Performance gym and got in his black Hummer H2.

Beardon was sitting behind the wheel of a silver 2012 Ford Taurus he used when he was surveilling a target. When he wasn't working, he drove a 1995 Mercedes-Benz E320 convertible he restored, but for surveillance work he needed something that would blend in, and no one would notice.

He'd followed Jackson from his home that morning to the gym. When he was inside, he slipped out of the Taurus and planted a LandSeeAir 54 GPS tracker on the Hummer.

After retiring from the NYPD, where he worked for the Counterterrorism Bureau with Mark Holland on his surveillance team, he retired and kept busy restoring classic cars and playing golf. But living alone as a widower when his wife died, he found that his hobbies weren't enough anymore, and he'd jumped at the chance to work for Mark Holland again and put together a first-class surveillance team for him.

Parked nearby were his first two hires, men he knew from the NYPD who also were retired and wanted to supplement their retirement income. Getting them to say yes, when he called and asked them to join his team and move away from the chaos of New York City had been easy. That gave him a small, experienced team to begin working with while he continued looking to poach younger surveillance experts from other agencies and law enforcement.

When he saw the Hummer's taillights go on, he called both cars he was working with. "He's leaving the gym, black Hummer H2 Washington plate number AMZ 5950."

Beardon watched the Hummer leave the gym's parking lot and turn east on Puyallup Avenue.

"Going east on Puyallup Avenue," Beardon reported. "He's yours, Two."

"Roger that," Two replied. "I have him in sight."

From the gym, they followed the black Hummer, leap frogging it as a team, all the way to Jackson's security business compound where it was parked in front of the company's office building until noon.

At noon, Jackson came out of the office alone and drove to a nearby sports bar for lunch and didn't return to his office until six o'clock that evening, when he left and returned to his home.

The second day, he followed the same pattern; gym, office, sports bar, office, home.

Beardon and his team changed the clothes they wore, the cars they drove each day, and the order in which they followed Jackson. The routes he took on both days were exactly the same, as was the time he reached each of the places he visited before returning home.

On the third day, he maintained his pattern until he stayed at work after six o'clock, when his Hummer remained parked in front of his office until dark at seven forty-five that evening.

Beardon was parked a block away from the security gate of the security company's compound, eating a deli turkey wrap he'd picked up on his dinner rotation, when Jackson's Hummer drove out of the compound, followed by the only other vehicle left in the parking lot, a late model Chevrolet Silverado pickup.

"He's on the move and there's a white Silverado pickup following him," Beardon said. "One, you take him first."

"Roger that."

The GPS tracker showed Jackson and the Silverado heading to downtown Tacoma, and then driving to the Port of Tacoma and the warehouse district there.

When the tracker stopped moving, Beardon told the other two men to hold position, that he was going in on foot. "If he leaves, follow him and I'll catch up."

He parked the brown Honda Accord in the shadow of the nearest building and reached back onto the rear seat to grab a black watchman's cap, a dark-green rain slicker and a large flashlight. When he had the cap and the slicker on, he got out and walked quickly down the dark alley toward the location of the tracker when it stopped moving.

The alley ended at the intersection ahead and Beardon estimated Jackson's Hummer was half a block away to the right. When he reached the intersection, he moved close to the cement wall of a warehouse and looked around the corner.

Jackson's Hummer and the Silverado pickup were parked in front of a warehouse's overhead door fifty yards away. To the left of the overhead door was a single door with a window and a flood light mounted above it. The window was frosted white, but he could tell the interior of the warehouse had lights on inside.

Beardon walked past the front of the warehouse and turned right at the corner and walked along its dark side to the rear of the building. There were no windows on that side of the building, or at the rear he saw when he looked around the corner.

The area at the rear of the warehouse had two shipping containers sitting on a paved pad and an old yellow forklift parked beside a padlocked windowless door. A yellow flood light was mounted on a pole at the other corner of the warehouse that provided light for the rear of the warehouse and for the other side of the building.

The purpose of the surveillance was to find out if Jackson had any involvement with the Chinese cartel and someone called "Viper", and being caught snooping around the warehouse would likely keep them from accomplishing that.

Beardon walked back along the back wall of the warehouse and down the other side, until he came to the front of the building where the Hummer and pickup were parked.

He started to walk out onto the alley when he heard the overhead door start to open and stepped back into the shadow. He heard the doors of the Hummer and the Silverado open and the two vehicles drive away.

He looked around the corner of the warehouse and saw an older Ford Expedition drive out and follow the Hummer and Silverado. Beardon didn't have time to move around and see inside the warehouse before the Expedition was out of sight and the overhead door closed, but he was able to get a good look at the Silverado's license plate as it drove away.

THIRTY-SIX

Thursday morning, Casey stopped by Drake's office to let him know the Director General of the New Zealand Security Intelligence Service had sent information about the men in the video they sent her.

Casey dropped his lanky frame down into one of the chairs in front of Drake's desk and said, "Looks like were dealing with China again. The consulate official from China's Tijuana consulate is Zhu Chao. He's posted as a defense attaché. New Zealand says his real name is Peter Deng and that he's really a spy from the Second Bureau of China's Ministry of State Security.

"This gets even more interesting because the other man in the video is Chen Huang. He's a former PLA Navy Marine Corps Sea Dragon commando. The NZSIS doesn't have any idea why he's in Mexico or what he's doing there."

"This all adds up to a real Chinese trifecta; a Chinese spy, a Chinese commando and a Chinese drug cartel in Mexico," Drake said. "What in the world are those three up to?"

"We don't know they're working together," Casey said.

"They are. We just don't have all the pieces of the puzzle to prove it yet."

Casey got up and asked, "Have our friends in Mexico learned anything about the new jefe of Los Zheng?"

"Not that I've heard. I'll let Ramirez know about the spy and the commando."

Drake looked out the window at the dark sky and heavy rain clouds. It was feeling like *deja vu* all over again. Last year China used a proxy to move against America; a Chinese triad and a Chinese drug cartel working together to flood the U.S. with fentanyl. This year, it looked like an emboldened China might be putting its own players on the field. But for what purpose?

He shook his head and turned back to stare at the open file on his desk. He was missing something.

A knock on his door interrupted his train of thought.

Mark Holland poked his head in and asked, "Have a minute?"

"Sure, come on in."

Holland sat in the chair Casey had just left and said, "Wayne Beardon, our new surveillance team leader had a fruitful night. They followed Jeff Jackson for two days before he broke from his daily pattern. He stayed at his office, instead of going home at six o'clock, and drove to a warehouse at the Port of Tacoma to meet someone. Beardon didn't see who he met with at the warehouse, but an older SUV left the warehouse after Jackson left.

"Beardon got the license plate and found out this morning when he ran the plate the registered owner is an export company that sells T-shirts and footwear to South America. The warehouse is also owned by the export company."

"Exporting and importing clothes and shoes to South America where there are no tariffs is one of the ways the cartels launder money," Drake said. "So, the export/import company may be laundering money for a cartel."

"Certainly possible, but there's more," Holland said. "Remember the guy on the motorcycle who had an unfortunate accident the other night? Kirkland Police identified him as a Chinese national, who just happens to work for the T-shirt and footwear exporter, T-City, in Tacoma."

"Who owns T-City?" Drake asked.

"A man named Ruben Fang. Chinese."

"Pieces of the puzzle. Are we sure Jeff Jackson was the one at the warehouse last night?"

"It was his black Hummer. He's the only one we've seen driving it."

"Could Ruben Fang be the "Viper" Colonel Walker is looking for?"

"It's possible," Holland said. "What do you want me to do?"

"Put a surveillance team on Fang and T-City. I'll have Kevin pay T-City's IT system a visit see what that will tell us."

"Anything else?"

"I think it's time for Colonel Walker and me to have a chat with Jeff Jackson."

Before he called Colonel Walker, he needed to let Pete Ramirez and the Las Sombra gang hear what he knew about the consulate official and the man he met in Mexicali.

Drake used Signal Private Messenger, as he had instructed his friends in Mexico to use when contacting him, and sent an encrypted message to Ramirez.

Have confirmed the name of the official from Tijuana.

He's posted as a defense attaché, one Zhu Chao. He really is a Chinese spy from the MSS by the name of Peter Deng.

The man he passed the USB drive to is a former PLA Sea Dragon commando by the name of Chen Huang.

Find out where Huang is and what he's doing here.

Drake walked down the hall to the executive floor breakroom to get a bottle of water and when he was on his way back, his phone signaled that he had a message.

We know Huang. He's the new leader of Los Zheng. Haven't found his hideout, but his helicopter was at the old sulfur mine south of Mexicali last week.
What directions re: Tijuana consulate and the spy?

Drake didn't want to get Las Sombra directly involved with China and someone in Mexico with diplomatic cover. But he couldn't resist learning more about what China was up to if there was an opportunity to do it without an American footprint all over it.

Do you have someone who works at the consulate, or could get a job there, and learn more about this spy?

I WILL CHECK **and get back to you.**

IF YOU DO, **let's meet and talk before we set sail on this.**

Whatever they did in Mexico would always have an element of risk involved but the risk was worth taking to find out.

THIRTY-SEVEN

After calling Colonel Walker and arranging to pick him up at the Woodmark in thirty minutes, Drake slipped on his blazer and took the stairs down to the PSS armory to see Master Sergeant Peters. The Kirkland Police Department still had his Kimber Ultra Carry II handgun, due to their ongoing investigation about the attempts last year by the Chinese triad to kill him. He wasn't going to confront Jeff Jackson unarmed, with everything he was learning about the man.

The Master Sergeant had insisted that he try shooting a new Staccato C2 compact pistol, and he found it to be the most accurate handgun he'd ever fired. Within a week of shooting it on their indoor range, and then at an outdoor shooting range in Redmond, Washington, he was shooting consistent one hundred yard shots in sub four seconds.

The pistol was a 2011 evolution of the classic John Browning 1911 design. It had a double-stack 9mm magazine, instead of a single-stack ACP 45, and a polymer grip and trigger guard bolted into an aluminum forward frame and slide on top. The Staccato was the

Porsche Turbo of the gun world and endorsed by over two hundred law enforcement agencies.

Master Sergeant Peters was in the supply room when Drake stepped to the counter and called his name.

"Be there in a second," Peters said. When he saw who it was, he returned to the supply room and came out with Drake's new Staccato C2 in a black leather OWB holster and handed it to him.

"I cleaned it for you," he said. "It's loaded with a magazine full of the Federal HST 124-grain ammo you like. Do you think you'll want to carry it when they return your Kimber?"

"This a sweet gun, but my Kimber's an old friend," Drake said. "We'll see, but having sixteen plus one round capacity, twice that of the Kimber, is nice. Thanks for cleaning it, Mitch."

"The pleasure was mine, Adam."

Colonel Walker was waiting at the hotel's main entrance when Drake pulled under the porte-cochere in Liz's Cadillac CT5-V.

Walker was wearing a black leather bomber jacket Drake hadn't seen before, jeans, a gray Henley shirt, and black alligator cowboy boots.

When he opened the door and got in, Walker said, "I wasn't sure where we're headed. Do I need a suit?"

"After we talk a bit, I thought we'd pay Jeff Jackson a visit. You're dressed appropriately to shake him up a bit, especially with those boots. Have you had lunch?"

"No, I was headed out to find something when you called."

"You like seafood?" Drake asked. "There's a great food truck on the way to Tacoma and I've been hungry for good fish and chips."

"That sounds good. How's your wife doing?"

"She's amazing, colonel. She had one rough week and since then, you wouldn't know she's pregnant. She's working, same as before, exercising and having fun trying to figure out how she wants to decorate the nursery."

"You're a lucky man."

"Don't I know it."

"Have you learned anything about the guys on motorcycles that came after me the other night?"

"That's one of the things I want to talk about," Drake said, as he slowed down to exit I-405 South. A green and yellow food truck was parked in a strip mall and was visible from the freeway

When they had two orders of wild Alaskan Cod fish and chips wrapped in food safe newspaper, English-style, and bottles of water, they sat under the truck's awning at a redwood picnic table to eat.

Drake dipped a cod filet in the tartar sauce, took a bite and smiled. "Tell me that's not the best fish and chips you've ever had," he said, nodding toward Walker's order still unwrapped in newspaper.

Walker took out a filet, salted it and sprinkled malt vinegar on it before taking a bite. "It's good, thanks. Now, tell me about the guys who came after me the other night."

"The one who died is a Chinese national. The other one fled and the police don't know anything about him, but I think he's also Chinese."

"Why?"

"His dead partner worked at a T-shirt shop, owned by a Chinese export company in Tacoma. The owner's name is Ruben Fang."

"What does Jackson have to do with the guys on the motorcycles?"

"We're working on that," Drake said. "We think Jeff Jackson knows Fang. Our surveillance team followed him to a warehouse at the Port of Tacoma. It's owned by Fang's export company."

"What is Jackson's relationship with Fang?" Walker asked.

"We don't know. That's what I'm going to ask him."

"Is this what Jackson's hiding, something to do with Fang?"

"Could be that, but there's more. Jackson and some of his employees have been spending a lot of money on expensive weapons and equipment. They're spending more money than we can see that they're earning. They could be getting it from Fang."

"For doing what?"

"I don't know, for sure," Drake admitted. "But exporting clothing and footwear is one of the ways cartels launder their money. Jackson could be protecting Fang's street dealers in the neighborhoods Jackson is protecting, like some of the community policing groups in Mexico. They strike a deal with one cartel to keep a rival out of their community and, in return, get money from the cartel to finance their policing activity. If Fang is working for a cartel, that could be where Jackson is getting money for the stuff he's buying."

Colonel Walker shook his head. "Jackson isn't going to tell you he knows Fang."

"I don't expect him to, but what he does after we leave might."

THIRTY-EIGHT

Before leaving the fish and chips food truck, Drake called Wayne Beardon, the surveillance team leader, to see if Jeff Jackson was still at his security company's office.

"His black Hummer is parked in front of the office," Beardon said. "He left, after we talked this morning, and returned an hour later."

"My ETA is twenty minutes to his office," Drake said. "Let me know if he leaves."

"Roger that."

"We might not get to see him," Walker said. "We had to bluff our way in when Paul and I didn't have an appointment."

"I think he'll see us when I mention Rueben Fang's name."

Twenty-two minutes later, sitting in Liz's white CT5-V in front of the security gate at the Northwest Security and Protection Services compound, Drake was correct. They were buzzed in when he said he was there to see if Mr. Jackson knew anything about a man named Fang that could help his investigation.

When they parked in front of the office building next to the black Hummer, Jackson's right-hand man, Jody Russel stood at the bottom of the steps leading to the front door. The scowl on his face matched the disdain in his voice when he asked Drake to explain again why he was there.

"I'm interested in knowing everything I can about a man named Rueben Fang. He may have something to do with the two motorcycle assassins who tried to kill Colonel Walker the other night," Drake said.

"Why do you think Mr. Jackson would know anything about this man?" Russel asked.

"He's in the security business, and I think he'd know about someone like Mr. Fang if he's operating here in Tacoma."

"Why, who is this Fang?"

"I believe he's a drug dealer and a member of the Los Zheng cartel," Drake said.

"What's your interest in him, if he is?"

"My Porsche is in the shop for repairs one of his employees is responsible for. I want to know more about the man and if he is cartel, before I go ask him to pay for the repairs."

Russel shook his head and said, "Mr. Jackson can't help you with that. It's time for you to leave."

"I'll leave when I've talked with Mr. Jackson."

Russel lifted his T-shirt and pulled a smartphone out of a brown leather holster on his belt with left hand. Drake saw he was also carrying a Sig Sauer P320 in a black Kydex IWB/appendix holster.

Thirty seconds later, four men rushed out from the office and stood in a line across the front porch of the building, with AR-15s held down along their right legs.

"Like I said, it's time for you to leave," Russel said.

Drake smiled and turned to Walker. "Remind you of Afghanistan?"

"Except they don't look as tough as the al-Qaeda and Taliban we faced," Walker said.

"Gentlemen, we'll leave, but I expect we'll see each other again. Tell your boss to call me, if he remembers anything I should know about Fang and his cartel," Drake said, and tossed his business card on the ground.

When the gate pulled back and Drake drove out of the Northwest Security and Protection lot, he called Wayne Beardon. "He's all yours, Wayne."

"If he leaves, do you want me to keep a team here?"

"I'm only interested in Jackson," Drake said. "Watch him for the next twenty-four hours. If we don't learn anything, we'll reassess. Keep the other team on Fang for the same amount of time, and let's see if they meet."

"Roger that."

"What will you do if they don't?" Walker asked.

"It depends on what we learn about Fang and his company. We know about his warehouse and his T-City business. I'd like to send someone into both places and have a look around."

"Are you doing all of this just to help me?" Walker asked.

"At first, yes. But I think there's something else going on that your man Nathan Arnold and his son got caught up in. I guess I'm just suspicious, after my experience with the Los Zheng cartel last year. There was no reason for someone to try to kill you because you were asking questions about a street dealer selling Adderall to kids. When they tried a second time, I knew this was about something else.

"There are things going on, in another part of the world, I'm not at liberty to talk about things that might be connected. I have to find out if they are," Drake said.

"Does this have anything to do with Mexico?"

Drake kept looking straight ahead and asked, "Why would you think there is?"

"Paul Benning told me about last year, that it involved this same Mexican cartel."

Drake thought back to Australia, being abducted and tortured, and chasing down the leaders of the Los Zheng cartel and its Chinese triad partners.

"I hope it isn't, colonel. But if it is, this will just be a piece of a much bigger puzzle. China was involved last year. If they're up to something again, they're making a big mistake. President Ballard sent them a message that was meant to tell them something like it had better not happen again. If it does, China's risking a war, and it won't have anything to do with Taiwan."

THIRTY-NINE

Jeff Jackson listened to Jody Russel recount his conversation with Colonel Walker and the attorney, Adam Drake, with a clenched jaw.

"I should have listened to you, Jody. Fang was a mistake," Jackson admitted. "The relationship worked for a while, but something's changed. He's doing things he would never have done before this colonel showed up. This kid wasn't the first of his clients to overdose and won't be the last. There was no reason to kidnap the kid's girlfriend to keep his dealer from being identified.

"You've seen the video from Puyallup. Something else is going on because those guys weren't sicarios from his cartel. They were too disciplined and well-trained. Four explosives detonating almost simultaneously on that farmhouse requires military precision. Fang's guys aren't that good."

Russel sat in the chair in front of Jackson's desk and asked, "If they're not his guys, who are they?"

"We need to know, before they come after us. Fang warned me that if Walker came after him, he'd come after me and that I wouldn't want that. If these are his guys, or someone he's hired, they'll be the same guys he sends after us."

Jackson leaned down and took out a bottle of Jack Daniels and two shot glasses from a desk drawer. "It's time to be preemptive."

He filled the shot glasses and pushed one across the desk to Russel. "How can we get rid of Fang?"

"Do we seriously want to take on Fang's cartel? That's what getting rid of Fang will mean."

"I think we've already crossed that bridge. Fang is Los Zheng. He takes orders from someone and that someone will come after anyone who takes out his guy. We saw how they operate in Puyallup," Jackson said. "We'll have to make sure they don't find out who's responsible for taking him out."

"How, by framing the Sinaloa cartel?"

"That's one possibility."

"Is there another?"

"Colonel Walker and his friend, possibly."

Russel pushed his shot glass back across the desk and waited for Jackson to fill it.

"I don't see Chaplain Walker taking out Fang. He has Special Forces training, sure, but he's a chaplain. He'd help law enforcement do the job, but I don't see him getting involved personally."

"He doesn't know what we know about Fang," Jackson said. "The police and FBI have left Fang alone because they don't have anything on him. Walker might suspect that Fang's cartel, but if he had something, he'd have taken it to Tacoma PD by now. I would know about it."

"What if we give Chaplain Walker what he needs to get Tacoma PD or the FBI to take out Fang?"

"You mean use the video?"

"Why not? Fang doesn't know we have it. We could send it to Walker anonymously."

"There's nothing on the video that links the attack at that farm to

Fang," Jackson said. "The Los Zheng's appetite for violence might point to Fang, if it's known he's Los Zheng, but it wouldn't be enough to prove Fang was responsible."

"Then let's think of something else we could feed Walker that would work."

Jackson refilled his shot glass, took a sip, tilted his head back and stared at the ceiling.

"There is something," he said. "We know the location of the stash house he's using. We could plant a copy of the video there and let Walker know it's location. The police would link the video to Fang."

"Knowing the location of the stash house isn't the same as planting the video without Fang knowing about it. They don't leave the stash house unprotected."

"Yeah, you're right," Jackson said and got up and paced across the office and back, before walking to the dart board on the side wall and pulling out three darts from the board.

His first dart scored a triple eighteen, the second twenty, and the third landed in the outer bullseye for twenty-five. When he turned back to Russel, he said, "Why don't we post the video online, like the cartels do as a warning to other cartels, along with something that does point to Fang?"

"Can it be done in a way that can't be traced back to us?"

"I'm sure it can."

"If it's posted online, the Sinaloa cartel will be the one that takes care of Fang for us," Russel said. "But that doesn't get Walker off our back."

"Let's take care of one problem at a time, Jody. If the chaplain continues being a problem, we'll think of something."

"Fang wants us to take care of Colonel Walker. To keep on his good side until the Sinaloa cartel can take him out, he should be told that Walker was here again. Tell him you have something planned and you'll take care of things. That will keep him from coming after us, until he's dead or fighting with the Sinaloa cartel."

"Sure, I can do that," Jackson said. "Before I go see him, find someone who can post the video without it being traced back to us. If one of our guys isn't confident that he can do it, find someone who is."

"It might not be cheap, to get someone like that to do it."

"It will be worth it, to get rid of Fang."

FORTY

Jeff Jackson left his office compound along with his day-shift employees and deviated from his normal pattern of travel for a second time.

Wayne Beardon noticed the new route he was taking on his dash-mounted Samsung Galaxy S22 Ultra with its SilverCloud app that provided real-time GPS tracking.

"I have Position One," he told the other three members of his surveillance team, who were also tracking Jackson on their smartphones. "Rotate positions on my command."

Since the night Jackson visited the warehouse at the Port of Tacoma, he had traveled the same route each day to and from his home. For a man who owned a security and protection business, Beardon thought it was odd that he didn't vary his routes from day to day. The bodyguards that were hired to protect Northwest Security and Protection Services VIP clients surely did.

The first indication Jackson was using a preplanned surveillance detection route was when he drove through a bank's parking lot and exiting onto another street before doing a U-turn at the next intersection. He then drove north toward downtown Tacoma in the direction he'd been headed before.

From there, Jackson stopped twice, going into a liquor store with darkened windows facing the street and a 7-Eleven. Each time, he came out with something in a small paper bag.

After driving slowly through the Tacoma Mall parking lot, Jackson drove to South 38th Street headed east and got in the exit lane onto I-5 South, before suddenly swerving back onto South 38th Street at the last moment.

The surveillance team, with Beardon in his old silver Ford Taurus, and the others driving a Toyota Camry, a Honda Odyssey minivan, and a ten-year-old Chevy Silverado pickup, changed places eight times in forty minutes following Jackson. He finally stopped at a strip mall in southeast Tacoma and parked in front of T-City, a T-shirt retail and custom print shop.

Owned by the man who owned the warehouse Beardon had followed Jackson to the other night, the man they believed was called Viper.

Beardon told his team to hold their locations while he called Drake.

"Jackson didn't want to be followed," he told Drake. "He took us on a long SDR to his present location at a strip mall. He parked in front of T-City and went inside. What do you want us to do?"

"Switch surveillance to Ruben Fang, if he's there," Drake said. "Fang drives a 2017 black Ford Expedition, license AXP7559. If it's there, Jackson's meeting Fang. If they leave, together or in separate vehicles, find out where they go."

"I don't see Fang's SUV out front. If it's not around back and Jackson leaves, do you want us to keep following Jackson?"

"No need, break off for the night. We've established that Jackson knows Fang. We'll decide where we go from here tomorrow," Drake said. "Good work, Wayne."

"Thanks, but we're just doing the job you hired us to do."

"Still, nicely done and thanks."

Beardon passed along the accolades from Drake to the team and had them take up positions around the strip mall. Fang's black Ford Expedition was parked behind the T-City shop, he learned, and Jackson was still inside.

He moved into a parking spot with a clear view of the front door of the T-shirt shop and took out his Canon EOS R5 digital SLR camera from the camera bag on the floor and attached a 100-500mm telephoto lens. If Jackson and Fang came out together, he wanted a picture of them.

He didn't have to wait long and hurriedly threw the cup of coffee he'd just poured from a thermos out the window and picked up his camera. He focused on their faces and kept the camera on continuous shooting mode.

From the looks on faces, Jackson and Fang were arguing about something. He lost focus on Jackson when he walked around the front of his Hummer to get behind the wheel, but Fang was still in view as he opened the door and pulled himself up into the passenger's seat of the Hummer.

Fang was saying something angrily when the door of the Hummer closed. It stayed closed for eleven minutes, before opening and Fang marching back into his shop without looking back.

Jackson and Fang might know each other, Beardon thought, but it didn't look like they were friends.

He alerted the team that Jackson was leaving, but their surveillance was switching over to Fang if he left the shop.

When they were in position to monitor every possible route away from T-City, Beardon waited another hour before sending everyone home for the night. He considered having a tracker put on Fang's Expedition, until he was told the back parking area behind T-City had two amber flood lights and an outdoor security camera above the rear door directly in front of Fang's SUV.

Before leaving, he drove from one end of the strip mall to the other, and then around to the back of the stores and restaurants. When he drove past the yellow-lighted parking area behind T-City, he spotted several places where they could place the Reconyx Hyperfire outdoor covert IR cameras they used for round-the-clock fixed place surveillance.

When the cameras were in place, they would know when Fang arrived and left his place of business, making it easier to plant a tracker on his SUV without being detected.

If Fang was the Viper, he would be careful and alert and dangerous, like most of the men Beardon had followed in his career. But he was good at his job and welcomed the opportunity to show his new employer just how good that was.

FORTY-ONE

When Drake got to PSS headquarters early Friday morning, Wayne Beardon was waiting for him in the executive floor conference room, with a coffee mug setting in front of him.

"I apologize for asking you to come in early," Beardon said. "I thought you would like to hear about last night as soon as possible."

Drake waved off the apology and said, "I've been up since five, had a run with my dog and fixed my wife an omelet. We're good. What did you want to talk about."

"We followed Jeff Jackson on a long surveillance detection route last night to a meeting with Reuben Fang," Beardon said.

"Where did they meet?"

"At Fang's T-shirt shop in a strip mall. I have pictures of them together. I'll get you copies."

"Tell me about Fang's shop."

"It's an end unit of a strip mall in south Tacoma," Beardon said. "The front windows are darkened and barred, and the metal front door has a commercial-grade keypad-operated door lock. It's the only unit that has that kind of security. Around the back, there's a small parking area with yellow LED flood lights. The back door has the same kind of door lock as the front door. There's one outdoor security camera over the door, and no windows at the rear of the unit."

"When Jackson left, how long was it before Fang left?"

"I didn't stay around long enough to find out. I thought I would place some outdoor IR security cameras around the back where he keeps his Ford Expedition, to monitor his movement. Unless he parks somewhere that gives us a chance to plant a tracker on his SUV without being seen, that's the best I can come up with."

"Do both, Wayne," Drake said. "I would like to get into his shop this weekend and have a look around. If Fang is "Viper", and his cartel was involved in kidnapping the girl we're trying to find, I want to know it as soon as possible."

"Consider it done."

"If we do visit his shop this weekend, I'll need your team to be lookouts around the strip mall, so we don't get caught with our pants down."

"I'll let the team know," Beardon said and left the conference room.

Drake followed him out and turned right to walk the short distance to Mike Casey's corner office. As usual, the PSS CEO was already at his desk working.

Casey looked up when he knocked twice on the open door and said, "I saw Wayne Beardon sitting in the conference room. Was he waiting for you?"

Drake sat in the chair in front of his friend's desk and said it was.

"How's he doing?"

"Wayne's a pro, and he's put together a good team. He wanted to meet early this morning to tell me about the surveillance I asked him to do. He followed Jeff Jackson, the private security company owner in Tacoma Colonel Walker thinks knows something about Madison Sanchez, the girl he's looking for. It looks like Colonel Walker might be right."

"How so?"

"Colonel Walker has a source who identified the Los Zheng

cartel in Tacoma as being involved in sex trafficking. The head of the cartel in Tacoma is someone called "Viper". Walker thinks he's a Chinese man by the name of Reuben Fang, the Chinese owner of a custom t-shirt company in Tacoma. Beardon followed Jackson on a long SDR last night to a meeting with Fang."

"And because Jackson knows Fang, he might know if Fang was involved in kidnapping Madison Sanchez."

"Correct."

"How are you and Colonel Walker planning on proving it?" Casey asked.

"By getting into Fang's shop and having a look around this weekend."

"Is Mark Holland in on this?"

"I haven't talked to him yet."

"This is close to home. Are you sure a B&E and risking getting caught is worth it, to help Colonel Walker?"

"It's a close call, Mike," Drake admitted. "But I have a hunch there might be more to this. Jeff Jackson and some of his men have been arming themselves with expensive weapons and equipment, at a level their income doesn't support, according to the information Kevin could find. Jackson has a connection to a known militia organizer and his employees are all former military. If Jackson has something going on with Fang and his cartel, I'd like to know what it is."

"All right," Casey said. "Have we heard anything new from our friends in Mexico?"

"Not since we told them who the consulate official and new head of Los Zheng is. They're trying to get someone hired and inside the Chinese embassy in Tijuana to see what Zhu Chao's doing there. When they do, I told them to check back, and we'd discuss what to do next."

"I sure don't like hearing that the new head of Los Zheng is a former Chinese commando," Casey said. "Especially when we know he's in contact with someone who's a Chinese MSS spy."

"President Ballard didn't like hearing it either.

"Did he give you any idea what he wants us to do, if they get someone inside the embassy and find out what China's spy is doing in Mexico?"

"No, he only said he doesn't want a U.S. footprint on anything that Las Sombra is doing there," Drake said. "If they do find out that China's up to something, he'll be between the proverbial rock and a hard place. He'd have to explain how he learned about it, and that would lead to having to explain about the money that Las Sombra is receiving from us."

"I don't envy the president and the decision he might have to make, if the Sombras find out what China's up to."

"After the warning he gave them last year about their role in flooding the U.S. with fentanyl, whatever he decides will have to hurt China's aggression more than it did last time," Drake said. "And we both know where that could lead."

FORTY-TWO

It was a quarter to twelve when Drake's phone pinged to tell him he'd received a text from Pete Ramirez in Mexico.
Found a person at the embassy who wants to help.

DOES **person know defense attaché Chao?**

HAS OFFICE AT CONSULATE. **Advises and buys Mexican Indigenous Art for the consulate. She's an art historian with a master's from San Diego State University and speaks Mandarin. Says she knows who he is.**

WHY DOES **she want to help? Do you trust her?**

. . .

SON WAS TAKEN **by Sinaloa cartel and never seen again.**

Divorced, with ex living in Mexico City. Best friend's mother is one of ours.

WHAT DOES SHE NEED?

A WAY TO **help us get rid of the cartels. That's all.**

WHAT DO **you need from me?**

ADVICE. **Never done this before.**

I'LL SEND **someone to San Diego who has. I'll be in touch.**

ROGER THAT.

DRAKE TAPPED in Mark Holland's extension on his phone console. If he knew anyone who could help Ramirez run a spy in the Chinese Consulate in Tijuana, it was Holland. As the head of the NYPD's Counterterrorism Bureau, he directed counterintelligence operations for years against spies and terrorists in New York City.

While he waited for Holland, he called Liz.

"How are you feeling?" he asked.

"I'm fine."

"Has the dizziness gone away?"

"Yeah, I laid on my side for a couple of minutes and it went away. I'll be there in an hour or so."

"Liz, why don't you stay home," Drake said. "It's Friday. Whatever you have on your desk will be there on Monday."

"I'll think about it, thanks."

She'd been talking about feeling more energy and not feeling tired the last couple of weeks, but this morning's episode of dizziness had surprised them both. He'd checked the web for symptoms during the second trimester of pregnancy and found that dizziness wasn't uncommon, but Liz was seeing it as a major setback. He'd have to think of something special for the weekend to lift her spirit this weekend.

Holland rapped twice on his door and opened it.

"Come in, Mark, and close the door," Drake said. "I have something I'd like you take to care of for me."

"Sure, how can I help?"

"First, I need for you to not mention this to anyone else," Drake said. "It involves something that only two other people in the office know about. Our friends in Mexico asked for our help when they were given a video of a Chinese Consulate official handing a USB flash drive in Mexicali, Mexico, to a person we now know is a former Chinese Sea Dragon commando and the head of the Los Zheng cartel. I agreed. Will you be comfortable with helping them, as well?"

Holland's eyebrows arched and he asked, "What kind of help?"

"Telling one of them how to run a spy in the Chinese Consulate in Tijuana."

"Isn't this something the FBI or the CIA should handle?"

"The president asked us to look into it, after our involvement with the Chinese and Los Zheng last year," Drake said. "We're a private intelligence contractor now and he's authorized us to find out what China's doing in Mexico."

"All right, who's the spy?"

"She's an art historian with an office at the consulate and speaks

Mandarin. She wants to help our friends get rid of the cartels in Mexico. Her son was taken by Sinaloa, and she never saw him again."

"Is she an American citizen?"

"I don't know," Drake admitted. "She has a master's degree from San Diego State, but that doesn't mean she's a citizen."

"Who will she be spying on at the consulate?"

"A man by the name of Zhu Chao, real name Peter Deng. He's the defense attaché there, and spy from the Second Bureau of the MSS."

"How did we come by this intel?" Holland asked.

"New Zealand intelligence knows him."

"Does this art historian know what she's getting into? Spying in a Chinese consulate on a Chinese spy is beyond dangerous."

"I don't know. That's why I'd like you to go to San Diego and meet with Pete Ramirez. He'll arrange a meeting with her. Find out if she's capable of doing this."

"If she is, how much help are we going to be able give her?"

"We'll decide that once you've assessed the situation," Drake said. "You know how Mexico stripped foreign law enforcement of immunity and restricted the way they can operate. The president doesn't want a U.S. footprint anywhere in Mexico on this, until we know a lot more."

"Okay, I'm willing to do whatever you need me to do."

"Good. There is one more thing. I want to see what the local head of Los Zheng is doing in Tacoma. I'd like you to go with me this weekend, tomorrow night or Sunday night, and help me get into his shop and office, like you did in Canada."

Holland smiled. "In Canada, the president said he'd call in favors if things went upside down to protect us. Should I assume this time that won't be the case?"

"You would be correct to assume that. But I don't think Ruben Fang, who owns the t-shirt shop we're going to break into, will call the police. He knows were trying to find a girl Colonel Walker is looking for, and he knows by now that we think he and his cartel are responsible."

"Do we have any information about this t-shirt shop?"

"Wayne Beardon is setting up covert IR cameras tonight," Drake said. "We'll have what we need before tomorrow night."

"Who's going along on this joyride?"

"You, me, and Lancer. Beardon's team will post lookouts at the strip mall where the t-shirt shop is located. Piece of cake."

"Says the man who wants to break into the shop of a Mexican cartel known for its love of violent brutality."

FORTY-THREE

Ruben Fang returned to T-City from his warehouse at the Port of Tacoma, after overseeing the distribution of product to the Hilltop Gangsters for the weekend and dismissing T-City employees for the day. He needed to have a little quiet time in his office, alone and without the possibility of being disturbed.

He didn't use drugs, he didn't gamble, but he did have one vice; he loved watching porn video with sex slaves and their masters. When Los Zheng had expanded its business beyond prostitution into the sex slave trade, he'd become addicted watching the videos of auctions the cartel held around the world. He considered watching them to be training for understanding the kind of young women the market desired but couldn't stop watching them.

Someday, when he could afford his own villa on one of the Can Dao Islands in Vietnam, he would have his own harem of sex slaves.

Fang unlocked the bottom drawer on the right side of his desk to take out an USB drive loaded with the last two years of Los Zheng's' sex slave auctions, including the Mexican auction being held in a couple of weeks, when his Xiam Ultra smartphone with a SIM card and app for quantum encrypted calls from Huang started vibrating.

He closed the drawer and raised the phone to his ear. "Yes, Huang."

"Have you seen the video?"

"What video?"

"The video of my men taking care of the Sinaloan. I told you to make sure the man you used to find him wasn't watching the farm any longer."

"I told him to stay away," Fang said. "Maybe it was someone else."

"Who else could it be, Fang? Who else would be watching the farm? The police? The FBI? They wouldn't put the video up on the internet for the world to see. My men wouldn't have made it out of the country if they had the farm under surveillance."

"What do you want me to do?"

"Make sure the man you trusted wishes he'd never betrayed us," Huang said. "Then get out of town. The Sinaloa cartel thinks we're responsible. They sent sicarios to kill six of our men already and they will come after you. "Go to the mattresses", as they say in the movies, until I decide how to handle this."

"What if wasn't him?"

"It won't make any difference. By the time you've convinced yourself it wasn't him, you'll have to kill him anyway."

"Understood," Fang said. "What do you want me to do?"

"Nothing. Do what I told you to do and don't jeopardize our business in the Northwest any more than you already have."

Fang dropped the phone on the desk and yelled. Huang had no idea what he was talking about. He was the cartel's business in the Northwest. He was the one who built the business and put together the alliances with the street gangs in Tacoma, Seattle, Olympia, and Vancouver. Huang was the one jeopardizing the business with his commandos and the plan to frame the 412s for an attack on America's power grid.

He understood one thing, however. It was time to look out for himself and make plans for his own future. And that meant wiping away any trace of his relationship with Jefferson Jackson and the video that he'd posted on the internet.

Jackson knew about the massacre in Puyallup and the only way he could have known was if he had someone there. That was what Jackson had been shouting about the other day, that he knew what they had done, and wasn't willing to risk losing everything by helping them with their dirty little business any longer.

He didn't need to know the truth about a video being posted on the internet. He needed Jefferson Jackson dead.

Fang picked up his phone to call Jihao, his enforcer, and decided to find the video online first and see what Huang was talking about. It didn't take long. A search using "cartel violence in Washington" located the video in seconds.

The video captured it all, from the explosions that destroyed the farmhouse, to the commandos running across the field, to the heads being slammed down in a line on poles facing the road for everyone to see.

Fang called Jihao and told him to come to T-City. He needed him to take care of something.

While he waited, he took the USB drive out and plugged it into his laptop on the desk. He had other thumb drives at his condo on Dock Street he liked to watch with female escorts he used that he'd take with him when he left town, but this thumb drive was his favorite to watch at the shop. It reminded him of the one side of the business he personally enjoyed.

He heard Jihao enter the shop from the rear entrance and walk to his office.

When his enforcer knocked on the door and was told to enter, Fang was feeding his pet viper a small white lab rat.

"Jihao, I want you to pick four men and make sure Jeff Jackson doesn't live another day. He's betrayed my trust and must pay the penalty. Do it somewhere there are witnesses. I want people to know he was dirty. If there are others with him, kill them as well. I don't care if they are his family, his friends, or his priest, for that matter. If he's at his company office, do it when he leaves or anywhere along his way home. I just want it done and done quickly."

"Yes, boss."

"I'm going out of town for a couple of days," Fang said. "You're in charge while I'm away. Tell the men to be extra careful. We may have the Sinaloa cartel making a move against us. Let's make sure they pay a price if they try."

"They will, I promise you," Jihao said with a salute and left.

FORTY-FOUR

The after-hours-tradition on Fridays at Northwest Security and Protection Services involved hauling out a cooler filled with ice and bottles of beer and three boxes of pizza from a local veteran-owned brewery to celebrate the end of the week.

Jeff Jackson stood next to Jody Russel with a bottle of beer in one hand and slice of pizza in the other. He was proud of his guys and wanted them to know it.

"Have any plans for the weekend?" he asked Russel.

"My son has his last game tomorrow at the round-robin basketball tournament they play to finish the season," Russel said. "They all get ribbons, so I'm sending my wife to watch it. As a tradeoff, I will be on the sideline at my daughter's soccer match getting wet and listening to the parents yelling at their kids. Sunday's all mine, why?"

"Come to my house in the afternoon. We need to decide what we're going to do about Fang."

"I thought posting the video was what we decided to do."

"It was but I don't think that's going to finish it."

"I still think we should let sleeping dogs lie," Russel said.

"If they'll stay asleep, yeah. I'm just not sure they will. Think about it. Maybe we can come up with something that will keep the peace."

Jackson and Russel split up and made the rounds, checking in with the clusters of employees enjoying the beer and pizza and joking with each other.

At seven o'clock, when the last dayshift employee had left and the pizza was boxed up and in the breakroom refrigerator for the weekend skeleton crew, Jackson walked out to his Hummer to drive home.

It was rainy and cold, and he sat in the Hummer to let it warm up. He loved the Hummer and all the extras he'd been able to afford to have installed on it. It was overkill he knew, but he couldn't forget the Hummers he'd seen in Iraq after encountering an IED. The streets of Tacoma weren't like Iraq, yet, but he still felt better knowing that if they ever were, he'd be protected.

To make sure of it, he'd added armor protection from a company called Amormax. The passenger compartment of the Hummer was bullet-proofed, the windows were ballistic glass, and the floor of the Hummer had bomb blankets to protect it from IEDs. In addition to having run flat tires, there was a switch that electrified the door handles to shock anyone trying to get inside and a switch to activate the smoke screen system.

If, for some reason, the security of the passenger compartment was breached, he had an M9 Beretta and a 12-inch Ka-Bar fighting knife in the center console.

Jackson selected a playlist from his phone and synced it with Bluetooth to the custom sound system in the Hummer and drove out through the security gate of the compound.

It was raining hard, and he turned the wipers on to full speed, and looked ahead to where two cars were stationary with emergency lights flashing. A man and a woman stood under an umbrella exchanging information.

He slowed as he approached behind the first car and waited. A car in the other lane had stopped to help and was keeping him from pulling around to drive past the accident.

Jackson reached into the pocket of his jacket for his phone to switch to another playlist and when he looked up, he saw four men walking toward the Hummer. They were all carrying AK-47 rifles.

He shifted the Hummer into reverse and accelerated back without looking and slammed into something he hadn't seen pull up behind him. He turned to look back and saw a tractor cab of a semi-truck blocking him.

When he looked back, the four men on the sides of his Hummer and aiming their rifles at the windows. Ahead on the road, the drivers that had looked to be exchanging information were gone, as well of the driver of the car that had stopped to help.

He'd driven to an ambush and there was only one way out of it; straight ahead through the gap between the two cars with their emergency lights flashing and the car beside them in the other lane.

With rounds from the four AK-47s pitting the bullet-proof windows of the Hummer, Jackson shifted into first gear and hit the gas, fish tailing on the wet pavement and side swiping the two gunmen on the right.

He aimed for the gap, steering more to the left to miss the greater mass of the two cars with emergency lights flashing, and kept his foot down on the gas pedal when he hit between the three cars.

The Hummer's heavy brush guard bumper tore off the right rear quarter panel of the first car and smashed into the driver-side door of the car in the other lane. The weight and taller size of the Hummer lifted the smaller car up on its side and pushed it left, letting Jackson break through the cars blocking the road.

When the Hummer fish tailed again, Jackson saw another man standing ahead in the middle of the road with a rifle raised. In a flash of memory, he recognized it as an AK-74 with a GP-45 40mm under barrel grenade launcher attached.

He ducked to the right when he saw the flash of the grenade

launching and prayed the ballistic glass was strong enough to repel the grenade.

The explosion rocked the Hummer upwards and dropped it back down onto the road on all four wheels. The fifth man had fired the grenade under the Hummer to explode it as an airborne IED, not knowing the Hummer had bomb blankets underneath to protect it.

Jackson looked for the man ahead and saw him trying to reload the grenade launcher as he flashed past.

I saw your face, Jackson smiled. "*If it's the last thing I do on this earth, I will put you in the ground.*

FORTY-FIVE

The weather forecast for Seattle Saturday morning was for scattered showers in the morning and clouds in the afternoon, but the weatherman got it wrong. Scattered clouds with patches of blue sky early on turned to a clear springtime blue sky, with sunshine that warmed your face as well as your winter-wearied spirit.

Drake surprised Liz with a shopping spree for the nursery that he thought would begin and end at Ikea, but Liz had other plans. They started at the Pottery Barn, then on to Nordstroms, The Land of Nod, and West Elm before she was ready to stop for lunch.

Her list of things for the baby's nursery had a crib, a changing table and dresser, a rocking chair and hamper crossed off, but Drake saw there were still a number of items on the list.

By the time he drove her back to the condo after stopping at her favorite deli for a Dungeness crab roll, it was after three in the afternoon before he got to PSS headquarters with Lancer to organize the visit to Fang's T-City shop that night.

Wayne Beardon had called while he was at the deli with Liz to say his team had set up the covert outdoor IR cameras and found the locations where they would station themselves as lookouts when they were inside the shop. Beardon also let Drake know he had one member of his team go into the shop that morning to identify the shop's security system and that he could disarm it before it had time to signal an intrusion. The security system was old and not very sophisticated, which surprised Beardon, and Drake as well when he heard about it.

If Fang was "Viper", and the head of the Los Zheng cell in Tacoma, he didn't seem to be worried the police would find anything at the shop that could get him arrested.

Drake considered changing his plan, but he still wanted to know more about Ruben Fang. If he was the Viper, his office was bound to have something in it that would help prove Fang was responsible for the two attempts on Colonel Walker's life and find Madison Sanchez.

Beardon was waiting in Mark Holland's office, which was down the hall from Drake's office on the third floor, when he got there with Lancer.

"Mark told me you might bring Lancer," Beardon said. "Glad you did."

"We used to compete in Schutzhund, and he's won championships. He'll make sure no one's inside that will surprise us."

"Do you want me to come along for the alarm system?" Beardon asked.

"Of course," Drake said. "You'll be in communication with your team, and I'd like you inside with us. Mark can handle getting us in and I'll head for Fang's office. You two can search the rest of the place."

"What time do you recommend we do this?" Holland asked Beardon.

"There are two restaurants in the strip mall. They both close at eleven on Saturdays, so there will still be a few cars in the parking lot at that time. The other stores are closed by nine. If we wait until later, we'll be the only ones there, so I think sometime before eleven. Fang's shop is on the northern end of the mall. We can park a car or two just south of it and pretty much block the view of anyone from seeing us go in."

"Ten o'clock then," Drake said.

"How many of your team will be in cars, as lookouts?" Holland asked.

"Six, two at each end and two more in back on the alley."

"Do we ride in one or two cars?" Drake asked Beardon.

"Two cars will be best parked out front. The parking area behind the shop is well lit and there's a security camera over the door. The front doesn't have a security camera and the parking lot's flood lights will be at our backs at a distance. I'll drive my team car and you two can ride together."

"What kit are we taking?" Holland asked.

"Night vision, dark clothing, radios, and phones for pictures," Drake said.

"What about weapons?" Beardon asked.

"You haven't been here long enough to get your armed private security license," Drake said. "Mark and I will carry, to be safe, but I don't think we'll need weapons. Lancer will be with us."

"How long will it take us to get to the strip mall?" Drake asked.

"An hour and a half, if the traffic's good," Beardon said. "Two hours if it's not, but it's Saturday."

"One hour and forty-five minutes, then, to be safe. Let's meet here at eight o'clock in underground parking," Drake said. "Any questions?"

"Do we have a rally point afterwards?" Holland asked.

"Sorry, I forgot to mention it," Beardon apologized. "Rally Point One is the Tacoma Mall, half a mile to the north and the parking area on the west side of Nordstrom's. It has easy access to South 47th Street and then to I-5. Rally Point Two would be back here at headquarters."

"Am I forgetting anything?" Drake asked.

"What if the police happen to show up, what's our story?" Holland asked.

"Let me do the talking," Drake said with a smile. "I represent Colonel Walker and we're following up on a lead about a missing and presumed kidnapped girl. If we need more, I'll say it's a matter of national security and they should call the president."

FORTY-SIX

After a comm check sitting in their cars in the parking lot at the north end of the strip mall, Wayne Beardon's Ford Taurus and Drake's Cadillac CT5-V drove to the T-City shop and parked out front next to each other and turned off their engines and lights.

When Beardon's four spotters reported there was no activity in and around the shop, Drake got out with his night vision goggles flipped down and opened the rear door of the CT5-V to let Lancer out.

With Lancer at heel, he joined Holland at the front door.

"If Fang is cartel, I expected him to have a better lock on this door than a mortise deadbolt and cylinder lock" Holland said and leaned down to open the door with his lock pick set.

"If his security is pair of pit bulls inside, Lancer would have let us know by now," Drake said. "There must be cameras inside."

Holland flipped his night vision googles down and opened the door. "I'll look for the security cameras DVR while you look around."

Drake gave Lancer the command to search and followed him down the main aisle of the shop past a sales counter at the entrance. The floor of the shop was taken up with tables, racks, and shelving along the left wall, displaying t-shirts and caps. On the right side of the shop was a long counter with two heat press machines behind it along the wall for printing custom t-shirts.

Holland moved silently along the counter to a door at the far end and stopped to listen, before slowly opening it to search for the DVR recorder for the two security cameras he spotted at each end of the shop high on the ceiling.

When he reached the end of the aisle, he moved left and stopped at a door next to a window with its blinds closed. Lancer was standing in front of the door with his ears up and his hackles raised.

Drake knew from his posture that Lancer hadn't caught the scent of someone hiding in the room, but something was causing his involuntary reaction to something.

"What is it, Lancer?" he whispered.

Drake leaned his ear close to the door and heard what Lancer had heard. It was a continuous scratchy, raspy sound coming from inside that he had heard before. It was the warning sound a saw-scaled viper made when it felt threatened. He heard it before in the Middle East when he and Mike Casey were looking for a sniper hide to provide overwatch on a mission.

He slowly opened the door and entered a small office. A glass terrarium was on a counter behind a desk with Fang's pet viper in it. Drake moved closer and saw the small green saw-scaled viper was coiled in S-shaped loops rubbing them slowly across its scales to make the sound warning it was prepared to strike. When he moved closer to look, the viper struck like a flash of lightning at the wall of the terrarium.

"So that's why they call you Viper," Drake said softly. "With a name like Fang, what else would they call you?"

He turned his back on the terrarium to search the desk and heard the viper strike against the glass again with his movement. Fang might be used to having a deadly snake a couple of feet behind him when he was sitting at the desk, but he knew he never would.

He pulled the top pencil drawer of the desk back and saw that it contained the usual collection of ink pens, paper clips and a dozen business cards, but nothing of interest. The drawers on the right side of the desk were both locked, so he pulled the pencil drawer open again and looked for a key. When he didn't find one, he took the new Benchmade 275 Adamas tactical folder knife he was carrying out of his pocket and forced the lock open in the top drawer.

Inside were three USB drives and an iPad. He put the drives in his front pants pocket and slipped the iPad in the right pocket of his black windbreaker.

He used his knife again to open the bottom drawer and found that it was filled with hanging file folders. He pulled up several of them and saw they were invoices, purchase orders and a file of accounts payable from a bookkeeper. He took out the most recent report from the bookkeeper and put it inside his windbreaker.

On the left side of the desk was a metal storage cabinet with locking doors. Drake moved around the desk and used his knife to open the door on the right side of the cabinet. The three bottom shelves were empty, but the top two had a collection of books on them. Drake pulled one from the top shelf and saw that it was written in Chinese. Another book from the second shelf was also written in Chinese.

He was surprised to find that Fang was a reader, or at least a book collector. Who knew that Chinese cartel drug dealers might have a taste for literature and refined side to them.

Then he smiled, reminding himself that it was dangerous to judge an opponent he knew nothing about.

Drake opened the door on the left side of the cabinet and found something more in line with what he expected to find in Fang's office. The bottom four shelves were lined with VHS tapes of Western Spaghetti Cowboy movies, but the top shelf had three pill containers sitting side by side, labeled Adderall, Oxycodone and Xanax.

He took the three pill containers and put them in the left pocket of his windbreaker.

"Time to go," he said to Lancer. "Let's find Mark and get out of here."

Holland was at the front of the shop looking through the shelves under the sales counter when Drake and Lancer came out of Fang's office. When he stood and saw them headed his way, he raised his hand above his head and moved it in a tight circle.

Drake signaled okay and walked with Lancer to join him and leave the t-shirt shop.

FORTY-SEVEN

At two in the morning that same night, Jeff Jackson and Jody Russel, Jackson's number two, were driving slowly toward Fang's warehouse at the Port of Tacoma in Russel's pickup. A slatted wood vegetable crate with four Molotov cocktails was on the floor at Jackson's feet.

Fang wasn't answering his phone and Jackson wasn't going to live looking over his shoulder for the rest of his life. It was time to take the fight to the man who sent one of his men to kill him.

"Park in the shadows in the alley across the street from his warehouse," Jackson said. "From the roof of the pickup, you can get onto the roof of the shipping container. You'll have a one hundred-eighty-degree view of the front of the warehouse and the street in each direction."

"Why don't you let me take them from there?" Russel asked. "At that range, even you couldn't miss."

"Very funny, sniper man. This is personal, that's why. I want Fang to know it's me and not the Sinaloa cartel paying him back for Puyallup. And besides, with my 300 Blackout AR-15 and two thirty round mags, a Kel-Tec KSG Bullpup shotgun on a sling with sixteen

12-guage shotgun shells available, and the Sig Sauer P320 in my drop leg holster, I think I have the firepower to take care of these two schmucks."

"When do I get to join the party?" Russel asked.

"If, and only if, Murphy shows up and I need your help. You're overwatch tonight."

Russel circled the block and drove down the alley and let Jackson out, before he pulled as close to the side of the shipping container as possible. When he was in position up on the top of the shipping container with his own 300 Blackout AR-15, he signaled Jackson that he was ready for him to cross the street with two of the Molotov cocktails.

There were no cars parked along the street that ran past Fang's warehouse and the frosted white window next to the front door was dark and there were no lights on inside. They didn't expect Fang or Jihao to be there, but that didn't mean Fang's men or members of his street gang couldn't be.

Jackson ran across the street with the wicks lit on the improvised incendiary devices and broke the glass in the window with the butt of his shotgun. When enough of the glass was smashed, he threw one cocktail after the other inside and ran back across the street and ducked into the shadows of the shipping container in front of Russel's pickup.

There were two more cocktails in the pickup, if they were needed, but the whoosh of ignition when the flames spread inside the warehouse was enough to tell Jackson he didn't need to run back across the street again.

Fang's condo on Dock Street was on the west side of City Waterway from the Port of Tacoma and Jackson estimated it would take Fang and Jihao ten minutes from the time the alarm went off in the warehouse to get there. With the business Fang was in, he doubted that the alarm in the warehouse would alert the fire department or the police about the fire. At least, that was what he hoped. If they go there before Fang and Jihao, he'd just have to find another place and time to even the score.

Twelve minutes later, when he heard a vehicle rapidly approaching without its siren blaring, he knew he was going to get his chance.

A black Chrysler 300C slid to a stop fifty feet from the overhead door of the warehouse and Jihao, Fang's enforcer, jumped out, circling around to approach the window next to the front door for a look inside.

When he was directly in front of the window twenty feet away, Jackson moved behind him and shouted, "Beautiful, isn't it?"

Jihao spun around and stared at Jackson and the AR-15 aimed at his chest.

"You missed, Jihao. That's your bad. I won't. Where's Fang?"

"Somewhere you won't find him."

"Maybe not tonight, but I will."

"What do you want?" Jihao asked and took a step forward. "More money?"

"Why did Fang send you to kill me?"

"He was ordered to."

"Why? What did I do?"

"Nothing. It was what you might do."

"Tell the police he's Los Zheng and doing business here? I'm sure they know or suspect that. It has to be something else."

"You knew about Sinaloa being on the farm in Puyallup," Jiaho shrugged his shoulders. "You put the video on the internet about what happened there. Maybe that's why."

"Whatever," Jackson said and smiled. "It doesn't make a difference now."

"He's going to make you watch him chop your wife and kids into little pieces before he kills you, you know that. You're making a big mistake, Jackson."

"Not as big as the one he made when he sent you to kill me."

"Whatever," Jihao said, shaking his wrist and dropping a

throwing knife into his hand from the sleeve of his black quilted tang jacket. With a blur of his hand, he sent it flying at Jackson's chest in an underhanded throw.

Before it struck point first into his body armor, Jackson cut Jihao down with a dozen rounds from his AR-15.

"We have to go," Russel shouted as he jumped down from the shipping container into the bed of his pickup. "Someone's coming."

Jackson scrambled to pick up his brass and jumped into the pickup when Russel pulled beside him in the street.

"I almost dropped him myself," Russel said. "I didn't think you we're going to get him in time."

"I had all the time in the world," Jackson said and pulled the zipper down on his leather bomber jacket to reveal the body armor he was wearing. "I never come to a knife fight without a gun and body armor."

FORTY-EIGHT

When Drake got back to the condo Sunday morning after his run with Lancer, he found a note on the island in the kitchen that read "I'm on the rooftop deck. Join me."

He poured a cup of coffee into the double wall glass coffee mug she'd left out for him and headed up to the rooftop.

Liz was standing at the railing looking out over Lake Washington through a light misty drizzle and turned to greet him with a smile on her face. "I'm beginning to like this place," she said. "I think we should stay."

He put his left arm around her and asked, "Seattle or the condo?"

"Both of them. We can find a place after the baby is born. I want to enjoy the next couple of months."

"I'll call the realtor and let her know," Drake said. "Anything special you'd like to do today?"

"I'm hungry for some seafood. Let's go to Pike Place Chowder for lunch and bring back salmon for dinner. How does that sound?"

"Wonderfully perfect," he said and pulled her closer to kiss her cheek. "What about breakfast?"

"Didn't you smell it? There's a spinach and mushroom quiche in the oven."

"Again, perfect," Drake said. "Need a refill of coffee?"

"No, I'm ready to go in, thanks."

Drake walked with his arm around her to the stairs leading to their bedroom on the third floor and heard her humming a tune he didn't recognize. "What is that?"

"Something my mother used to hum to get me to sleep when I was a baby. Brahms, I think," she said.

He followed her down the stairs and smiled at the thought of her humming a lullaby to get their baby to sleep.

After enjoying two slices of quiche and another cup of coffee, Drake went down to the office on the first floor to call Kevin McRoberts, while Liz was showering and dressing for their outing to Pike Place.

When he got back to PSS headquarters with the others the night before, Kevin was still in his office. He offered to take the USB drives and the iPad from Fang's office and find out what was on them. Drake was anxious to hear what he discovered.

"Good morning, Kevin. Did you sleep last night?"

Kevin was spending more and more time in his office, and Drake was worried about the number of nights he was spending sleeping there.

"Not a lot," he said. "I made the mistake of watching what was on the USB drives and the iPad. That's a sick man."

"What did you find?"

"A lot of porn."

"Did you find anything to help us find Madison or explain why Fang tried to kill Colonel Walker?"

"I might have," Kevin said. "Two of the USB drives just had porn on them, but the third one had a string of videos from what looked like trailers for sex slave auctions. I'm trying to locate the site on the dark web where the trailers came from."

"That might explain why Madison was kidnapped. What about the iPad?"

"I haven't cracked the password on that yet."

"Can you tell where the girls for sex slave auctions are being held? I expect the auction itself will be on the internet, but the girls are being held somewhere. If Madison is one of them, we might have a chance to rescue her before she's delivered to some buyer."

"I'll take a closer look at that third USB drive. It might have something on it that will tell us where they're keeping the girls."

"All right, call me if you find anything."

"I will, Mr. D."

Mr. D was the new name Kevin started using for him. Drake didn't mind, with the stellar work he was doing for the company. It was just one of many quirky things he loved about the kid.

When Liz came down and met him in their chef's kitchen on the second floor, she had on a black Nike hat, a black Nike maternity pullover, black leggings and pink Nike Pegasus running shoes that complimented her cheeks that were still pink from her shower.

"You like?" she asked and pirouetted for him.

"Are the shoes new?"

"Of course, along with the rest of the outfit. I had to have something to wear when we go out on a weekend."

"Yes, I like. Very sporty, very chic," he said. "Very..."

"Stop while you're ahead and take me to lunch."

Their first stop at Pike Place was at Pike Place Chowder for bowls of New England Clam Chowder, and then the Pike Place Market for Northwest King Salmon filets at the Pure Food Fish Market.

It was three in the afternoon when they got back to the condo, after deciding to invite Colonel Walker for dinner, when Kevin McRoberts called Drake.

"I think I found something," Kevin said. "One of the promotional trailers for a sex auction on the third USB drive had "La Chinesca 47" scrawled on a brick wall in the background. La Chinesca is what they call the underground Chinatown in Mexicali, Mexico. Chinese immigrants dug a network of tunnels under the whole city. During prohibition, La Chinesca was a center for casinos, bordellos, and bars. It still is."

"Can you identify the bordello's location?"

"Not yet, but it won't be long. I'm using AI to see if it can locate where "La Chinesca 47" is scrawled on that brick wall."

"Good work, Kevin."

"There's more, Mr. D. I figured out the password for the iPad. It was easy. He used "My Green Viper". The next sex save auction is this Wednesday, and there's a girl on the selection carousel of young virgins named Madison. I don't have a picture of her, but it could be the Madison Colonel Walker is looking for."

"Keep digging. We don't have much time if the auction is three days from now. I'll get a picture of Madison for you within the hour. Colonel Walker has one and he's coming for dinner. I'll ask him to come sooner."

FORTY-NINE

Colonel Walker rang the chimes at the door of Drakes' condo at four in the afternoon. He held out a bottle of wine to Drake when the door opened.

"The sommelier at Como said Sauvignon Blanc pairs well with salmon," Walker said.

"You didn't need to bring wine, Colonel," Drake said, "But the sommelier is correct and this a good one. Come in."

Drake led the colonel up the stairs to the main living area and kitchen, where Liz was stirring risotto in a saucepan.

"Hello, colonel," Liz said. "Glad you could join us."

"I am too," Walker said.

"I know he needs to talk with you. Have him pour you a drink. I'll call you two when dinner's ready."

Drake took a white marble wine chiller out of the freezer for the bottle of Sauvignon Blanc and then poured a generous amount of Pendleton Whisky into two tumblers.

"It's from their new 2023 Military Edition to show support for military personnel," Drake said. "Do you want ice?"

"Neat's fine, thanks.

Drake led the way into the living area to a pair of yellow armchairs by the window.

"There's good news and not-so-good news," Drake began. "We think we may have found Madison. The not-so-good news is she might be in Mexico, held as a sex slave for an online auction of young virgins."

"You said "may have". What does that mean?"

"There is a girl by the name of Madison on a selection carousel for the auction. We'll be able to confirm it's her from the picture of Madison I asked you to bring. We think it probably is her. The auction is run by the Loz Zheng cartel, the same cartel in Tacoma that tried to kill you and may have kidnapped her for its sex trade."

"What's the not-so-good news?"

"The auction is being held this Wednesday."

"Can we go get her?" Colonel Walker asked.

"We're working on that, but it isn't going to be easy. We don't know her physical location and she'll be guarded by the most violent cartel in Mexico."

Walker got up and raised his empty tumbler. "Do you mind?"

"Help yourself, colonel."

Drake knew that the colonel had been involved in planning Special Forces missions in Iraq and Afghanistan and gone with the soldiers on those raids. Most of the raids had been to capture a terrorist leader and return with him for interrogation. But some of them had been to rescue an Iraqi or Afghani suspected of collaborating with the U.S. before they were tortured and killed. Those missions were often not successful.

Colonel Walker returned with a refilled tumbler and a furrowed brow. "What assets do we have to go rescue her?"

"We have friends in Mexico who might be able to help," Drake said. "As soon as we confirm that it's Madison, I'll ask them if they can find where she's being held and if they think we can get her out."

"Not trying to get her out is not an option," Walker said firmly. "I'll go myself, if I have to."

"If we find where she is, I think you'll probably have to. Our Mexican friends will need someone to bring her home. There is another option. If we can't find her before the auction, we might have a shot at getting her back from the person who buys her."

"How will we know who that is?"

"I have someone who might be able to find out."

Walker set his tumbler down on the glass-topped round table between their chairs and asked, "May I ask how you found this out? Is this something SSIS was able to do?"

"In fact, it was. Why?" Drake asked.

"I have friends in the Defense Intelligence Agency. If you ever need someone to talk to there, I'd be glad to put you in touch with them."

"Thanks, colonel."

"What now?" Walker asked.

"Is Madison's picture on your phone?"

"Send it to me. I'll get it to Kevin, and we'll find out if it's your Madison."

Walker took out his phone and sent the picture to Drake. As soon as he had it, he sent it to Kevin.

"Gentlemen," Liz called out from the kitchen, "Dinner is ready."

While Liz brought their plates of pan seared salmon filets, asparagus and tangy cucumber salad to the table, Drake opened the bottle of chilled Sauvignon Blanc and poured each of them a glass.

When he sat across the table from Colonel Walker, he asked him if he'd say grace.

"Of course, Adam," the colonel said. "Father, thank you for your bounty from the sea that provides us this meal, and thank you for these friends I get to share it with. As we move forward, I ask a special blessing on the efforts we're about to make to see that justice is done and rescue Madison Sanchez. Amen."

"Thank you, colonel," Liz said.

Drake raised his glass to try the wine and before he took a sip, his phone buzzed in his pocket. When he saw that it was Kevin, he excused himself to take the call.

"Mr. D, there's no question. The Madison on the auction carousel is the Madison Colonel Walker is looking for."

"I'll let him know. Go home and get some sleep."

"No time, Mr. D. I haven't found where they're holding her yet."

FIFTY

Drake was waiting at seven o'clock Monday morning in the third-floor conference for the team he called to arrive and put together a plan to rescue Madison Sanchez.

Mike Casey was the first to arrive, followed by Mark Holland, the director of Sound Security and Information Solutions, Dan Norris, the head of the PSS Hostage Rescue Team, and Marco Morales, a member of Drake's Special Operations Division and former Army Long Range Reconnaissance Patrol (L.R.R.P) soldier.

"Some of you know or may have met Colonel Thomas Walker, the Special Forces chaplain Mike and I served with in Iraq and Afghanistan. He's been trying to find a young girl named Madison Sanchez who was kidnapped in Tacoma a couple of weeks ago.

"We have evidence that she's in Mexicali, Mexico, and about to be sold as a sex slave by the Los Zheng cartel in an online auction the day after tomorrow. We're going to go get her before that happens.

"I called our friend in Mexico, Peter Ramirez, and his freedom fighters to help us. They'll do the heavy lifting when we find out where they're holding Madison.

"Our end of this rescue operation is to locate Madison's exact location, figure out how to get in and out of there with her, and then get her safely across the southern border to Calexico, California.

"We know she's somewhere in Mexicali's Chinatown called La Chinesca, that has an underground complex of basements and tunnels where Chinese immigrants lived in the early 1900s. They were brought here from China to work on a railroad and irrigation project for the Colorado River Company. When the project was finished, many of them stayed in Mexico to avoid persecution and harassment in America.

"Mexicali once had the largest Chinese population in Mexico and there are over two hundred Chinese restaurants in Mexicali today. I mention this because we will stand out, except maybe Marco because they're used to seeing Mexicans, if we cross the border to Mexicali.

"The Asian mafia, not only Los Zheng, control the sex trade in Mexicali and Tijuana, and use those locations to bring young girls there to be trained before they're sent back to cities in the U.S. or abroad. That's why Madison is probably there before she's auctioned off.

"Kevin is using AI to pin down the location of something he saw scrawled on a brick wall in the background of a video of a previous sex slave auction held by Los Zheng. It could be an underground brothel in Chinatown. That's what we'll need to recon and help Pete's guys get in and rescue her from the Los Zheng cartel members who will be guarding her.

"Let's hear some ideas about how we're going to do this," Drake said.

"Are we ruling out our direct involvement?" Norris asked.

"Yes, unless we think getting involved is the only way we can pull this off," Drake said.

"I asked because this is what my guys are trained to do," Norris said. "Two or three days isn't enough time to train Pete's men to do what we can do."

"You've met them, Dan. You've seen what they're capable of.

Let's develop a plan and then figure out if they can be successful without our help."

"When we come up with a plan, how are we going to brief them on how to carry it out?" Holland asked.

"Pete suggested meeting them in Calexico and laying it out," Drake said.

"When we get her out, how do we get her across the border?" Casey asked.

"Colonel Walker said he's willing to go and bring her across. He knows the head of an organization that rescues sex trafficked girls all over the world. He met him at a conference they held for the Army Chaplain Corps and got to know him. He'll call him and get him to make sure he's recognized as one of their volunteers if he gets called out at the border crossing."

"If she's being held in an underground brothel, how are Pete and his men going to gain access to it and get out of there without leaving dead bodies behind," Holland asked. "If Mexicali is as corrupt as the rest of Mexico, won't this brothel have police protection?" Holland asked.

"Pete says they have what are called "zonas de tolerancias" where prostitution is allowed and police protection isn't necessary," Drake said. "Sex trafficking is against the law, but it's concealed by the cartels and the Asian mafia running the brothels. That will be where the local police might be involved. Pete will do some undercover work and find out if the police will be a problem."

"Adam, until we know where Madison is being held, there's not much we can do to plan a rescue," Norris said.

"Yeah, I hoped we'd hear something from Kevin by now," Drake said. "Dan, will you go down and ask if he'd found anything yet?"

"Sure thing," Norris got up and left.

"While we wait, is anyone beside me hungry?" Casey asked. "I can order something?"

Morales raised his hand and Casey left for his office to order something.

Drake stood up and asked Holland to join him out in the hall.

"Pete would like you to meet with the woman helping us in the Chinese consulate in Tijuana. She's not getting anywhere, and he doesn't feel comfortable telling her how to get closer to the defence attaché. If he can arrange it, will you go to San Diego and see her?"

"Before Wednesday?"

"No, after we fly to Calexico to brief Pete on our plan. We can swing by San Diego on our way home with Madison."

"Sure thing," Holland said.

Drake saw Norris coming down the hall signaling with a thumbs up. "Kevin found it."

FIFTY-ONE

The PSS Gulfstream G280 landed at the Calexico International Airport at 2:41 p.m., PDT Monday afternoon with Adam Drake, Colonel Tom Walker, Mark Holland, Dan Norris, and Marco Morales on board.

By 3:30 p.m., the five men were joined by two more men, Pete Ramirez, and Dan Vasquez under the blue umbrella of a poolside table at the Holiday Inn Express in Calexico, California, two miles north of the U.S. border.

It was 106 degrees Fahrenheit and condensation droplets dripped down the sides of their beer bottles.

After the two leaders of Las Sombra were introduced to Colonel Walker and Mark Holland, who hadn't met the two Mexicans the year before, Drake briefed Ramirez and Vasquez on what they knew about Madison Sanchez and where they thought she was being held.

"Kevin has identified the location of a Chinese restaurant in Mexicali that has an online gambling lounge and a basement. We think the restaurant's gambling lounge leads to a basement that connects it with the underground tunnels running under La Chinesca.

"What we haven't been able to confirm is the exact location of the underground brothel run by the Los Zheng cartel, where we believe Madison Sanchez is being held.

"We need to recon the restaurant and the gambling lounge, as soon as possible, and learn how we get to the brothel in the tunnels," Drake said.

"What's the name of the Chinese restaurant?" Ramirez asked.

"The Golden Imperial Palace in Chinatown."

"The busiest time for the brothel will be later tonight," Vasquez said. "That's when it will be easier to get someone inside. Who's doing the recon?"

"Who volunteers?" Drake asked.

"Does it matter if it's a Mexican or a gringo?" Norris asked Vasquez.

"It doesn't. There are plenty of gringos who cross the border to visit the "zonas de tolerancias". But it might be easier for one of us to get someone talking about how to get to the brothel."

"I'll go," Morales volunteered.

"I'll go with you," Vasquez said.

"What are we going to do when we confirm her location?" Ramirez asked.

"That will depend on who we have to go through to get her and how we get her out of there when we do," Holland said. "Colonel Walker will get her over the border when we find a place other than the restaurant to get out of the tunnels."

"I can help with that," Ramirez said. "The owner of the Chinese restaurant, who gave us the video of the Chinese consulate official meeting with Chen Huang, runs tours of the underground tunnels from his restaurant's basement. He might not know where the brothel is, but he'll have a tour guide who knows the tunnels and the basements that connect to the tunnels. I'll go see him."

"Excellent," Holland said.

"La Chinesca is not that big," Ramirez injected. "As soon as we hit the brothel, Los Zheng will be all over the place. We're going to have a fight on our hands."

"Can you handle it?" Drake asked.

"We can, but I don't want innocents killed when we leave the zona."

"If we can make it to your friend's Chinese restaurant, can we leave there in something the cartel's muscle won't recognize? A delivery truck or something?" Norris asked.

"I'll see if we can arrange that," Ramirez said. "Are you going with us?"

"I planned on going. Am I?" he asked Drake.

Drake looked at Ramirez and Vasquez and shook his head. "We can't leave a U.S. footprint on this. Marco's recon of the Chinese restaurant won't lead back to us, he's just a hungry American visiting Mexicali. After we have Madison, Colonel Walker's involvement can be explained by the rescue organization he's volunteering to help."

"Then why did I come?" Norris asked.

"To help us plan," Drake said. "You're former FBI HRT, Dan, and you know better than anyone how to plan something like this."

"I'll need more information than we have, if I'm going to be responsible for a rescue plan."

"You'll have it by tomorrow, once Morales, Vasquez, and Ramirez report back."

"When are we planning on doing this?" Ramirez asked. "The auction is Wednesday. Do we know when?"

"Kevin said the auction's website on the dark web says all bids have to be in by midnight Wednesday," Drake said.

"And that's 12:00 a.m. Thursday?" Ramirez asked to clarify.

"Correct."

"How many of your men will be available to help with this, Pete?" Holland asked.

"We have twenty men assembled in and around Mexicali. We won't be able to take a big number down to the brothel, say four or five in twos and threes. The others will be available to help us get to the exfil location in the tunnels and then out of La Chinesca to the border crossing."

"A gunfight in the tunnels will attract a lot of attention," Holland said. "Do your men have suppressed weapons?"

"They all have Dead Air Sandman suppressors on their AR-15s and Dead Air Wolfman suppressors on their Sig Sauer P320 pistols," Ramirez said.

"What about flash bang grenades, smoke grenades and night vision for the tunnels? You might need them to get out of there," Holland suggested.

"They'll have M-84 flash bang grenades, M18 smoke grenades, and ENVG-Bs night vision goggles," Ramirez said proudly. "I think we've got it covered."

"I'm impressed," Holland said. "You seem to be well equipped and obviously well-funded."

"We are," Ramirez said without looking across the table at Drake.

"Is there anything else we need to cover for now?" Drake asked.

No one said there was, so they agreed to meet at eight o'clock for dinner at Palominos, a steakhouse just across the border in Mexicali that Vasquez said had steaks from Sonora, Mexico, that were rated above prime and prepared over Mesquite charcoal.

FIFTY-TWO

Drake, Colonel Walker, Mark Holland, and Dan Norris were waiting on the terrace and studying their menus at the Palominos when Morales, Vasquez and Ramirez arrived.

"You can sure pick 'em, Danny," said Norris. "This place is terrific and expensive! I'm glad Drake is picking up the tab tonight."

"He'll be okay doing it when he's tasted his steak, trust me."

"Did you three learn anything helpful that will justify what this is going to cost me?" Drake asked.

"Yes and no," Ramirez said. "We'll have a delivery van available at the China House Restaurant to get her out of La Chinesca, if we need it. But I think we should revise our plan a little, after looking at the available routes to the border crossing. There are too many bottlenecks where they could block us if they think that's where we're heading. I suggest we book three rooms for you four and Madison, at one of the bigger hotels in Mexicali and not try to leave directly that night."

"All right," Drake said. "What did you learn that isn't helpful?"

"I talked with the man that leads the tunnel tours. There are forty eighty basements in restaurants and shops in La Chinesca that used to have access to the underground tunnels. When I told him the brothel we're looking for is somewhere near where "La Chinesca 47" is written on a brick wall, he knows where that is. It's on a wall that blocks off the entrance to the basement of the Golden Imperial Palace restaurant. If we want to use the tunnels to get to the van at China House, instead of fighting our back out through the gambling lounge and the Golden Imperial Palace, we're going to have break through that brick wall."

"Can it be done?" Drake asked. "You were our breacher in Delta."

"Sure, it can be done. But if the timing isn't right, we'll never get to a hole in the brick wall before they cut us off."

"What do you need to get the job done?" Drake asked.

"Ideally, the Army's new Selectable/Scaleable/Breacher, the SSB. It can make a hole big enough for a man to get through concrete masonry, triple layer brick and double reinforced concrete with a single shot. It's still in the testing stage, but without something like that I'll have to guess how big a charge to use because we don't know if that brick wall is reinforced or has a concrete supporting wall on the other side."

"I'll see if I can come up with one," Drake said, causing three of the men to turn and look at him.

"How?" Dan Norris asked.

"Maybe later," Drake said. "The men who go in after Madison will have APX NEXT two-way radios you told me, Pete, to signal the breacher when they're coming out, so timing shouldn't be a problem."

"The guys in the brothel can't be seen with two-way radios," Holland said.

"They won't have to," Ramirez said. "Our two-way radios have the RBX app that allows them to make and receive phone calls from smart phones."

Norris was still looking at Drake with his head tilted to one side, ready to ask another question, when their waiter arrived to take their orders.

So far, he'd been able to keep the arrangement to assist Las Sombras and their mission to rid Mexico of the cartels to President Ballard, Mike Casey, his wife and himself. He knew that tight circle of people who knew what they were doing was going to have to get bigger soon, to keep the trust of the men he was relying on to do the things they were doing.

Drake handed his menu to the waiter and ordered a Tomahawk steak, medium rare. "Anyone care to join me?"

Only Vasquez and Ramirez declined the invitation and ordered grilled octopus and grilled salmon instead.

After allowing Colonel Walker to order wine for their meal, Drake asked Morales about their visit to the Golden Imperial Palace restaurant and its gambling lounge.

"We had a drink at the bar and learned from the bartender the gambling lounge closes at two in the morning," Morales said. "He was guarded when we asked about the brothel, but Danny got him to open up. You pay a cover charge to get into the gambling lounge and there's another charge when you're allowed to leave the lounge and go to the basement.

"When you get there, you negotiate with the madam and tell her what you're looking for. You pay her when you decide, and then go to another room where you can have a drink and make your selection from among the girls who are available at that time. If you've been there before, you can pay extra to reserve a girl for the night."

"Did he say how many girls are working in the brothel?" Colonel Walker asked.

"Forty," Morales said.

"Good lord," Walker said. "How can we find where they're keeping Madison?"

"The Asian mafia-run use brothels here in Mexico to train young girls before they move them to cities across the U.S. and around the world," Holland said. "If Los Zheng does the same thing, Madison will be on display at some time each night. When she is, one of you will have a chance to leave with her and find a way to get back out of there."

"Aren't we overlooking something," Norris asked. "The guards will be armed. If they search anyone entering the brothel, which I'm sure they will, our guys are going to be screwed because we can't send them in carrying."

"Don't worry, amigo," Ramirez said. "We've got it covered. Danny and I will use the weapons we'll take from the guards."

FIFTY-THREE

It was six degrees Fahrenheit warmer Tuesday afternoon than it had been the day before, when Drake was driving back from the airport in Calexico to the Courtyard by Marriott Mexicali, where they'd booked three rooms.

After calling the president the night before to borrow an Army SSB breacher, one had been flown to the Calexico International Airport from Butts Army Airfield at Fort Carson, Colorado, where the 10th Special Forces Group was based.

Pete Ramirez, who had been a Special Forces trained-breacher and served with Drake and Casey in Iraq and Afghanistan, was teaching one of the Las Sombra men, who would be in the tunnel on the other side of the brick wall, how to use the SSB in an auto repair garage on the outskirts of Mexicali.

Danny Vasquez, a former Navy SEAL, was taking a private tour of the underground tunnels with the tour guide from the China House Restaurant to examine the brick wall they had to breach and mark an exfil escape route back to the restaurant and the delivery van for Colonel Walker and Madison Sanchez.

Kevin McRoberts at PSS headquarters in Seattle continued to

monitor the dark web site for the sex slave auction, leaving Drake, Holland, Norton, Morales, and Colonel Walker nothing to do, except go over and over the plan to rescue Madison and worry about what could go wrong.

While the Las Sombras men prepared for the evening, the five men met in the hotel's bar to pass the time until Ramirez and Vasquez returned to meet them for dinner.

"How will Madison know we're the good guys?" Norris asked.

"Her dad gave me her drivers license and picture with him in their backyard on his last birthday," Colonel Walker said. "Ramirez or Vasquez can take them to show it to her."

"What if she's not wearing much?" Morales asked. "Do we need to get her something to wear when she leaves the tunnels?"

"I'll get her something from the hotel gift shop," Walker offered. "That will make it easier to get her to my room when we get back to the hotel."

Drake sipped his beer, looking at the television monitor high on the wall at the end of the bar showing a multi-car accident on Highway 5 leading to the border. He pointed to the monitor and asked, "What do we do if something like that happens, and we get stuck in traffic with her on the way to the hotel or the border?"

"It shouldn't be a problem late at night," Morales said.

"But if it is?" Drake asked and looked around at the others. "We should have a backup plan, just in case."

"I'll bet some of the Sombras guys ride motorcycles," Holland said. "Ramirez could ask a couple of them to follow the delivery van. The colonel and Madison could get out and get a ride with them."

"Dan, are we overthinking this?" Drake asked Norris. "You planned hostage rescues with HRT."

"No, I think this is good. We're depending on Pete and Danny's guys to pull this off. We don't know anything about the experience or training any of them have. The more help we can give them the better."

"You mentioned a backup plan," Colonel Walker said. "If we don't get her out of there tonight, what do we do?"

"Kevin thinks he can access the auction website and get enough information to identify the buyer," Drake said. "We'll go after her."

"That will take it to a whole different level," Colonel Walker said. "Are you willing to go that far?"

"We won't have to do it by ourselves. We'll have enough information to get the president to call in the Hostage Recovery Fusion Cell, that has specialists from the FBI, the State Department, the Department of Defense, and other agencies, to rescue American citizens in international kidnappings. They'll get her back if we miss her here."

Dan Norris set his beer bottle down and stood up. "I need to burn off some nervous energy. Anybody up for a walkaround to see what's going on in the neighborhood?"

"It's 109 degrees, gringo," Morales grinned. "You sure you're up to that?"

"People say I have ice water in my veins. I'll be fine."

Morales got up to leave with him and was heard saying to Norris, "Let's grab some bottles of water, just in case you aren't," as they left the bar.

Colonel Walker stood and said, "I think I'll call Madison's father and let him know we may have an idea where his daughter is."

"Don't tell him too many specifics, in case this goes sideways," Drake said.

Walker nodded and said, "I won't."

When he walked away, Holland asked, "You mind if I ask you something?"

"It depends on what it is."

"Why are we being so careful to not leave footprints here? Is there something I should know about, in as much as I am the director of our intelligence contractor division?"

"What do you think that might be?"

"I see how well-funded and equipped Las Sombras are and how easy it was for you to come up with the Army's new breaching device that was in final testing not that long ago. Is the U.S. involved with Las Sombras?"

Drake shook his head and said, "You don't miss much, do you? Technically, the U.S. is not involved with Las Sombras. We are. The president has authorized us to investigate the options he has to deal with the Mexican cartels and the drugs coming across the border. There's a ten-million-dollar credit line attached to the intelligence contract to provide him with one or more options that we come up with. The credit line can be increased if needed. Las Sombras is one option we're exploring."

"This sounds a lot like the mess Oliver North and the Contras in Nicaragua got us into," Holland said.

"There are similarities," Drake admitted. "But here we're protecting ourselves against a criminal and terrorist group operating out of Mexico, like we did in Afghanistan with the Taliban. We're not funding a revolution in a foreign country."

"Mexican officials in the government who are being bribed and looking the other way may not see it that way."

FIFTY-FOUR

After a short meeting in Drake's hotel room, Pete Ramirez and Danny Vasquez left at eight o'clock that evening to brief the Las Sombras men on the final plan for their mission to rescue Madison Sanchez.

Drake and Colonel Walker waited another hour before leaving the hotel to have a leisurely dinner at the China House restaurant and be on hand when Madison arrived. Drake was wearing a Motorola APX3000 P25 two-way radio on his belt and a Bluetooth wireless earbud in his ear to monitor the transfer of Madison to the restaurant's delivery van with Colonel Walker.

Dan Norris and Marco Morales were leaving the hotel in the black Chevrolet Suburban Drake rented when Ramirez and Vasquez planned on entering the underground brothel at eleven o'clock. They were going to park somewhere close by China House in case they were needed to get everyone across the border in a hurry from the restaurant.

Mark Holland was remaining at the Courtyard by Marriott Mexicali to greet Colonel Walker and Madison in the lobby when they arrived. His role was to be there to reassure the hotel staff, with a

"To whom it may concern" letter from the nonprofit rescue organization that identified Colonel Walker as one of its volunteers and explained that the colonel had a legitimate reason for taking the young woman to his room.

When Ramirez and Vasquez finished with their dinner at the Golden Imperial Palace restaurant and paid the five hundred pesos fee to spend an hour in the gambling lounge, they paid another five hundred pesos fee, along with a two hundred pesos tip to the bouncer, to be admitted to the underground brothel.

Wide black marble stairs with red walls on either side decorated with black dragons fighting one another led down to a hostess station. A beautiful young Chinese woman wearing a white silk kimono asked for their credit cards and said she was opening a tab for them for the night's entertainment. When she finished, she handed them a white card and a black marker pen and led them to a large viewing room with subdued lighting. Small round tables and chairs filled the open area in front of a raised stage with dark red curtains that were drawn.

Ramirez counted twenty-nine men at the tables, joking and laughing and being served drinks by half a dozen young Chinese women, wearing skintight black sheer Hong-Kong-style cheongsams slit up the sides to their hips. Most of the men, perhaps twenty or so, were young Chinese men.

Two Chinese bouncers wearing black tuxedos stood at the ends of the stage facing the clientele, with two more bouncers in tuxedos standing at the back at the viewing room.

Ramirez and Vasquez sat a table near the stage and waited for one of the Chinese women to come to their table.

"I'm surprised most of these guys are Chinese?" Ramirez said quietly. "I expected more Americans and Mexicans."

Vasquez nodded and said, "They all look to be about the same age. Reminds me of being in a port with sailors on shore leave."

When one of the young Chinese women came to their table, Ramirez asked her, "What are these white cards for?"

"When you select a girl, write her number on the card and hold it up," she said in decent Spanish with a Chinese accent. "Would you like to order something to drink?"

"How long do we have before the next viewing?" Vasquez asked.

"Maybe ten minutes?" she said.

"Then we have time," he said and ordered two Coronas for them.

"What do we do if another man selects the same girl?" Ramirez asked before she left.

The woman smiled and said with a wink, "Madame will meet with you to decide which of you wants her the most."

"No wonder they have so many bouncers," Vasquez said.

"Yeah, I can see how it might get ugly real fast."

While they waited for their beers, Ramirez touched the PTT button under his black embroidered Guayabera shirt and whispered, "At the wall?"

"In position," he heard Miguel say in his wireless earbud.

Vasquez laid two five hundred pesos notes on the pewter serving tray to pay for their drinks and told their server to keep the change. When she left, he asked Ramirez how long he thought it would be until he was ready to head to the brick wall after he was alone with Madison.

"I'm hoping that it will just be a few minutes after I show her the picture with her dad at his birthday and her driver's license that Colonel Walker gave me. If it takes longer to make her understand I'm here to help her, you'll have to improvise and find an excuse to keep your pants on until you hear from me."

"Then be quick about it," Vasquez said. "I don't want someone yelling for help because she thinks I'm some kind of pervert and there for the wrong reason. I need time to slip out and find you before a bouncer comes to find out what's going on."

"Relax, this will be over soon," Ramirez said when the lights went off and on to signal it was time for the next review.

The red curtains opened slowly to the tune of Henry Mancini's *Bolero* from the movie "10" and ten young girls with their hair braided in corn rows like Bo Derek and wearing open sheer white cover ups, black bikini bottoms with a red number attached, and nothing else.

Madison was the last of the ten girls to walk onto the stage and the oldest. Before she stopped and turned around slowly to face the men in the audience, Ramirez wrote "10" on his card and help it up. Madison's number was "10".

FIFTY-FIVE

One of the Chinese women wearing the black cheongsams tapped Ramirez on his shoulder and motioned for him to follow her.

He patted Vasquez on the shoulder, saw him nod and write a number on his white card.

Ramirez followed the woman to a door at the back of the viewing room that was held open by one of the bouncers. Beyond the door was a long corridor with brightly colored doors on each side and another bouncer standing at the far end.

He counted fifteen doors on each side as he followed his escort with *Bolero* playing more loudly in the corridor than it had been in the viewing room and saw a door open near the end of the corridor, where Madison was standing with her head bowed.

When she stepped inside, the escort motioned for him to enter the room and closed the door behind him.

Red sheets hung on the walls and a bed with black silk sheets occupied the center of the room. A small gold revolving disco ball hung from the ceiling above the bed.

Madison was standing with her eyes downcast on the right side of the bed and started to take off her sheer coverup when Ramirez quickly said, "Madison, stop."

She looked up with her eyes wide open and he saw that she was having trouble processing what she heard him say.

Ramirez raised a finger to his lips and held out the picture from her dad's birthday party. "I'm here to take you home."

She started swinging her head from side to side and moaned, "No, they'll hurt me, no."

"I won't let that happen."

"Who are you?"

"A friend. We need to go. Will you trust me?"

She stared at him but didn't say no.

Ramirez pushed his PTT button and asked, "Danny, where are you?"

"In a room at the end of the corridor."

"We're in a room on the right side, three doors from the end. Can you take out the bouncer?"

"I may not have to. I think he's standing with his back to the door they closed up that we're going to breach.

"Miguel, are you ready with the breacher?" he asked.

"Tell me when."

Ramirez held out his hand to Madison, who was staring at him, and motioned for her to join him.

She stood still for a long moment before quickly walking to his side.

"When I open the door, run to the end of the corridor. Someone will be there to help you through a hole in the wall. Go with him and do what he tells you to, okay?"

Madison nodded twice and squeezed his hand.

Ramirez pushed his PTT button again and said, "Breach on one. Three. Two. One!"

The explosion from the breaching charge rattled the door and started the disco ball swinging from side to side.

Ramirez threw open the door and saw the bouncer at the end of the corridor was lying face down ten feet away, covered in chunks of cement and red brick.

When Vasquez threw open his door on the other side of the corridor, Ramirez ran holding Madison's hand along their side of the corridor to a gaping hole wide enough to step through.

"Go with Danny," he yelled above the screams and shouting coming from the other rooms.

Ramirez ran back to the bouncer lying in the corridor and pulled a Glock G21 with an extended magazine from his waistband holster. He stood up with just enough time to fire twice at the bouncer running toward him from the other end of the corridor with a gun in his hand.

When he saw the man fall, he turned and ran to the hole on the wall and stepped through it. Miguel was waiting for him with his AR-15 aimed down the corridor and his night vision goggles raised above his eyes.

"Go," Ramirez shouted.

Miguel handed him a SureFire tactical flashlight and started running down the dark tunnel after Vasquez and Madison. When they were fifty yards from the breaching hole and heard shouts coming from the corridor, Miguel waited until Ramirez ran past and pulled the pin on an M18 smoke grenade.

As the tunnel filled with green smoke, someone started firing blindly down the tunnel at them. Miguel took a MK 20 MOD 0 flash bang grenade from his pouch and threw it back through the smoke and ran.

When he reached the basement door of the China House, the restaurant's tunnel tour guide was there waiting for him, and quickly closed the door behind him.

"They left in the delivery van," he said. "Your friend is waiting for you in the bar."

"Gracias, mano," Ramirez said. "We couldn't have done this without your help."

"Anything for Las Sombras," the man said with a smile and

handed him a black polo shirt with the restaurant's logo on it to change into.

The owner of the restaurant was sitting at the back of the restaurant's bar when Ramirez slipped in through the kitchen. A bottle of Patron Añejo Barrel Select Tequila and two tequila glasses were on the table and Vasquez was sitting there wearing a white polo shirt like the one Ramirez was wearing.

The owner got up and said, "Bueno trabajo, amigos! I'll be at the front door; in case anyone comes here looking for you."

Vasquez filled their glasses and handed one to Ramirez. "I thought that went well."

"It has so far. I'll relax when they get her to the hotel."

Vasquez was savoring the smoky finish of his first sip of the tequila when he saw the owner hurrying their way.

"Four Chinese men with guns just arrived asking if I'd seen two men wearing guayaberas coming out of the tunnels," the owner said. "They didn't believe me when I told them no, I hadn't. They're going from table to table showing your pictures on their cell phones. Go to my office at the back of the kitchen. There's a shotgun in the closet and a door I use to leave by the alley."

Ramirez and Vasquez walked quickly to the door of the kitchen and crossed through it to the owner's office.

When Ramirez opened the closet and grabbed the sawed-off shotgun, he said over his shoulder to Vasquez and said, "Make sure no one's waiting for us in the alley."

Vasquez pushed the PTT button under the black polo shirt and called Miguel outside, "We need to leave the restaurant. Make sure the alley out back is safe."

FIFTY-SIX

When Miguel gave the all-clear after a pickup with two men standing in the back AKS-74Us on slings drove through the alley, Ramirez and Vasquez ran to the corner and jumped in the back of one of the Las Sombras Jeep Wrangler Sports they had in Mexicali for the rescue mission.

The cargo area of the 2-door Jeep was limited for the two men, but the darkened rear windows kept them from being seen by any of the men on the street searching for them.

"Miguel says there are four late model Chevrolet Silverado pickups with armed men looking for us," Vasquez reported, "and Chinese men on foot all over La Chinesca."

"Do they fit the description of the men we saw in the brothel?" Ramirez asked.

Vasquez asked Miguel and said, "Yes, Chinese men in their twenties and thirties, with short military-cut hair that look to be fit and in a hurry. Why?"

"Chen Huang is Chinese, Los Zheng is a Chinese cartel, and these might be his men. We need to follow them and see if they lead us to their hideout. Check and see if Colonel Walker made it to the hotel with Madison."

Vasquez used his Bluetooth-capable APX3000 P25 radio and called Drake at the hotel.

"She's safe," Drake said. "Colonel Walker and Mark Holland are with her. She's fragile and withdrawn, but physically okay. Are you and your men, okay?"

"We are, for the moment. There are Chinese men going from place to place, with pictures of us they must have taken off the CCTV in the brothel, looking for us but we're on our way out of La Chinesca."

"Are they Los Zheng men?" Drake asked.

"We think so. We're going to follow them when they stop looking for us. and see if they'll lead us to their hideout."

"If they do, let me know. When Colonel Walker and Madison are in the air back to Seattle, Mark Holland and I are driving to San Diego tomorrow for the meeting with the art historian Pete arranged. I'd like to know what you have planned for Chen Huang and Los Zheng, if you find their hideout."

"Roger that."

"And tell your men thank you for what Las Sombras pulled off tonight."

"I will, thanks."

When they reached the rally point on the outskirts of Mexicali, a school's parking lot, and waited for other members of Las Sombras to join them, Ramirez and Vasquez jumped out of the back of the jeep and fired up two Cohiba Robustos cigars to celebrate the night's mission.

"If we do find the hideout, what will we do?" Vasquez asked Ramirez.

"Rid Mexico of Los Zheng, that's what we do."

"That won't be easy. If it's in the mountains, they'll see us coming a mile away."

"Drake might be able to help with that." Ramirez said.

"Remember that nano drone Morales was always bragging about last year? If we could get Drake to lend it to us, we could recon the hideout and find out where they're vulnerable."

"Or give him the coordinates of the hideout and ask him to use the satellite surveillance used before."

"Let's find the hideout first and then find a way to attack it."

When they finished their Cohibas, the other Las Sombras men began arriving thirty minutes later, one vehicle at a time. Except for two of their Jeep Wrangler Sports.

Miguel was the last to arrive and hurried over to Ramirez and Vasquez.

"They left in a convoy and headed west," Vasquez said. "Mateo and Raul are following them in one vehicle and Enrique and Javier in another."

"How many of them were in the convoy?" Ramirez asked.

"We counted twenty, riding in the four pickups."

"That's how many I counted in the brothel," Ramirez said.

"I wonder why they were all at the brothel tonight, traveling in a group?" Vasquez asked.

"It could be because none of them speak Spanish," Miguel offered. "One of our men asked two of them who they were looking for in Spanish and they just shook their heads and gestured that they didn't understand."

"If they're members of a Chinese cartel operating out of Mexico, you would think they'd know a little Spanish," Vasquez said.

"Unless that's not why they're here," Ramirez said. "If they were here as labor to reopen that old sulfur mine, they wouldn't need to speak Spanish."

"The Chinese company that bought the rights to the mine pulled out, those guys aren't staying at the man camp," Miguel said. "We've kept an eye on the place. There's no one there."

"How many men did you say were there at one time?" Ramirez asked Miguel.

"There was portable housing for at least a hundred men. We

never saw that many of them, but they could have been inside the buildings. They weren't outside working to reopen the mine."

"If there were a hundred of them at one time, where are the other eighty?" Vasquez asked. "At the hideout?"

"If they are, and the twenty who were in town tonight are joining them at the hideout," Ramirez said, "We'll need reinforcements if we're going to take them on."

Vasquez motioned for Ramirez to walk with him. When they were away from the others he said, "We need to talk with Drake. Maybe he can supply us with something that will make the fight a little more even."

"Like what?"

"I don't know. I just think we should ask him. He seems to be on good terms with you know who."

FIFTY-SEVEN

After seeing Colonel Walker and Madison Sanchez lift off from the Calexico International Airport in the PSS Gulfstream G280 Wednesday morning, Adam Drake and Mark Holland were driving to San Diego in a black Mercedes-Benz AMG C63 Drake rented for the day.

They were meeting Elena Alba, the art historian working at the Chinese consulate in Tijuana, for lunch at the Prado restaurant in Balboa Park. Ms. Alba said she would tell the consulate she was going to San Diego to see an exhibit of Latin American Art at the San Diego Museum of Art.

There wasn't much to see on the one hundred twenty-two-mile drive and Drake was enjoying the power and handling of the AMG C63.

"We don't need to be there until noon," Holland reminded Drake when he noticed the speedometer creep up over one hundred miles an hour.

"I know, sorry. It's hard to keep this beast at the speed limit. I was thinking about what Elena might tell us about Zhu Chao."

"She'll have something for us. I just hope she's been careful."

"Did she seem nervous about what we were asking her to do when you met with her?" Drake asked.

"Just the opposite. She was eager to get started."

"Does she have access to Chao or his office?"

"She didn't when we met, other than seeing him from time to time at the consulate," Holland said. "But when she finds a piece of indigenous Mexican art that she thinks will look good in the consulate, she's able to buy it. She's been looking for something to put in Chao's office. If she found something, she'll have access, but Chao isn't there all the time. She hopes she'll be able to be in his office often enough to hear something important."

"I hope she does," Drake said. "China's up to something. Ramirez briefed me on what they saw last night. He thinks the Chinese men at the brothel might be a part of larger group of Chinese they'll find at the Los Zheng hideout. He asked if there was something I could provide to even the odds, if they attack the hideout."

"How many Chinese men is he talking about?"

"As many as one hundred. That old sulfur mine the Chinese company bought the mineral rights to south of Mexicali had a man camp that could house that many."

"What kind of something is he asking for?"

"Las Sombras is well-armed. I think he wants something more than what they already have."

"Do we have something like that?" Holland asked.

"We might. I'll have to think about it."

They entered the city limits of the eighth largest city in America at ten thirty that morning and parked the AMG C63 in the Casa de Balboa parking lot near the Visitors Center. With plenty of time before they were meeting Elena Alba for lunch, they began exploring the twelve-hundred-acre historic urban park before deciding there was too much to see in the short amount of time they had.

"Seventeen museums, a zoo and gardens, I'm going to have to come back some day when I have more time," Holland said, reading from the map he'd picked up at the Visitors Center.

"You picked a good place to meet Elena," Drake said. "The restaurant is within walking distance from the Museum of Art."

"The restaurant is in the historic House of Hospitality that was built in 1915 for the Panama-California Exposition to celebrate the opening of the Panama Canal," Holland said, reading from the Guide to Balboa Park he purchased at the Visitors Center.

"The building was demolished in the 1990s for structural reasons and reconstructed later using the original model with its beautiful Moorish and Mexican architecture, artwork, and fountains.

"I made reservations at Prado, however, because the food is said to be excellent, expensive, and you're paying," Holland said and laughed. "Actually, Elena recommended it."

Holland had reserved a table on the terrace overlooking the Casa del Rey Moro Garden. When they were seated, he ordered two glasses of the restaurant's signature sangria.

"Elena also recommended the sangria," Holland said.

"And we're just demonstrating that we trust her, I imagine," Drake said.

"Absolutely."

Holland was studying his menu when Drake saw a classy looking woman wearing a white pants suit, with shoulder length light brown hair and sunglasses, walking toward them.

Drake asked softly, "Is that Elena?"

Holland looked and stood up to greet her. "Yes."

Elena Alba held out her hand to Holland and asked, "Who is this?"

"This is Adam Drake, Elena. He's the man I told you about."

"Mr. Drake," she said and held out her hand to him as well.

"Please call me Adam, Elena. Thank you for meeting with us."

Drake moved around and held out the chair for her. "How was the art exhibit?"

"A little disappointing, I'm afraid. It wasn't the best example of Latin American Art I've seen."

"Elena, the sangria is excellent. Would you like a glass?" Holland asked.

"Yes, please."

"Do you come to San Diego often," Drake asked.

"I lecture at my alma mater a couple of times a year. When I first started working for the consulate, I was followed everywhere. I try to limit my travel across the border now."

"Do you think you were followed here?" Holland asked.

"No, I think they trust me now."

"Would you like to order something to eat?" Drake asked.

"I would, thank you. I have their paella whenever I'm here. You should try it."

Drake signaled for their waiter and with a nod from Holland, ordered three paellas."

"How are things at the consulate?" Holland asked when the waiter left.

"Very quiet," she said. "They've added to the Chinese staff at the consulate. They keep to themselves and they're very secretive and nervous about something."

"Do you have any idea what they're nervous about?" Drake asked.

"It has something to do with what China's doing in Mexico, but I don't know what. There are a lot of Mexican officials in and out of the consulate."

"Who do they meet with when they come?"

"Zhu Chao."

FIFTY-EIGHT

Elena Alba took her sunglasses off and leaned forward with her elbows on the table, squinting her bright blue eyes in the sunlight shining onto her face.

"My office is on the second floor of the consulate, a floor below Zhu Chao's defense attaché office. After I met with Peter Ramirez, I asked the Consulate General for permission to replace some of the artwork on the upper floors to complement the artwork on the first floor. He agreed and I started with Chao's floor, because of the increasing number of Mexican officials who were visiting there.

"Chao's office has two old framed Chinese CCP poster for artwork in the reception area, where his assistant has her desk, and nothing on the walls of his office. Neither of them speaks Spanish, so I've been able to go in and out of there without having to talk with them."

"But I have been able to listen, as they talk openly to each other when I'm there. I learned to speak Mandarin in college because I was interested initially in ancient Chinese art. I grew up in Mexicali and one of my best friends was Chinese.

"I overheard Chao tell his assistant to make sure someone named

Huang had the men from the sulfur mine in place by the end of the month," she said. "I don't know who Chen Huang is and I don't know anything about this sulfur mine. I'm afraid that's all I have been able to find out so far."

"We know who Chen Huang is, Elena," Drake said. "He's a former Chinese Sea Dragon commando and the current leader of the Loz Zheng drug cartel in Mexico. Chao met with Huang in Mexicali recently."

"What business would Chao have meeting with this man Huang, and what does he have to do with the men from the sulfur mine?" she asked.

"We don't know," Drake admitted. "We were hoping you could find out."

"Elena, Chao is a spy from the Second Bureau of the Ministry of State Security," Holland said. "Does the consulate have just one defense attaché?"

"Chao is the only one I know about," she said. "There is a communications room next to his office. I've seen two men come in and out of there. They could be part of his team."

"You mentioned Mexican officials visiting the consulate," Drake said. "Do you recognize any of them?"

"The only one I recognized is a man from the Industrial Development Bank. My former husband in Mexico City works there. I don't pay attention to who comes and goes in the government."

When a server brought a large pan of paella to their table, with plates and utensils, they were silent as they served themselves and began to eat from the classic Spanish dish of seafood, chicken, and chorizo.

Elena helped herself to two more scallops from the pan after several minutes and asked Drake, "May I ask you a question, Adam?"

"I don't know if I'll be able to answer it, but yes, ask me whatever you like."

"What are you and Mark doing with Peter Ramirez and Las Sombras?"

Drake finished taking a mussel from its shell and eating it before he asked, "What do you know about the Sombras?"

"I know they are fighting the cartels," she said. "My friend's son is with them. I know they are like shadows, striking and disappearing into the night. No one knows who they are or who their leader is."

"But you know your friend's son and Pete Ramirez. Do you think they are doing the right thing, trying to liberate Mexico from the cartels?"

"Yes, I do. The government is too corrupt to do it. But they would need friends to get the job done. Is that who you are?"

Drake smiled and said, "A year ago, I was kidnapped by a Chinese triad in Australia. We followed them here to Mexico and found the triad, with the assistance of China, was responsible for most of the fentanyl flooding into America. Peter Ramirez and some of his friends helped us find and deal with the triad and its leaders. I'm trying to return the favor."

"Was China directly involved with the triad last year, as they appear to be now, if their defense attaché is meeting with the head of Los Zheng?" she asked. "If they are, isn't that something your government should be dealing with instead of you?"

"When we know more about what China's doing here in Mexico, perhaps it will," Drake said. "Elena, I don't want you to get the wrong idea about why Mark and I are here. We came here to rescue a young woman who had been kidnapped by the Los Zheng cartel and brought to Mexicali for the sex trade. She was going to be auctioned off online today, as a sex slave. Pete and his friends helped us get her back last night.

"Along the way, we found out that Zhu Chao had a meeting with Chen Huang, the leader of Los Zheng. We're trying to find out why. That's why we asked you to help us."

"Do you work for your government? Am I spying on China for the CIA?"

"I'm not the CIA, Elena," Drake said.

"But it amounts to the same thing, doesn't it?"

"If it did, would that bother you?"

Elena picked up her sunglasses and smiled. "I think the idea of being a spy is exciting. No, it wouldn't bother me."

"Elena, being a spy in a Chinese consulate itself is extremely dangerous," Holland said. "Doing it with Zhu Chao and the MSS makes it doubly dangerous. We're not asking you to do anything more than you already have."

"What if there is more that I could do?" she asked. "Chao isn't always in his office. What if I see something on his desk or on his assistant's desk? Do you have one of those little cameras I could use?"

Both Drake and Holland shook their heads, no.

"Elena, just keep your ears open," Holland said. "If you hear something, use the Signal app on your phone to get a text message to me and tell me about it. Otherwise, please don't do anything that could get you killed."

Elena's eyes took on a steely look when she said, "Sinaloa cartel took my son from me, Mark. If I can pay them back, I'm willing to risk it."

FIFTY-NINE

After saying goodbye to Elena Alba at the Prado restaurant, Drake and Holland drove back to Calexico, California, to return the AMG C63 to Hertz in Calexico instead of returning it in San Diego.

There was something else they needed to do before they returned to Seattle.

Ramirez sent a text message to Drake while he was at the Prado having lunch. The Sombras had followed the convoy of pickups the Chinese men from the brothel in Mexicali to a mountainous area south of Highway 20 where armed lookouts on the road forced them to turn around.

Ramirez asked Drake to get the satellite imagery that would confirm that they had located Chen Huang and his hideout.

"If the men from the sulfur mine are at this hideout with Huang, it won't be easy to get to him. Do we know how many men Pete has in Las Sombras?" Holland asked Drake as they were speeding east back to Calexico.

"Pete's never said, but I know their numbers have been growing. It's possible that what Elena heard Chao say something about making sure the men from the sulfur mine were "in place", he could have meant somewhere other than Huang's hideout."

"It might also mean out of Mexico or somewhere else," Holland said. "It's the "somewhere else" that bothers me. Huang's a Chinese commando with a hundred Chinese men at his disposable, hiding out just south of the border. Having them "in place" could mean moving them somewhere north of the border."

"It could, but why? Huang's cartel already has men all over the U.S. Why add to that number? The drug business isn't dependent on the number of men to move product. They rely on the street gangs to do that."

"Maybe this doesn't have anything to do with the cartel's drug trade?" Holland offered. "Maybe China is putting saboteurs in place for something it's planning. With our borders wide open, why wouldn't China take advantage of it? We would do the same if it was as easy there as it is here."

"That's a chilling thought," Drake said. "If Huang's men are already across the border, we'll never find them. The Border Patrol says the number of Chinese nationals illegally entering the U.S. has skyrocketed since 2020. Hundreds of them are military-age single men, who fly to Panama or somewhere in South America and then head north with other immigrant groups."

"If Huang is responsible for getting men "in place", he'll have information on where he's sending them. We need to help Ramirez get in there and find out where that is."

"That's what I'm thinking," Drake said. "Before we ask Pete and Las Sombras to take on Huang in his hideout, they'll need as much help as we can give them. Satellite imagery, Black Hornets for on ground surveillance, something to overcome the advantage Huang will have with his lookouts and other defensive measures and materiel."

"Like what?"

"We know the cartels have trucks with mounted .50 caliber machine guns, as well as their armored narco tanks, have .50 caliber

Barrett sniper rifles and grenade launchers, and use IEDs and bomb-dropping drones against each other and the police. They'll need whatever we can get for them."

Drake stared at the shimmering waves of heat rising from the road ahead, thinking about what was realistically possible to supply Las Sombras with that gave them a chance to win against Huang and his men.

"They'll have to have the element of surprise on their side," he said. "We can't supply them with anything Pete and Danny can't get on their own. They're well-armed. They need a way to incapacitate Huang's men and keep as many of them alive as possible, if we're going to find out where Huang has moved his men, if they've already left.

"I'm thinking they'll need something like the immobilizing searchlight Intelligent Optical Systems developed to be mounted on a drone. We used one on a ranch in Colorado a couple of years ago, before you joined us," he told Holland. "Maybe some of the puke sabers, the DHS commissioned for the Border Patrol to use."

"I read about those," Holland said. "Large flashlights with a cluster of LEDs emitting bright lights on changing wavelengths that incapacitate, confuse, and make a person vomit. But how do we get our hands on any of this, in time for Las Sombras to use. We need to move on the hideout as soon as possible."

"Mike can get us the searchlight and a drone, and Black Hornets by flying them down today," Drake said. "I'll have to make a call and see if the Border Patrol can get some puke sabers to us in Calexico."

"Will Pete's men know how to operate the searchlight drone and the Black Hornets?" Holland asked.

"Good point, I'll ask Morales to come, he flew the drone with the searchlight and the Black Hornets."

Holland turned to look at Drake and saw him roll his shoulders and clench his teeth. "Worried?"

"We're expecting them to do the impossible, Mark. Huang will know they're coming a mile away. He has the high ground and position his men to take advantage of it. Even with the toys we can get for them, Huang's a trained commando and knows how to defend his position."

"And you have training in attacking positions like the Taliban used in Afghanistan," Holland said. What would you do to make this an even fight?"

"With a little shock and awe," Drake said. "I think we have everything we'll need at PSS headquarters."

SIXTY

When they got back to Calexico, Drake returned the AMG C63 to Hertz and rented a Suburban to replace it, while Holland reserved two rooms at the Holiday Inn Express for the rest of the week.

While they were still on the road traveling east from San Diego, Drake had Kevin McRoberts order more satellite imagery of the mountainous area the Las Sombras scouts had followed the convoy of pickups to before they were turned back by the Los Zheng lookouts.

He also recruited Marco Morales and Dan Norris to return to Calexico in the PSS Gulfstream G280, with Mike Casey as its pilot, and a load of materiel to deliver the shock and awe he was planning for Huang and his hideout.

The equipment included the Black Hornet for Morales for recon, and four Penn Arms L640-1 40mm six-cylinder rifle launchers and rounds of 40mm Aerial Flash Bang 200-meter cartridges to incapacitate anyone at the hideout and let the Las Sombras fighters storm the hideout.

The PSS security team had used the aerial flash bang launchers and cartridges successfully to quell an Antifa riot on the Microsoft campus in Seattle the year before. Fired over the heads of the crowd as a warning, the flash bangs had dispersed the mob in a matter of minutes.

With four launchers firing six cartridges each from points around the hideout, Drake was confident the aerial flash bangs would provide the confusion and incapacitation they would need to take the fight to Huang's men.

If more was needed, the Las Sombras would have the puke sabers Drake had asked the president to have the Border Patrol get for him, as well as the strobing searchlight they had used before, available from the PSS armory.

To leave Mexico in a hurry with Huang or any of his men, Chinese commandos or Los Zheng cartel members who were captured alive, Mike Casey had chartered a Bell 412M helicopter that would be at the Calexico International Airport, if it was needed.

As the sun was going down that Wednesday, seven men were sitting under an umbrella at a poolside table at the Holiday Inn Express: Drake, Casey, Holland, Morales, Norris, Ramirez, and Vasquez. They were meeting to plan an assault on Huang's hideout.

Casey laid a stack of satellite images on the table. "We located Huang's hideout here, at the foot of this mountain south of Highway 20. There is only one road to the west that gets us anywhere near the hideout. The hideout is at the foot of these high rock cliffs and there's a cave here, a little to the east," he pointed out. "Huang has snipers above the hideout, here and here, and guards who are usually posted here, here, here, and here."

Morales picked up one of the images and studied it. "The terrain opens to the east, but it looks like the nearest road is here, maybe two miles from the hideout. That's tough, open ground to cross."

"We're used to terrain like that," Ramirez said. "We can handle it."

"How many men will you have for this?" Norris asked.

"By tomorrow night, forty."

"Do they have military training?" Holland asked.

"We were all in the army in different branches," Vasquez said proudly," and we all have U.S. citizenship because of it."

"I've seen them in action," Drake said. "They're good."

"How well equipped are they?" Casey asked. I wasn't here for the rescue at the brothel."

"AR-15s with suppressors, Sig Sauer P320s, night vision goggles, two-way radios," Ramirez reported. "We have Barrett .50 caliber rifles for our snipers and Benelli semi-automatic shotguns for close quarter urban fighting with the cartels. We all have KA-BAR knives on our battle belts."

Holland looked at Drake and smiled. "Sounds a lot like our Special Forces."

"That's who we copied," Ramirez said. "Having anything less effective against the cartels means we lose."

"What's our plan?" Morales asked.

"What do you see?" Drake asked. "You were long range reconnaissance in the army."

Morales leaned over one of the satellite images and studied it again. "They won't expect anyone from the north. Four men coming up behind the snipers at the top of the cliffs could eliminate that threat.

"Three scout teams from the south could take out the lookouts on the road east of the hideout. The rest of the men will need to move north from here and be close enough to rush the camp, when the aerial flash bangs are lobbed in."

"Dan?" asked Drake.

"The men will have to know when the flash bangs are used, or they'll be as blind as the men at the hideout. Someone in command will need to coordinate that," he said.

"How will we know the right time for the flash bangs?" Vasquez asked.

"I'll get someone up to speed flying the Black Hornet nano drone," Morales said. "The operator should be with whomever is in command, to advise him when the time is right."

"What about IEDs?" Holland asked. "Will Huang have them to defend his hideout?"

"I'll teach the man flying the Black Hornet to use its infrared to spot them," Morales said.

"Major, I know this is our fight but what do you recommend for the rules of engagement for this?" Ramirez asked Drake.

"I'm concerned about the possibility that Huang is moving men across the border for God knows what. We need to take him alive, and as many of his Chinese comrades as you can. We're hoping to find intel that will tell what he's up to, but if it's destroyed before we recover it, he's the next best thing. Beyond that, it is your fight. Set your own rules of engagement, but I want Huang alive and across the border, if that's possible."

"We'll do our best," Ramirez said.

"Get a good night's sleep, gentlemen," Drake said. "We'll all need it for tomorrow."

SIXTY-ONE

After spending hours going over the satellite imagery from the day before until noon that day, Ramirez agreed with the recommendation that the attack on the hideout should happen at two o'clock a.m. the next morning.

With the surveillance satellite's low earth orbit producing imagery every ninety minutes, they could see that the hideout went dark at eleven o'clock the night before and came alive again that morning at five o'clock.

Camouflage covering could be seen pegged down over two large areas and five smaller areas that were possibly assembly and mess hall areas, and the five smaller areas sleeping quarters for Huang's men.

Four worn straight paths from one of the large, concealed areas led to posts where guards were stationary 24/7, confirmed the likelihood that IEDs were buried around the hideout.

Ramirez and Vasquez left the hotel at four o'clock to meet with the Las Sombras fighters. They were assembling at a ranch west of Mexicali for a barbeque dinner and final briefing.

At ten o'clock p.m., forty men would leave the ranch in an assortment of personal vehicles and move to their assigned staging locations: one to the north of the hideout, two to the east of the hideout, and one a mile west of the hideout, off the road south from the small city of La Rumorosa.

Marco Morales and Dan Norris followed Ramirez and Vasquez across the border to the ranch in the Suburban from Hertz to continue training the Black Hornet operator. Before that, they dropped Drake and Casey off at the Calexico International Airport to be ready to cross into Mexico with the chartered Bell 412M helicopter and return with Chen Huang and any of his captured Chinese comrades.

"This is harder than I thought it would be," Drake told Casey as he followed him around while he did a preflight inspection of the chartered helicopter.

"What, being stuck here with me?"

"Not being with Pete and Danny when they hit the hideout."

"You can't risk being caught or killed and Mexico discovering that the U.S. is helping Las Sombras."

"I know."

"But there's something else, isn't there?" Casey said over his shoulder as he kept moving.

"What else?"

"Not being the tip of the spear this time."

"That's part of it, I guess," Drake said, stopping and patting the nose of the helicopter.

Casey turned back and faced Drake. "What's the rest of it? Knowing that sooner or later you're going to have to make the same decision I did and leave the heavy lifting to others?"

"No, it's more than that. It's being afraid I can't make the same decision that you did. I know that's what Liz expects me to do, and I know that's what I should do. We fought in Iraq and Afghanistan because the enemy waged war on the West in the name of Allah and attacked our country. I wanted to eliminate that enemy from the face of the earth so a 9/11 never happened again.

"We developed skills in the army that allowed us to take the fight to an enemy and that sets us apart, Mike, to take on the drug cartels, and the triads, and China, whenever they cross our paths here at home."

"But I left the army because our generals became politicians first and soldiers second and didn't support us when they threw us under the bus in Afghanistan. If it hadn't been for that, I'd still be a Delta Force operator.

"I don't go looking for enemies here at home Mike, you know that. But I can't stand back and wait for the government to do something when there's something I can do to keep people from dying.

"I know you feel the same way because we've talked about it. And I understand why you made the decision you made. There's just something inside me that won't let me do that right now and I'm afraid Liz won't understand it when I tell her."

Casey came to Drake and put his hands on his shoulders. "Liz will understand. She joined the FBI for some of the same reasons you joined the army. She's about to become a mother and doesn't want to worry that she might be alone to raise your child. Megan was the same way and I dealt with it by finding ways we could use the company to do the things you're talking about.

"You're the director of Special Activities and you'll keep using that and our new intelligence contractor division to deal with threats and answer the call when the president needs help. In time, you'll find a way to keep everything in balance," Casey said. "Right now, we have a job to do. What you need to be thinking about is what we're going do if this goes upside down when we fly in to get Huang back across the border. The helicopter is chartered in the company name. Mexico will know we're involved."

"I thought about that," Drake said. "We're here to help Colonel Walker, as a recognized volunteer of a nonprofit organization that rescues sex trafficked young girls and he's here to rescue Madison Sanchez. His paperwork from the nonprofit will support that. I'm his attorney and I can say he was trying to bring back her kidnapper to stand trial in the U.S."

"I'm not sure how that will explain why we flew a Bell 412 into Mexico and got involved in a fire fight between Las Sombras and the Los Zheng cartel?" Casey said.

"Then we'll have to ask the president to have our six, if we don't find evidence that Huang is moving Chinese saboteurs across the border," Drake conceded.

SIXTY-TWO

Drake and Casey left McDonald's in Calexico when it closed at 1:00 a.m. They were served a couple of surprisingly good late-night Quarter Pounders , with fries and coffee, then returned to the airport to wait for a call from Huang's hideout.

The call came over their APX radios at 2:30 a.m. from Ramirez.

"Huang left the hideout last night," Ramirez reported. "The men he left here didn't put up much of a fight."

"Did we lose anyone?" Drake asked.

"No, they lost half a dozen who refused to surrender."

"How many of them did surrender?"

"We have fourteen men who have Los Zheng tattoos, Madam Qim, who runs the cartel's brothel in Mexicali, and a man who identifies himself as Sergeant Major Kwan."

"Is the sergeant major a Chinese?"

"He is, and he's asking for asylum and protection in the U.S. Madam Qim is also asking for asylum and protection," Ramirez said.

"Why do they think the U.S. would be willing to grant them asylum and protection?"

"The sergeant major says he knows what Huang is planning, and Madam Qim says she knows where we can find Huang."

"Do you believe them?" Drake asked.

Ramirez chuckled and said, "We found Madam Qim in Huang's motorhome, where she says she stays when she visits him. She might know where Huang is and that he's on his way back to China. Sergeant Major Kwan says he was with Huang's soldiers at the sulfur mine. Of the two, Kwan is the most credible, I'd say."

"Did Kwan say the men at the mine were "soldiers"? Chinese soldiers?"

"He says he needs asylum before he says anything else."

"We need to get those two somewhere and find out what they know," Drake said. "We'll be there in fifteen minutes."

"That's not a good idea," Ramirez said. "Our men at the ranch reported the Federales from Mexicali are headed our way. They'll reach the hideout before you can get here."

"Can you get Qim and Kwan across the border to us?"

"Yes, we're leaving, and we can take them with us. We can get them to you in San Diego. It would be easier to get them across the border there than around here."

"Then Vaya con Dios, amigo. Call me when you're planning to cross the border and I'll tell you where to bring them," Drake said.

"Let's get out of here before anyone connects us with what Las Sombras did at the hideout this morning," he said.

"We can leave the helicopter here," Casey said. "The charter service flew it here and for a hefty price, agreed to let me fly it. They'll come and fly it back when I tell them we're finished with it."

"I'll call Dan and Marco and have them get our things and check us out of the hotel." Drake added.

On the way walking across the tarmac to the FBO's airport terminal building, Drake called Dan Norris and told him to meet them with the Suburban when they left the hotel.

"Pete didn't say anything about the men who were at the sulfur mine," Casey said.

"No, and if Huang's on his way back to China, it could mean the men at the mine are in the U.S. by now."

"The president's not going to like hearing that."

"Neither am I, because it's going to be up to us to find them."

"And find a way to explain how we know about them."

"The president knows," Drake said. "It's the FBI and the rest of them who will want to know."

"Should we get the Deputy Director involved?"

"Let's wait to call Kate Perkins until we know what Madam Qim and Sergeant Major Kwan tell us. If we turn them over now to the FBI, it will just slow us down when we go hunting for Huang's soldiers."

Norris pulled up in front of the FBO twenty minutes later in the Hertz Suburban and Morales rolled down his window.

"Where are we headed?" he asked.

"San Diego," Drake said and got in the seat behind him.

"What about the Black Hornet and the stuff we gave the Sombras?" Morales asked Drake.

"Let's leave it with them, if that's all right with you, Mike?"

"They'll find a way to pay us back," Casey said, as he got in the Suburban next to Drake and winked at him.

"Sounds like they had an easy time of it at the hideout," Norris said.

"They did," Drake said. "If Huang and his soldiers were there, it might not have been that easy."

"Do you think this sergeant major knows where Huang's soldiers are?" Morales asked.

"If China's behind this and Huang's the experienced and professional soldier we think he is, he might have kept that information to himself," Casey said. "If he didn't, and he trusted Sergeant Major Kwan with it, we might find out if he's granted asylum and protection."

"How are we going to get him asylum and protection?" Norris asked. "Isn't that something only the FBI and DOJ can grant?"

"Or the president," Drake said. "We might get your old girlfriend involved to help us, as soon as we know Kwan has something to trade."

Norris was quiet as he followed the GPS directions to CA-98 on their way to San Diego. Kate Perkins was the reason he left the FBI and Washington, D.C., when they ended their relationship. He'd regretted the decision every day since then.

If finding out what Sergeant Major Kwan knew about the location of Huang's soldiers meant there was a chance to see Kate again, he'd make sure the sergeant major told them everything he knew. Legally, of course.

SIXTY-THREE

On the way to San Diego, Drake called Liz in Seattle and asked her to find a place they could stay and question Madam Qim and Sergeant Major Kwan. She'd called back ten minutes later and gave him directions to her mother's home east of La Jolla.

The residence was a twenty-minute drive from the San Diego International Airport and would be available for as long as they needed it, she said. Her mother was on a month-long cruise to Antarctica with her Bridge night friends, and her father no longer had a key since their divorce.

The modern 5-bedroom home was on Mount Soledad with an amazing view of sunsets over the Pacific Ocean and all the privacy they would need. It was available at no cost to them on one condition; if she could fly down with her key to her mother's home and join them.

At five o'clock Friday evening, Drake, with Liz, and Lancer in the back of their newest Hertz rental car, a black Chevrolet Camaro SS, led the way to their destination on Mount Soledad with the other four members of the PSS team in tow.

Pete Ramirez and Danny Vasquez were bringing Madam Qim

and Major Sergeant Kwan across the border later that night and would join them to find out if the captives had any information worthy of asylum and protection.

When they reached the California modern home on the side of Mount Soledad facing the ocean, Drake parked the Camaro on the cement brick area in front of solid double mahogany doors with copper grab handles and said, "Wow! Is this where you lived?"

"They bought it after I graduated and joined the FBI," she said. "Dad was making good money by then."

Drake got out and walked around to open her door when Norris pulled up beside him in the Suburban with Casey, Holland, and Morales.

"How long did you say we get to stay here?" Norris asked Drake when he stepped out with Holland behind him on the driver's side of the SUV.

"As long as it takes to get some answers."

"My interrogation skills are a little rusty," Holland said and shrugged. "That could take a while."

Liz leaned down and pulled her seat back to let Lancer get out and said, "Before you boys start fighting over the bedrooms, someone will need to go to the store. Mom said the refrigerator's empty, and she doesn't drink beer."

"Mike said he's in charge of the kitchen," Morales said, "And I volunteered to help. We have it covered, Liz."

"All right," she said, taking a key out of the cross-body shoulder bag where she carried her Glock 26. "Let me show you around your quarters."

The house had five bedrooms, four and half bathrooms, a gourmet kitchen, several dining areas, a gym with weights, a game room with a pool table, and a patio deck with fire pit, a jacuzzi spa, and a covered grilling station with a grill and a pizza oven.

By the time she finished the tour their sleeping quarters had been divided between the six of them, with bedrooms allowed for Ramirez, Vasquez and the two captives. Straws were drawn for the shifts necessary to guard Madam Qim and Sergeant Major Kwan until they were turned over to the FBI, if they ultimately were.

The sun was a golden red orb slipping onto the edge of the ocean at seven o'clock that evening when Ramirez parked a Winnebago camper van out front. Vasquez jumped out and pulled the side door back to let Madam Qim and Sergeant Major Kwan step out.

They were quickly escorted inside, where Ramirez introduced them to their hosts and had them taken to the bedrooms where they would be kept and interrogated.

"Have any trouble getting them here?" Drake asked.

"One of our men lives in San Diego," Ramirez said. "He brought them across and then gave us the van for as long as we needed it."

"Are they saying anything?" Casey asked.

"Sergeant Major Kwan is waiting until someone tells him he has asylum."

"Does he know that isn't going to happen until he gives us something worthy of asylum?"

"Sergeant Major Kwan understands and says he'll wait until he's talking to someone with authority to grant asylum. Madam Qim hasn't stopped talking but she doesn't seem to know much about Huang, other than his sexual, and the cartel's sex trafficking business. She's in charge of training the girls they bring to the brothel."

"She did say one thing that might be helpful," Vasquez said. "I asked her if she'd seen anyone coming to the hideout when she was there, other than the cartel men and Huang's soldiers. I thought she might have seen the guy from the Chinese consulate. She did remember seeing a short cartel guy from up north who wore a hat with a snake on it and cowboy boots. She said she never saw anyone from the consulate at the hideout."

"Did she get his name, the guy from up north?" Drake asked.

"No, why?"

"It could be someone we know, a Los Zheng cartel member from Tacoma, Washington, by the name of Rueben Fang. They call him Viper."

"Why do you think it could be this guy called Viper?" Vasquez asked.

"The girl we rescued from the brothel was kidnapped in Tacoma," Drake said. "Fang could have been the one who brought her to Mexico."

"Do you think Fang might know why Huang had the Chinese men from the sulfur mine at his hideout?" Ramirez asked.

"He might. Let's find out if Sergeant Major Kwan knows anything about him."

SIXTY-FOUR

The Chinese Sergeant Major was sitting at an eight-player poker table with a green felt top in the game room, with Dan Norris watching him, when Drake and Holland came downstairs to talk with him.

He looked relaxed, with his hands folded in his lap, when Drake sat across the table from him, and Holland took the chair to the right of Drake. Kwan had calm brown eyes that moved from Drake to Holland and then stayed fixed on Drake.

It was hard to tell his age, but his weathered face and crow's feet at the corners of his eyes identified him as a man who didn't sit at a desk all day. His military bearing did that as well.

"Sergeant Major, my name is Adam Drake. This is Mr. Holland. I understand you're asking for asylum in the U.S., in exchange for information about Chen Huang and his soldiers who were at the old sulfur mine."

"Yes," Kwan said. "Do you have authority for granting me asylum and protection?"

"No, I don't. But the the FBI and the president do. I will speak with them, on your behalf, if we decide you have information that will help us understand what Chen Huang is planning."

"Why will they listen to you? Do you work for the FBI or the CIA?"

"I work for the president. He asked me to find out what China and Huang are doing in Mexico."

"Why do you think China is doing anything in Mexico?"

"Why else would a Naval Sea Dragon commando, with a hundred soldiers at his command, meet with an agent of the Second Bureau of the Ministry of State Security from the Chinese consulate in Tijuana?"

Kwan smiled and nodded. "You are well-informed, but that doesn't prove that you can arrange asylum for me."

Drake returned Kwan's smile and said, "I guess you'll have to take my word for that. Why don't you tell me something about Huang and find out what I can do for you?"

Kwan stared at Drake without blinking for a long minute before speaking.

"Chen Huang has moved men into the U.S. to create a diversion that will keep the U.S. from reacting when China invades Taiwan."

Holland's eyebrows shot up. "How's Huang going to do that?" Holland asked.

Kwan kept his eyes on Drake. "Is that enough for asylum?"

"Do you have evidence of that?" Drake asked.

Kwan nodded and said, "I prepared the men at the sulfur mine for their mission."

Drake returned Kwan's stare, searching his face for any sign of deception, and finding none, stood up. "Let me make a call."

He left the game room and took the stairs two at a time to the main floor and went out to the patio deck, with Liz and Lancer following behind him.

"What's happened?" she asked.

Drake turned back to face her and held up his smart phone. "I need to call the president. Sergeant Major Kwan says he trained men in Mexico to create a diversion that will distract us when China invades Taiwan."

"Did he say how?"

"He wants asylum before he says anything else."

"Do you believe him?" Liz asked.

"Yes, unfortunately."

Drake found the number the president gave him to use for private encrypted conversations in his contact list and called him.

"Hello, Adam."

"Good evening, Mr. President. I have some disturbing news and a request for asylum I'd like you to grant."

"What news?"

"China has soldiers inside the U.S. for some mission to keep us from reacting when China invades Taiwan."

"Say that again, please," President Ballard said slowly.

Drake repeated what he said.

"How do you know this?"

"I have a Chinese Sergeant Major downstairs who says he trained the soldiers in Mexico for the mission."

"How did you find this sergeant major?"

"Our friends in Mexico captured him when they raided the Chinese cartel hideout."

"The same cartel we dealt with last year?"

"Yes, Los Zheng."

"How is China going to keep us from reacting when they invade Taiwan?"

"Sergeant Major Kwan won't tell us until he's granted asylum and protection in the U.S.," Drake said.

"Do you believe him?"

"From what we've learned, I do. The new head of the Los Zheng cartel is a former Chinese Navy Sea Dragon commando by the name of Chen Huang. China bought the mineral rights to an abandoned sulfur mine in Baja California and built a man camp to house a hundred or more soldiers.

"Sergeant Major Kwan says he trained soldiers there for this mission in the U.S. We also know China has a spy from the Second Bureau of the MSS at the Chinese consulate in Tijuana who met with Chen Huang in Mexicali. We have video evidence of that meeting. I think it adds up, sir," Drake said. "I believe Sergeant Major Kwan should be granted asylum so we can find out what China has planned and stop them."

"I agree," said President Ballard. "Tell Sergeant Major Kwan he has asylum and will have our protection. I'll arrange for the FBI to take custody of him when you finish with him. Find out what he knows and get back to me as soon as possible. I'll have my national security team assembled and ready to deal with whatever you learn from him."

"Thank you, sir."

Liz was standing at his side and could hear what the president was saying on Drake's phone.

"I can't believe China is willing to put Chinese soldiers on American soil," she said. "They know that's an act of war."

"China's being preparing to take back Taiwan for years," Drake said. "They know when they do, if we will honor our treaty with Taiwan, it will be WWIII. If they can distract us for long enough to delay a military response, they'll have Taiwan, and it will be too late for us, or anyone else, to do anything about it."

SIXTY-FIVE

Drake returned to the game room and took his seat across the poker table from Sergeant Major Kwan.

"You have been granted asylum, if what you tell us proves to be true," Drake said.

"How do I know you're telling me the truth?" Kwan asked.

"The FBI will come and take you into custody when we've heard what you have to say," Drake said. "You have my word, sergeant major, that you've been granted asylum. The FBI will confirm it when they get here."

"I want it to be in writing."

"It will be," Drake said. "Mr. Holland is going to record what you tell us, and we will provide it to the FBI for verification. If what you tell is found to be untrue, or even partially true, asylum will be revoked. Is that clear?"

"Yes, I understand."

Drake nodded to Holland, who had his smart phone out and hit record, before he laid it on the table.

"Why don't you tell us who you are and what you were doing in Mexico," Drake said.

"My name is Ho Kwan. I am a Sergeant Major in the People's Liberation Army of China. I was in Mexico to train soldiers to carry out a mission in the United States."

"What is that mission?" Drake asked.

"There are ten power substations that will take down the U.S. energy grid if they are destroyed. I trained ten five-men teams to destroy those power substations."

"Are those fifty man the total force in the U.S. to carry out this mission?"

"There are another fifty men for security for the strike teams and other assignments when the targets are attacked."

"You're saying there are a hundred Chinese soldiers in the U.S. who have been sent to take down our energy grid?" Holland asked.

"Yes."

"How are they going to do it?" Drake asked.

"Each team will on command launch four kamikaze drones, like your Switchblade 300 unmanned aerial vehicles, with explosive warheads and GPS satnav systems preset with coordinates for the targets."

"Where are the ten targets?"

"I don't know the individual targets. Chen Huang kept that to himself."

"Is Chen Huang the leader for this mission?"

"Yes, he is Naval Sea Dragon Commander Huang. He came ahead of me to Mexico. He took the place as the former leader of the Los Zheng cartel as his cover, until MSS could arrange to buy the mineral rights of the sulfur mine. The mine was used as a base to train the commandos and prepare them for operating in the U.S."

"You're saying this is a Chinese PLA operation to infiltrate soldiers into the U.S. and start WWIII?" Holland asked incredulously.

"That is not the purpose," Kwan said. "The purpose is to distract America so China can take Taiwan without having to fight the U.S. to do it."

"How is sending Chinese commandos to blow up our energy grid going to distract America?" Drake asked. "As soon as the first commando is killed or captured, we'll know China's behind it and is starting a war with the United States."

"You will be distracted because you won't be looking for Chinese soldiers."

"Who will we be looking for?" Holland asked.

"One of the militia groups your government says is the number one threat to your national security," Kwan said.

"You mean a civilian armed militia group?" Drake asked.

"Yes, like the ones who attacked your capital after the last election."

"Do you know which militia group?"

"I only know that it's one that a Los Zheng cartel man in America learned about."

"Which cartel man? Do you know his name?"

"Yes, he visited Huang at his hideout. His name is Fang."

"Rueben Fang?" Drake asked.

"Yes."

"Did Fang identify the militia group?"

"Not by name. I heard him say it's someone he's done business with who is a member of the militia."

Drake looked at Holland. "I think we know who that is. Jeff Jackson."

"Why will we be looking for this militia group?" Holland asked.

"Because evidence of the group's plot to bring down the government by attacking the energy grid will be made public," Kwan said. "The militia men near each of the target substations will be found to have committed suicide after the attacks, with details of the plot in their possession."

"When will the attacks on these substations happen?" Drake asked.

"On your Tax Day, when anti-government sentiment is highest."

"When does China plan to invade Taiwan?"

"Shortly after your Tax Day, when America is paralyzed by the energy grid going down."

"You said Huang kept the location of these substation targets to himself," Holland said. "Do you know where Huang is now?"

"Back in China by now."

"Did he go to the consulate in Tijuana," Drake asked.

"Yes, the morning before the hideout was attacked."

"Do you know where Rueben Fang is now?" Drake continued.

"He returned to his home, wherever that is," Kwan said.

Drake looked at Holland and then over Kwan's head at the dart board on the wall behind him.

When he looked back at Kwan he asked, "Can you think of anything else that might help us, sergeant major?"

Kwan shook his head and said, "No. Be ready for war. China is and won't stop until Taiwan is China again."

Drake left Sergeant Major Kwan with Holland to take him back to his bedroom and went upstairs to call the president. With only two weeks until April fifteenth, they needed to move quickly to find the Chinese saboteurs and a way to keep China from invading Taiwan.

As soon as he called the president and told him what Kwan said, he knew what he would be doing next. Find Jeff Jackson and the location of the power substations his militia group had targeted.

SIXTY-SIX

After Drake called the president and told him everything Sergeant Major Kwan said he knew about China's plan, he found everyone in the kitchen, except Morales who was making sure Madam Qim and the Sergeant Major Kwan stayed in their bedrooms. They were standing around the large white granite island in the kitchen, with a beer or glass of whisky or wine in their hands, except Liz who had a glass of orange juice.

"Mark told us what Kwan's saying about Huang and his commandos," Casey said. "What are we doing about it?"

"Kwan doesn't know the location of the ten power substations they're targeting," Drake said. "But I think I know who does. The man Rueben Fang has done business with has to be Jeff Jackson. We thought he might be a militia member when Kevin saw all the money he was spending buying expensive guns and equipment. We need to find Jackson and get him to tell us about his militia and what they were planning on doing that China found out about."

"What about Fang?" Norris asked. "Won't he know about Jackson's militia and China's plan?"

"We need to find him as well," Drake said. "If he's learned about the raid on Huang's hideout, he'll be harder to find, but we should look for him as well."

"Huang knows where he sent his commandos," Ramirez said. "We should look for him too."

"Kwan said Huang left his hideout and went to the Chinese consulate in Tiajuana. He's on his way back to China," Holland said. "If he's still at the consulate, we won't be able to get to him."

"Maybe we can't," Ramirez said, "But I know someone who's crazy enough to try, the Sinaloa cartel. They're offering a million-dollar reward for anyone who knows who is responsible for the massacre of their men shown in the video that was posted online. They suspect it was the Los Zheng cartel. If we tell them it was Huang and suggest they send sicarios to kill the leader of their rival cartel, they'll get him. Maybe not at the consulate, but he has to make it to the airport."

"Will they buy that?" Norris asked.

Ramirez shrugged his shoulders. "It's worth a try."

"We might be able to help with that," Drake said. "Fang had a copy of the video of the massacre of the Sinaloa men in Puyallup, Washington. It isn't the original, but it was pulled off the internet. We'll get it to you to show your Sinaloa contacts. It should convince them."

"What are we going to do with Madam Qim and Sergeant Major Kwan?" Casey asked.

"The FBI is coming to take custody of them," Drake said.

"Do we know who's coming?" Norris asked.

"Which FBI agent would you like it to be?" Liz asked with a teasing smile. "I'll need to tell them how to get here. I could call Kate and give her the address."

"Whatever," Norris said with a grin.

"Mark, call the surveillance team looking for Jeff Jackson and Rueben Fang and asked if they've found them," Drake said.

"Dan, call and organize your HRT guys so they're ready to roll as soon as we locate Jackson and Fang? You and Marco stay here with our guests until the FBI get here, since you used to work for them. I don't expect you to lead the HRT team, but I want them prepared for what they might run into. Jackson and his militia men might put up a fight when we go after him."

Norris crossed his arms over his chest and started to say something, then changed his mind and just nodded.

The tight-lipped grimace suggested the decision Drake had made for him to stay until the FBI arrived, and not return to Seattle and lead his men, was one he understood but was having a hard time agreeing do. Norris wanted to see Kate Perkins again, Drake knew, after having chosen his career with the FBI over a relationship with her years ago and wanting a second chance. But he also knew Norris would want to do what he'd trained to do most of his adult life.

Drake hoped he was making the right decision for his friend.

"Adam, does Madam Qim have asylum as well as Sergeant Major Kwan?" Ramirez asked.

"Not yet, I thought we'd let the FBI sort that out."

"She doesn't deserve it. She's been training kids and sending them off to live in hell for the rest of their lives. Maybe we should take her back to Mexico and let the families of the little ones she sold as sex slaves give her a measure of rough justice," Ramirez said. "If she gets asylum she won't be prosecuted, they'll let her go after she tells them what she knows."

"If she gives them enough to bring down the Los Zheng trafficking network, Pete, we have a chance to find where they are and rescue a lot of kids," Liz said. "Like you did for Madison Sanchez."

"I understand," Ramirez said. "But people like her make me sick."

"They make all of us sick," Liz said. "I'll make sure Kate knows you were at her brothel and saw the young kids that were there."

"Is there anything else we can do before we leave here?" Drake asked.

Holland shook his head and reached for the bottle of Jack Daniels, refilled his glass, and raised it high. "May the good Lord bless our efforts to defeat an enemy that was foolish enough to invade our land!"

"And when the gun smoke settles," Norris said raising his glass, "We'll raise our glasses against evil forces, singing whiskey for my men and beer for my horses."

SIXTY-SEVEN

The PSS Gulfstream G280 descended on approach to Boeing Field in Seattle after leaving San Diego and flying one hour and fifty minutes Saturday morning through bumpy and turbulent air.

Wayne Beardon was waiting at the airport to take the party of five directly to headquarters, where the PSS HRT men were assembled and ready to leave for the Hood Canal, where Jeff Jackson had a secluded cottage on Liberty Bay.

Beardon had the doors open on the white PSS GMC Yukon XL when the G280 stopped next to it. Drake helped Liz into a seat in the second row, with Lancer standing outside her door, and returned to help Casey and Holland with their luggage from the plane.

Beardon walked with him. "Jackson hasn't left the cabin since arriving there last night. There were three men with him in his Hummer. We can't tell if there are others in the cottage."

"Are his wife and two boys still at home?" Drake asked.

"Yes, with two of his company's tan Chevy Colorado ZR2 pickups his men drive parked out in front of the house."

"He's expecting trouble."

"Looks like it," Beardon said.

"Then why leave his family behind and go to his cottage?"

"Maybe to draw the threat away from his family to himself."

"Who is he afraid of?" Drake asked. "He put together a small army at his company."

"If I had to guess, I'd say it's Rueben Fang," Beardon offered.

"Why Fang?"

"His men have started calling the police when they find Fang's kids selling in the neighborhoods he protects, according to news reporting. Fang has a reason to be angry."

"Especially if Jackson was protecting those kids before," Drake said. "Have you been able to find Rueben Fang?"

"He hasn't been at his T-shirt shop in a week," Beardon said. "One of my team asked for him at the shop and was told he was on vacation. The clerk didn't say where. We found his condo, but he hasn't been there for a while."

"He was in Mexico," said Drake. "He could be anywhere or here, looking for Jackson."

When the bags were loaded in the back of the SUV, Drake opened the door for Lancer to jump up beside Liz and got in next to her. Holland was sitting on her right and Casey was riding shotgun on the ride to headquarters.

"Does anyone need to stop somewhere on the way to headquarters?" Beardon asked when he got behind the wheel of the Suburban.

"I'd like to go home," Liz said, "If that's okay. My stomach's still queasy from the turbulence and Lancer needs to go for a walk."

"I thought you looked a little pale," Drake said and took her hand. "I'll carry our bags up and take Lancer for a walk. You should rest. Mike and Mark can get things organized at the office."

"I have an upset stomach, Adam, that's all," she said firmly. "I don't need to rest!"

"Okay. I'll still take Lancer for a walk."

Liz withdrew her hand from his and brushed her hair back over her left ear with it, before staring straight ahead.

"Sorry," Drake said, reminding himself that Liz said she'd tell him when she wanted help. She'd handled two trimesters of pregnancy without a problem and couldn't see the third trimester being any harder.

It might not be any harder for her, he thought, *but it will be for me if I don't stop being so obvious when I'm trying to protect her.*

After walking Lancer and giving her a kiss on the cheek while she was unloading her red hardshell rolling suitcase open on their bed, Drake drove his Cayman GTS 4.0 to headquarters, now that it was repainted after colliding with rider and his motorcycle chasing after Colonel Walker.

Beardon had images on the large digital display screen on the wall at the end of the conference room when Drake arrived. Eight members of the HRT unit were seated at the conference table, wearing green forest camouflage Battle Dress Uniforms (BDUs). Casey and Holland were sitting with them.

"Jackson owns a secluded cabin on the Hood Canal south of Bangor and the Bangor Trident Base," Beardon said. "A creek runs through the property that covers nearly three acres, most of it forested, according to the realtor listing two years ago when Jackson bought it for a quarter of a million dollars. Access is from this road, Jupiter Trail, and a steep gravel driveway that runs down to the cabin. The property includes this small private beach."

Drake walked closer to the display screen and pointed to the image of the beach. "Is that big enough to land a helicopter?"

"It's narrow, looks like maybe eight or ten feet," Casey said. "Maybe a Little Bird, the AH-6, but it would be close. I can't tell how far the branches from the trees at each end of the beach extend out over it. If we land a helicopter there, he'll know we're coming. We'd be sitting ducks."

"Not if he doesn't see us as a threat," Casey said.

"How do we do that?" Drake asked.

"I've fished the Hood Canal on the same charter a number of times and know the captain," he said. "We could drive close to the beach in his boat and fake engine trouble or something. Then come ashore in a dingy asking for help."

"Will Jackson be used to seeing a fishing charter this time of year?" Beardon asked.

"The winter salmon season closes at the end of this month," Casey said. "He'll see people fishing offshore for another three days."

SIXTY-EIGHT

At twelve twenty p.m., three PSS white Yukon XLs left Seattle on the Walla Walla ferry toward Bremerton, Washington, across Puget Sound.

Drake and Casey were in one SUV, and Holand and eight HRT team members were in the other two SUVs.

Casey had been able to reserve Captain Jimmy Matson's Hewescraft Pacific Cruiser 240 for an afternoon of winter salmon fishing, after Matson returned from his morning charter.

Captain Matson wasn't told about the plan to fake a reason to come ashore on Jackson's beach. Casey was sure he would go along with it once he understood why they wanted to talk with Jackson. Matson was a retired Seattle police sergeant and a friend. He knew about Casey's service as Tier One Special Forces sniper, and he'd been a Marine fighting in Iraq.

When they reached Bremerton, Drake and Casey would drive to Captain Matson's dock and start toward Jackson's beach in his fishing boat.

The two Yukon XLs would drive from Bremerton north on Highway 3, detour west to Olympic City, then north on Turtle Road to NW Jupiter Trail and Jackson's driveway. Once there, they would park near the start of the driveway leading down to Jackson's cabin and wait. When Holland received the signal from Drake, the HRT men with Holland in tow would slip into the forested area and come down behind the cottage.

The plan was for Drake to leave Captain Matson's boat in the small inflatable boat he used for his clients to get ashore for clamming, after they finished fishing for the day.

Captain Matson was going to fake needing to get to a hospital by collapsing in his boat, and needing medical attention Drake and Casey weren't qualified to provide him. While Casey stayed on board with the captain, Drake would head ashore and plead for Jackson's help to get Matson to an emergency room.

At three thirty that afternoon, Captain Matson's boat suddenly veered left seventy yards offshore and headed toward Jackson's beach. Drake and Casey could be seen rushing into the pilothouse to help Matson. The outboard trolling engine stopped, and the boat drifted toward the shore.

Drake and Casey rushed out of the cabin to the rear deck and took an eight-foot-long inflatable boat down from the top of the pilothouse and set it on the portside gunwale. Working together, they attached a small electric motor to the transom mount, and when it was in place, lowered the inflatable into the water and Drake dropped down into it.

As soon as he got the inflatable underway, Drake started waving his hand above his head to draw the attention of anyone in the cabin and steered the inflatable toward the strip of gravel beach.

"Two men with AR-15s are running to the beach," Drake heard Casey say in his earpiece.

"I see them," he replied.

"Private beach," one of the men shouted and waved his hands. "Turn away!"

Drake was twenty-five yards from the beach and shouted, "The captain's had a stroke or something! He needs to get to a hospital!"

"We can't help you," the other man shouted. "Go to Bangor. That's the closest hospital."

Drake turned off the motor when he was ten yards from shore and let the inflatable drift closer.

"Don't get out of that boat, mister," the first man warned.

When the inflatable slid onto the beach, Drake jumped out and saw that both men's rifles were pointed at him.

"Easy, gentlemen," Drake said. "The captain doesn't really need a hospital. I wanted you to hear what I have to say before you started shooting. Your boss is in danger, and I need to talk with him while there's still time."

"Who are you? Did Fang send you?" the second man asked angrily.

"My name is Drake, Adam Drake," he said calmly, not able to avoid copying the way James Bond introduced himself in the movies. "Fang didn't send me and I'm not law enforcement. But I know about Fang and your boss needs to hear what I've learned about him."

"Raise your hands, Drake, and turn around. Are you armed?" the first man asked, raising his rifle upwards.

"There's a holstered Sig in a belt holster, right hip, under my jacket," Drake said, raising his hands and turning around.

He felt his jacket being lifted and his pistol pulled from its holster. Then he was patted down for other weapons he might have forgotten to mention.

"Turn around, slowly," he was told. "How did you know Jeff was here?"

"There's a tracker on his Hummer," Drake said.

"Then you have some explaining to do, mister," the first man said. "Let's go see what Jeff has to say about you putting a tracker on his Hummer."

Drake walked ahead of the two men up a slope toward the cabin when he heard Mark Holland quietly tell him in his earpiece that trouble was headed his way.

"Two black Chrysler 300s just turned off the road. They're

headed down the driveway to the cabin," Holland said. "The windows are tinted I can't tell how many are inside."

"Are you expecting visitors?" he asked the men.

"Why?" the man behind him said.

"Two black Chrysler 300s are coming down your driveway."

Both men started swearing and running toward the cabin, leaving Drake out in the open on the slope above the beach.

"Mark, send the men down. I think it's Fang," Drake said and took off running after the men.

The familiar sound of gunfire from AK-47s erupted from the first of the black cars, as it raced out of the forested area into the open on the driveway south of the cottage. The car's side windows were down facing the cabin and the AK-47s were firing wildly on full auto.

The second black Chrysler 300 slid to a stop in the gravel. Four men jumped out and took cover behind their car.

Drake saw they were wearing body armor, as he sprinted up the slope. Gunfire started up from within the cabin, slamming into the cars in the driveway.

Drake ran with his head down, wishing he had his gun to return fire with, if the gunmen saw him out in the open with nothing to hide behind.

SIXTY-NINE

When he reached the front porch of the cabin, Jackson's man from the beach was firing over a river rock half wall at the end of the porch with an AR-15.

"Stay here until this is over," he told Drake.

Drake nodded and asked Holland for a sitrep.

"Both teams are in the trees at the edge of the forested area. What do you want them to do?"

"Where are you?"

"With H1 on the side of the driveway behind the cottage."

"Have H1 and H2 neutralize Fang's men," Drake ordered.

The man next to him behind the wall ejected the thirty-round magazine from his rifle and slapped in another. "Who were you talking to?"

"I brought backup with me, just in case," Drake said. "You'll see them in just a minute. Tell your guys inside they're friendlies."

"My name's John," the man said, taking Drake's pistol out of his waistband and handing it to him. "I'll be right back. Keep them busy."

Drake nodded and peered over the half wall.

He saw the head of a man looking over the roof of second car explode in a red mist. Another man ran around from behind that car to get behind the first car and met the same fate, from a shot fired from the cabin.

When Fang's men realized they were taking fire from uphill, they moved around to the front of the first car. Before they could acquire a target, Drake dropped two of them with head shots from twenty yards away.

John returned with Jeff Jackson, who dropped down beside Drake.

"When this is finished, we need to talk," Jackson said.

"We will," Drake said. "Any idea why Fang came after you?"

"Why do you think these guys are Fang's?"

"Because I know he has a reason to want you dead."

The gunfire stopped suddenly, and the only sound heard was a moaning sound coming from behind the first black Chrysler 300.

Jackson stood and motioned for John to go out to the car and have a look.

Drake stood up beside Jackson and watched John run around to the back of the car. A moment later, one shot was fired and the moaning stopped.

"It was going to be hard enough to explain this without one of Fang's men being allowed to confuse things," Jackson said. "You might want to get your guys out of here. It will take them some time before the police get here from Bangor, but someone will report hearing gunfire. I can explain why Fang's men came after me. It might be harder for you to explain why you were here and got involved."

"That's what we need to talk about, why I'm involved," Drake said. "I know Rueben Fang is working to frame you for an attack on the U.S. power grid by Chinese commandos. Come out to the fishing boat with me. We can talk without your men hearing what I have to say."

"Sorry, I don't know you and I'm not getting in your boat,"

Jackson said. "Why do you think Fang is working to frame me for an attack on the power grid?"

"Because he knows about your militia's plan to hit ten key power substations in the U.S."

Jackson looked over his shoulder and then back at Drake. "We can talk down on the beach."

Drake followed behind him, holstering his weapon on his way down the slope. When Jackson reached the gravel and turned around, he had a Colt 1911 .45 in his hand pointed at Drake's chest.

"I holstered my Sig. I suggest you do the same," Drake said.

"Why should I do that?"

"Because my friend in the boat is a former Delta Force sniper and his rifle is aimed at you, probably at your head. That's what he's known for, head shots at three thousand yards."

Jackson turned around enough to look out and see that Drake was telling him the truth; Casey was standing at the rear of the pilothouse with Casey's favorite heavy-barreled and scoped Winchester Model 70 aimed at him.

Jackson turned to face Drake and holstered his pistol. "What's this about me being in a militia and why would Fang want to frame me for anything?"

"You may or may not be in a militia, but Fang thinks you are and so do I. Fang is a Los Zheng cartel member and takes orders from a man named Chen Huang, a Chinese Naval Sea Dragon commando. Some friends of mine raided Huang's hideout two days ago in Baja California and captured Huang's second in command, Sergeant Major Kwan. I spoke with Kwan, who's now in the custody of the FBI, and he confirmed what I'm telling you.

"Rueben Fang visited Huang's hideout and was heard to say that he has a source in a militia that is planning on taking down the U.S. power grid by attacking ten key power substations," Drake said. "You are Fang's source and I believe you're a member of Lt. Colonel "Bull" Browning's militia. How am I doing so far?"

"Go on," Jackson said.

"From a base camp outside Mexicali, Baja California Huang has sent a hundred Chinese commandos across our border to attack the ten power substations your militia planned to attack. After they do, your militia men who were supposed to carry out the attacks are going to commit suicide, with enough evidence planted to convince the FBI that your militia was responsible."

"Why would China try and do something like this?" Jackson asked.

"China is going to invade Taiwan. Taking down the power grid is meant to distract us and delay a military response from the U.S., so China gets what it wants, a united China, without fighting a war with the U.S."

Jackson's eyes narrowed and Drake saw the color drain from his face.

"No," Jackson said. "This can't be. How would Fang...?"

"Find out?" Drake finished for him. "You've been working with him. He's gotten close enough to penetrate your militia's security somehow."

"Does the FBI know all of this?"

"Not yet. I wanted to get to you first and find out where these ten targets are and stop these Chinese commandos. The government tends to take its time figuring out what they want to do in a crisis."

"Then you have a problem," Jackson said. "I only know about one target."

SEVENTY

Jackson wanted a deal, and Drake explained what it would take for him to get it; tell them everything he knew about the militia he was a member of, and everything he knew about Reuben Fang and the Los Zheng cartel.

If he did, Drake promised to do everything he could to get him a grant of immunity for his involvement with his militia. Any crime or crimes he'd committed outside of his involvement with the militia would not be a part of the deal.

Jackson agreed and left his cabin with Drake and four men from the HRT unit as security to return to Seattle and PSS headquarters. Holland and the rest of the HRT unit stayed behind to remove any sign of a PSS presence, leaving Jackson's men to decide how they wanted to deal with the bodies of the eight cartel assassins.

On the way back to the Bremerton ferry, Jackson told Drake what he knew about the 412 militia and its "someday" plan to take down the government. If conditions became so critical to the democracy that a new beginning was needed, the plan was to attack the energy power grid and create enough chaos to allow the military to take control of the country without any resistance from the citizens.

Jackson explained how the 412 was compartmentalized, with no individual member knowing any of the other members, except how to communicate with the other members of the cell he belonged to and the target that cell was assigned to destroy. Members were only known by their member numbers and only used the military-grade Nokia XR20 smartphones they were provided to contact one another. There were no meetings.

It was a secret militia society, with each member personally recruited by Lt. Colonel "Bull" Browning, who knew each member personally at one time or another, from the member's service in the U.S. Army.

The only member who knew all the details of the "someday" plan was "Bull" Browning, the founder of the 412 militia.

When Drake was on the M/V Walla Walla ferry leaving Bremerton at 6:40 PM Saturday night to return to Seattle, Drake left Jackson in the custody of the other PSS men and went to the upper deck to call President Ballard.

"Give me a minute to get out of bed and go to my study," the president said when he answered.

"Sorry for the late call, Mr. President."

"I'm usually up late, don't worry about it. What have you learned?"

"I have a member of the militia China wants to frame for the attack their commandos are planning," Drake said. "He's asking for immunity for telling us what he knows."

"Is he an active member of the plan to attack the power grid?"

"He is and he isn't," Drake said. "The militia exists, but the plan is something they planned on doing sometime in the future, if they felt it was necessary. There is no active plan that's being acted on."

"How did China find out about this plan? Are they sponsoring it?"

"There's no evidence of that, sir. "I think they learned about the militia somehow and penetrated the militia's security to learn about the plan."

"And appropriate it for their own and blame the militia," the president said.

"That's what it looks like."

"Does this man know which power substation the commandos plan on attacking? Deputy Director Perkins says the Chinese Sergeant Major you turned over to the FBI doesn't know."

"He only knows the substation his cell was supposed to take out," Drake said. "He says the only person who knows the details of the entire plan is the founder of the militia."

"Do we know who that is?"

"Yes, it's Lt. Colonel "Bull" Browning. He's been on the FBI's radar as a militia organizer in the South, living in South Carolina."

"I'll tell Kate to bring him in for questioning," the president said. "If he only knows the targets of his plan, that won't help us find these Chinese commandos running around the country and carrying it out for themselves. How do we find them?"

"The militia man we have may know where the the cartel member is who learned about the plan," Drake said. "If we can find him, he may know enough to help us find the commandos. And if we get "Bull" Browning to tell us where these power substations are, the commandos will probably be somewhere in the vicinity."

"Tell your militia man he'll get immunity, if he helps us," the president said. "And Adam, do whatever it takes to find this cartel member. We're running out of time. I need the world to know what China's done, and have the evidence to prove it, if we're going to stop China from invading Taiwan."

"Yes, Mr. President."

"God speed, Adam."

"Thank you, sir."

Drake found Jeff Jackson sitting between two men from the HRT unit, silent and staring out the window, and replaced the man on Jackson's right.

"You'll have immunity, as we agreed," Drake said. "It will be in writing, from the FBI. But you'll have to continue cooperating with us until we find these Chinese commandos."

"How am I supposed to do that?" Jackson asked.

"You can start by helping us find Rueben Fang."

SEVENTY-ONE

Jeff Jackson's recorded interview at PSS headquarters revealed that Jackson and his men had been looking for Fang, since Fang tried to kill him. Leaving for the weekend and going to his cabin on Hood Canal was set as a trap for Fang to come after him to finish the job. Unfortunately, Fang didn't come with his men.

Jackson said Fang hadn't been seen at his T-shirt shop or his condo in several weeks, but that members of his cartel had been followed to a motel on Pacific Avenue in Tacoma. The motel was owned by an offshore LLC registered in Panama, but Jackson was sure it belonged to the Los Zheng cartel, as its rooms were regularly used by the cartel's prostitutes. If the Chinese commandos were allies of the cartel, Jackson thought it was possible they might be staying in the motel.

The reason he thought it possible was because the substation his militia cell was responsible for taking out was a Bonneville Power Administration substation in South Tacoma.

By midnight Saturday, Wayne Beardon's surveillance team confirmed that prostitutes were seen entering and leaving the motel Jackson identified. The two-story motel had forty-eight rooms, twenty-four rooms on two floors on each side of the motel's office that was located between them on the ground floor.

The rooms on the southern wing of the motel appeared to be used by the cartel's prostitutes, with men arriving with young women and being taken to a room without having to check in at the motel's office.

Beardon also reported that Uber drivers were seen making late-night pizza deliveries to five rooms on the ground floor of the northern wing. One man who opened his room's door wide enough to be seen when the pizza was delivered was Chinese.

At four o'clock Sunday morning, four PSS white Yukon XLs with twenty members of Dan Norris's HRT unit were parked a block away in the parking lot of a Mexican restaurant. The men were wearing black military-style combat uniforms, black boots and hats, and body armor. Their weapons were the same as the ones the HRT men carried at Jackson's Hood Canal cabin; Sig Sauer Rattler MCX personal defense weapons chambered in .300 Blackout ammo and Sig Sauer P320 AXG suppressed pistols.

A fifth Yukon XL was parked at the head of the line, with Adam Drake, Mark Holland, Dan Norris, and Marco Morales inside. Norris would lead the HRT team when they raided the motel, after Morales finished his recon of the motel with the Black Hornet nano drone.

Drake and Holland would follow the HRT team, looking for Rueben Fang and any evidence of the commandos' planning to attack the power grid. Morales was assigned to go to the motel office after storing the drone and keep the motel manager from calling the police.

Morales powered up the Black Hornet and held it outside his window to launch it into the air. Using the joy-stick control on the base unit resting on his lap, he guided the nano UAV weighing thirty-two grams across Pacific Avenue toward the motel at a speed of twenty-two miles per hour.

When it crossed the parking lot in front of the motel, Morales guided it down from an altitude of thirty feet to fifteen feet and watched the live video feed on his control panel to fly it to the front of the first motel room they thought the commandos were staying in.

He moved it slowly forward until it hovered a foot away from the top of the window, with a view into the room through the gap above the top of the blind.

"Two Chinese men are watching TV, each on a twin bed to the right of the door. They're wearing T-shirts and briefs, no sign of weapons on the dressers or nightstands. Couple of night owls," Morales said and moved the drone left to the window of the next room.

"Lights out in the second room from the right," he said. "Night vision in the nose of the drone shows two men, asleep under the covers on their twin beds. Can't see their faces. Again, no sign of weapons. Doesn't mean they don't have guns under their pillows, but nothing I can see.

"Next room's also dark, two men in bed asleep like the last room, no sign of weapons. Moving to room four, dark, but light coming from the back, probably a bathroom. One man in bed, no sign of weapons.

"Next room, second from the end on the left, room is dark, two men in bed under the covers, no sign of weapons.

"Last room, the light is on one man sitting up in bed watching something on an iPad," Morales said. "There's a glass tank on the dresser under the TV, can't see what's in it. No sign of weapons."

"Bingo!" Holland said. "That must be Fang. He had a snake terrarium in his office when we were there."

"You see anything else we should know about before we go in?" Drake asked Morales.

"Let me check the office and see what the manager is doing."

Morales moved the joy-stick control to fly the drone down the row of rooms

and stopped it outside the front window of the office. He used the control and zoomed in on what the manager was leaning forward in his chair and staring at large CCTV screen.

"The manager won't be a problem," Morales said. "He's watching what's going on in the rooms their prostitutes are using. He might have a weapon under the front counter, but I'll be in there before he has a chance to get to it."

Drake hit his PTT button at his waist for his two-way radio to talk with the HRT unit men. "Be ready to move, as soon as surveillance gives the all-clear."

"Command," Beardon said, "You have all-clear. I say, all-clear."

"Remember everyone," Drake said, "We're here for Fang. Anything you find in the rooms, laptops, phones, maps, anything that's evidence of their plan leaves with us. Wear the balaclavas and don't say anything, just move fast, get them down and restrained. The FBI will come and get them when they're called. No one gets hurt, not us, not a civilian, just like we talked about. In and out in five minutes, tops from right now.

"Let's go," Drake said and drove the lead Yukon XL out of the restaurant's parking lot.

SEVENTY-TWO

Drake pulled off Pacific Avenue into the parking lot of the motel and turned off the Yukon's headlights as he slowed down enough to let Morales jump out. He kept the Yukon rolling until he stopped behind a blue gray Mercedes cargo van parked in front of room number five.

The four Yukons behind him stopped and twenty members of the HRT unit fanned out to run to the five rooms, where the Chinese commandos were staying.

Drake, Norris, and Holland jumped out and ran to the sixth room and stopped, standing on either side of the door, with their pistols held at the high ready position.

Wayne Beardon had supplied each of the men responsible for breaching the motel room doors with a dry erase marker. It was repackaged with an Arduino microcontroller in its hollow shell that could open any motel room door equipped with Onity brand key card locks in seconds. Onity made the locks used by most of the hotels and motels in the U.S. The device could be made for less than fifty dollars, using off-the-shelf hardware and a little programming knowledge.

With Drake on the right side of the door and Norris on the left side, Holland inserted the barrel jack that replaced the dry eraser's felt tip in the power jack at the bottom of the lock. When the door clicked open, he stood aside to let Drake and Norris enter.

Drake opened the door and moved to the left near the dresser at the foot of the bed . Norris followed moving to the right near the window. Rueben Fang was sitting up in bed, leaning back against the headboard with an iPad on his lap.

Fang flung the iPad Frisbee-style at Norris, skipping it across the bed at Norris and jumped to his feet on the far side of the bed. He was wearing a pair of black silk pajamas and had a large black and red dragon tattoo on his chest.

"Keep your hands where I can see them and move to the foot of the bed," Drake ordered.

"Who are you?" Fang hissed but didn't move.

"Move," Drake said.

Fang smiled and shuffled forward a step. "If Jackson sent you, I will pay you more than he ever could."

"Keep moving," Drake said, reaching with his left hand to take hand restraints from a pocket.

"Where are you taking me?" Fang asked.

"To a place where you're going to tell me what Chen Huang is planning. Now move."

Fang's eyes narrowed as he took another step and then stumbled when his foot struck the bedpost at the foot of the bed. Dropping his left hand to the bed to keep from falling, he straightened up with a butterfly knife flicked open in his right hand and lunged at Drake.

Drake reacted by leaning forward and grabbing Fang's wrist with his left hand and deflecting the knife down and away. He followed the move with a groin kick with his right foot that brought Fang's head down and slammed his black Staccato 9mm pistol hard into the side of his head.

Fang dropped to the floor like a sack of rocks.

Drake holstered his pistol and moved around to pick the unconscious man up and throw him face down on the bed.

"Search the room," he told Norris as he pulled Fang's hands back behind his back to restrain him.

"What's that sound?" Norris asked, jumping back as he pulled open a dresser drawer.

Both men looked at the snake terrarium where Fang's saw-scaled viper was moving in its S-shape coil scraping sections of its body over each other.

"Fang's pet," Drake said. "I'm tempted to take it with us to get him talking."

"Good idea, but if you do, I'm riding with someone else," Norris said. "If that thing got loose in the Yukon, it has enough venom to kill all of us."

"Only fitting then, if we put his pet next to him and he's one of them," Drake said. "I'll let you tell the others why you want to swap a ride with someone."

"Won't bother me. I'm man enough to admit I don't like snakes, especially ones that can kill you."

The only things Norris found searching the room were Fang's wallet, some keys on a ring, and the iPad Fang had thrown at him.

"See if the keys belong to the cargo van," Drake said. "I'll send someone else back to get the snake."

"Roger that," Norris said. "Thanks."

Drake rolled Fang over to his back, lifted him up and put him over his shoulder. When he got to the door, he opened it enough to see if the way was clear to the lead Yukon.

Men from the HRT unit were jogging back to the other SUVs when he came out and the lights were flashing on the Mercedes cargo van beside him. He looked back and saw Norris holding up Fang's keys.

"Bring the van with us," Drake said, "I'll have someone put the snake terrarium in the back. You'll be fine."

Norris raised the key fob in his right hand with one finger extended skyward and opened the door of the cargo van.

Four minutes and forty-five seconds after stopping behind the blue gray Mercedes cargo van, Drake led the PSS convoy out onto Pacific Avenue heading north and back to the PSS headquarters in Seattle.

SEVENTY-THREE

Drake stood back with Mark Holland watching the man called "Viper", sitting on a green army surplus folding chair in the cement-walled basement storage room next to the PSS firing range. His hands were duct taped behind his back and his ankles were taped to the legs of the folding chair.

Drake stepped forward and pulled the black balaclava off Fang's head. They had turned it around backwards so he couldn't see where they were taking him. Fang inhaled audibly and flinched when the balaclava was removed. The blood on the side of Fang's head had dried and was matted with some of the wool of the balaclava.

Fang blinked several times and turned his head around and saw boxes of ammo and paper targets, hearing protection earmuffs hanging on pegs, and shooting glasses on the shelves of the storage room. He also looked down at the floor and quickly looked away. His terrarium was on the floor next to his left foot and his pet viper was staring up at him through the glass wall.

Drake and Holland wore balaclavas and stood silently in front of him with their arms crossed over their chests.

"Who are you, police?" Fang finally asked.

"It doesn't matter who we are," Drake said. "The only thing that matters is the decision you make when I ask you a question."

"I have nothing to tell you," Fang said. "I don't know anything."

"That's not true, is it? We found you hiding out with ten Chinese commandos at a motel your cartel owns, with a cargo van parked outside. In it were eight kamikaze drones, AKS-74U assault rifles, Glock pistols, and U.S. Army Woodland pattern battle uniforms in it. The keys to the van were in your room."

"I don't know anything about kamikaze drones or the other stuff."

"Yes, you do," Drake said. "Reuben, I don't have time to play games with you, so I'll tell you how this is going to end. If you tell me what I want to know, you will leave this room alive.

"If you don't tell me what I want to know, your pet viper is going to accidentally escape the terrarium and I'm going to leave you alone to deal with it."

Fang tried to smile and said, "I don't believe you."

Drake went to the terrarium and kicked the side of it. The viper raised its head with its little tongue darting in and out of its mouth and began moving in its S-shaped coil making its warning sound.

Drake leaned down and said softly, "Last chance, Reuben. You leave this room alive, if you tell me what Chen Huang and his commandos are planning. I'll turn you over to the FBI and you can work something out with them.

"If you don't, my friend is going to open that door for me and I'm going to kick this terrarium over and run like hell. I'll bet your snake gets to you before I get to the door."

Fang took a deep breath and stared at Drake. "The commandos are going to shut down your energy grid, okay. That's all I know."

"Do you know where the other commandos are?" Drake asked.

"I only know the ones Huang asked me to find a place for them to stay."

"How does Huang contact you?"

"He calls me on a special phone."

"The phone in your motel room?"

"Yes."

"How did Huang's commandos get into the U.S.?"

"We smuggled them across the border. That was easy. It's our business. Getting them into Mexico was harder."

"Do you know the substations Huang wants to take out?" Drake asked.

"He never told me the details."

"How did Huang become the head of your cartel?"

"When someone shows up with a hundred Chinese soldiers and takes over, you don't ask questions."

"Is there anything else you know about Huang's plan?"

"The commandos know this is a suicide mission. They don't expect to make it back to China."

"We'll make sure they don't," Drake said. "Sit tight until the FBI gets here. They'll have more questions than I have time to ask you now but be prepared to tell them everything. That's the only thing that might keep you from being executed as a Chinese enemy combatant found on U.S. soil."

Holland walked with Drake to the door of the storage room and said, "Send someone down to replace me. I don't like snakes any more than Norris does."

"On it," Drake said. "Before Kate Perkins sends someone to get this guy, take his phone and iPad up to Kevin. See if there's anything on it that identifies the other targets. It might take a while to find the head of Jackson's militia, time we don't have."

"We should move Fang out of this room and get rid of his snake," Holland said. "We don't want the FBI to get the idea we tortured him to get him to talk."

"Good idea, I'll let you take care of that."

"Thanks a lot."

"You're welcome but it was your idea to use the snake to get him to talk."

"An idea I now regret."

Drake left Holland in the basement and took the stairs to his office to call the president.

With ninety Chinese commandos somewhere in the U.S., armed and equipped to carry out their mission, this was far from over. Unless they found the 412s founder, Lt. Col. "Bull" Browning, quickly and got him to identify the other nine power substations in his latent insurrection plan, they wouldn't know where to start looking for the commandos.

Then Drake remembered something Jeff Jackson had said when he was being interviewed. He said the 412 militia members only used Nokia XR20 smartphones to communicate. The XR20 was a rugged military-grade smartphone, he knew, and it was made in China.

China had found a way to breach the 412s security and learned about their plot. What if China had accomplished it by using a backdoor built into the Nokia smartphones the 412s used?

Drake stopped halfway up the stairs and called Kevin McRoberts on his personal phone number.

"Kevin," he asked when his sleepy IT genius answered, "Are you in your office?"

"Yes, sir."

"I told you to go home and get some sleep, Drake said. "Never mind. If there's a backdoor in the smartphone we recovered from Jeff Jackson that he used to communicate with his militia buddies, would you be able to find it?"

"I think so. Why?"

"I think that's what China used to learn about the militia's plot. If China used it, maybe we can too, and identify the other members of the 412 militia and the power substations they were planning to hit."

SEVENTY-FOUR

Drake made a list of the information they learned and called President Ballard at ten o'clock Sunday morning, Pacific Time.

"We just got back from church, Adam," the president said. "Hold on a minute and let me get to the other room."

Drake used the time to order the items on his list by assigning each a number.

"Fire away," the president said.

"Sir, Jeff Jackson, the militia man I told you about, led us to a motel in Tacoma where we found ten of the Chinese commandos early this morning. The ten men are restrained in four motel rooms and will need to be picked up by the FBI."

"I'll tell Kate Perkins to call you for the address of the motel. Did you learn anything from them?"

"Not from them, but we also found the Los Zheng cartel man who's been helping them. His name is Reuben Fang. We have him here at PSS headquarters, along with the Mercedes cargo van that was parked outside his motel room. It's loaded with the weapons they were going to use to take out one of the power substations."

"Which one?"

"The South Tacoma BPA substation."

"What were they going to use to do it?"

"There are eight Switchblade 300 kamikaze drones concealed in backpacks in the van," Drake said. "They're missiles with a warhead, launched from tubes, with GPS targeting that can hit a target with precision as far away as seven miles away."

"Are they Chinese?"

"No sir, they're made here. Our military has used them in Afghanistan, Iraq, and Syria."

"Something the militia could be expected to get their hands on," the president said.

"There were army surplus camo BDU's in the van for the commandos to wear that would identify the attackers as Americans."

"Do you have any information about where the other commandos are?"

"No, sir," Drake began when there was knock on his office door and Kevin McRoberts stuck his head in. "Sir, would you hold on for just a minute?"

"Take all the time you need, Adam."

"I have "Bull" Browning's phone number," Kevin said.

"How?"

"Jackson had a uMobiz surveillance app on his Nokia XR20. It monitors social media, like the WhatsApp the militia used for text messaging. When Jackson received a text from Browning, it recorded his phone number."

"Great job, Kevin," Drake said. "Mr. President, we found the phone number for Lt. Colonel "Bull" Browning. When we arrest him, he'll know where the other targets are located."

"Excellent, Adam," President Ballard said. "I'll have Kate pick him up. Is there anything else I need to know right now."

"No, sir. That's all I have for now."

"I need you to bring my security team up to speed on all of this. How soon can you get to the White House?"

Drake looked at his watch and said, "I can be there by five o'clock tonight."

"I'll have the team waiting," President Ballard said. "God speed, Adam."

"Thank you, sir."

Kevin McRoberts was still standing at the door, listening to Drake talk with the president.

"Kevin, I want you to come with me to Washington. Bring Jackson's phone, Fang's iPad, and anything we found in Fang's office that you think might be helpful. Pack a bag for a quick trip to the capital. We'll meet here in an hour and drive to the airport."

"Yes, sir," Kevin said, grinning from ear to ear.

Drake found Mark Holland in his office and told him he was flying to Washinton to brief the president's security team. Someone needed to make sure Jackson and Fang didn't go anywhere until the FBI arrived to take them into custody.

"Dan Norris is still here," Holland said. "If Deputy Director Perkins is going to be involved in the handover, he'd probably like to be the one keeping an eye on those two."

"Trying to be a matchmaker or just trying to get away from being in the same building as Fang's viper?" Drake asked.

"Both, I guess."

"Sure, ask Dan if he wouldn't mind sticking around to meet with the FBI. If he has any questions, have him call me. I'm going to run home and tell Liz where I'm going. Tell Steve to get the Gulfstream ready to fly. I'm taking Kevin with me to the White House. He hasn't been there before."

"You don't need me to tag along, do you?" Holland asked.

"Do you want to go?"

"That would be nice. I haven't been to the White House either."

"That surprises me, with the work you did as the head of the NYPD Counterterrorism Bureau."

"I was too busy and always sent someone else when they called."

"Then let's make it a first for you and Kevin," Drake said. "Meet here in one hour and we'll drive to the airport."

Drake called Deputy Director of the FBI on the drive home to their condo and arranged for the handover of Jeff Jackson and Reuben Fang. He also called ahead to let Liz know the president asked him to come to the White House.

When he pulled into their underground garage and took the stairs two at a time to the master bedroom on the third floor, she was standing beside the bed with an open bag packed for him.

Drake put his arms around her and pulled her close. "I won't be away for more than a day or two."

"When you get back, we're going away for a vacation," she said. "I feel like I haven't seen you in weeks."

Drake kissed her and asked, "Where would you like to go?"

"Somewhere trouble can't find you."

SEVENTY-FIVE

PSS pilot Steve Carson announced they were on the final approach to Reagan National Airport in Washington, D.C., at four fifteen P.M Sunday afternoon.

Twenty minutes later, Drake led Holland and McRoberts pulling their rolling carryon luggage through the lounge of the Signature FBO located in Hanger 7 of the General Aviation Terminal, to a white Ford Explorer parked outside at the curb.

Staff Sergeant Nelsen had both doors open on the passenger's side of the SUV, wearing khaki pants, a white shirt, and a blue windbreaker. The same uniform he wore the year before when Drake had met with President Ballard at the White House.

Staff Sergeant Nelsen was a driver for the White House Transportation Agency. "It's good to see you again, Mr. Drake," he said as he walked to the back of the Explorer to help the men load their luggage.

After being introduced to Holland and McRoberts, Staff Sergeant Nelsen asked Drake if he would like to take a quick detour around the Tidal Basin. "It's the National Cherry Blossom Festival, sir."

"Maybe later, Staff Sergeant. I promised the president I'd be at the White House by five o'clock."

"Understood, sir. We'll be on our way."

Driving in light late afternoon traffic, Staff Sergeant Nelsen pulled to a stop outside the West Wing of the White House with time to spare, waving them on to a Secret Service agent waiting to take them to the president.

President Ballard was in the Oval Office on the phone, when they were escorted to the president's small study. The president's National Security Advisor Pat Jefferson and Congressman Matthew Bridge, and the president's best friend and political advisor, were sitting at the round cherry wood table, with tumblers of whisky raised to greet them.

Jefferson stood and shook Drake's hand and turned to Holland, "Mark, it's been a while. I heard you'd moved out west."

"I left New York last year," Holland smiled and said. "I had to escape the politics."

"Pat, I'd like you to meet Kevin McRoberts," Drake said. "He's the head of our IT division at Puget Sound Security."

"You must be good," Jefferson said and reached his hand out, "To head a division at your age. May I ask how old you are?"

"I'm twenty, sir." Kevin said.

Congressman Bridge stood and said, "Gentlemen, can I pour you a drink? He's talking with Deputy Director Perkins. It shouldn't be long."

"Yes, thank you," Drake said.

"Mark?" Congressman Bridge asked.

"Yes, thanks."

"Kevin, you're welcome to join us," Congressman Bridge said.

"I don't drink, sir."

"Of course," Congressman Bridge said, as President Ballard entered the study.

The president shook hands with Drake and Holland and said, "So, this is the young man you told me about, Adam."

"He is sir. This is Kevin McRoberts the head of our IT division."

"Thank you for coming, Kevin," the president said and shook Kevin's hand.

"Adam, why don't you tell Pat and Matthew what you've been telling me. I tried to summarize it for them, but they need the details."

Drake began with Lt. Colonel Thomas Walker arriving in Seattle asking for help finding the dealer responsible for the death of one of his soldier's son, to the rescue of the son's girlfriend who'd been sex trafficked by the Los Zheng cartel, and her rescue in Mexicali, Mexico.

"When we received a video of the leader of the cartel, Chen Huang, and found out that he was a Chinese naval commando and had met with an MSS agent from the Chinese consulate in Tijuana. We subsequently learned China was moving commando saboteurs across our southern border.

"The Chinese Ministry of State Security gained access to a plot of an American militia group to take down our power grid, in the future if they felt the country was going to hell and needed saving.

"China's plan was to take over the plot, make it look like the militia was responsible for taking down the power grid. The chaos that would result was supposed to prevent a military reaction from us until it was too late to stop China from invading Taiwan."

"Can we prove this?" Pat Jefferson asked.

"The FBI has custody of a Chinese Sergeant Major in the PLA who trained a hundred commandos at an abandoned sulfur mine in Mexico," Holland said. "We have a militia man involved in the plot and his Nokia-made-in-China smartphone with a backdoor the MSS used to learn about the plot. And the FBI now has ten of the Chinese commandos and the weapons they planned on using to take down a BPA power substation in Tacoma."

"What about the other ninety Chinese commandos?" Congressman Bridge asked.

"That was Kate Perkins I was talking with," the president said. "An hour ago, the FBI arrested Lt. Col. "Bull" Browning in South

Carolina. He's the founder of the 412 militia that's involved in this and knows all the substations they planned to destroy. He's asking for a deal. When we know where the other substations are located, we'll be able to round up the rest of the Chinese commandos."

"Do we know when China planned to take down our power grid?" the National Security Advisor, Pat Jefferson, asked.

"On April 15th, Tax Day, when anti-government sentiment is high and you might expect a militia to act," Drake said.

Jefferson and Congressman Bridge sat quietly, processing the information and the elephant on the table it presented; how to respond to China's reckless aggression.

"Pat, the National Security Council needs to be briefed on this," the president said. "Who do you think should do it?"

"I think we should let Kate Perkins and the FBI put it together for them," Jefferson said, looking across the table at Drake. "The council will want to know how we learned about this and why we didn't tell them about it before now."

"I understand," President Ballard said, "And I'm prepared to tell them. It's going to ruffle a lot of feathers when they find out Adam and his company did this without their help. We'll have to be prepared to deal with that, but if it gets them off their butts and doing the job we pay them for, so much the better."

"Yes, Mr. President," Jefferson said. "It would be helpful if Adam, Mark, and Kevin could stay around for a day or so to help me put this together."

"Adam?" President Ballard asked.

"We're here for as long as you need us, Mr. President," Drake said.

"That's it then," the president said and stood to leave the study. "I don't know if you were able to make reservations for a suitable place to stay tonight, so I asked the Hay-Adams to take care of you men. Put the room and other charges on your bill when you send it in."

"Thank you, Mr. President," Drake said, standing with the others and looking around at the smiles on the faces of Holland and McRoberts.

SEVENTY-SIX

Thursday morning, after flying home to Seattle late the night before, Drake surprised Liz with breakfast in bed, waking her up with a glass of orange juice and an English muffin with marmalade on a tray with a single red rose.

"Wake up sleepy head," he said, smiling at her as she rubbed her eyes and sat up. "We have a reservation at Salish Lodge and Spa for the rest of the week. I'd like to be on the road in time to check in by noon."

"Is this our vacation," she asked, taking the tray from him and balancing it on her lap.

"It was raining in Paris, so I looked for something closer to home."

"How did you know I wanted to go to the Salish Lodge and Spa?"

"I saw you looking at its website on your laptop," Drake admitted. "You're booked for a Mother-To-Be spa treatment every day, if you want to use it."

"What have I done to deserve all this?"

Drake leaned down and kissed her. "It's for loving me. I'll take Lancer for a run while you enjoy your breakfast."

When he returned from his run thirty minutes later, Liz's sand colored carryon luggage was half full. Drake's matching navy blue carryon was open and empty on the bed.

"I didn't know what you have planned while I'm being pampered at the spa, so I didn't start on your bag" she said.

Drake walked into his closest and came back with a pile of clothes over his arm. "I'll hike along the river with Lancer, check out the Snoqualmie Tribe's sacred site, buy something in the gift shop, or read a book. Don't worry, I'll find things to do."

"And when I'm not at the spa?" she asked with a lascivious smile.

"There will be time for that as well," he said and returned her smile.

They left the condo shortly before eleven thirty with Drake behind the wheel of Liz's Cadillac CT5-V Blackwing. The price he paid for being allowed to drive the Blackwing was his promise that under no circumstances would he unleash the car's hand built V8 engine and its six hundred and sixty-eight horsepower while she was in the car.

That condition, of course, allowed for the possibility of Drake going for a drive while she was at the spa.

Approaching the exit from I-90 onto the Snoqualmie Parkway a few minutes before noon, Drake asked Liz to turn on the radio to listen to the news at the top of the hour. He thought he knew what President Ballard was going to say in his press conference scheduled a few minutes later. The White House had let the media know the president was going to make an announcement of significance, but he wanted to hear if the response to China's aggression had changed since he left the White House.

"It should be on AM 770 KTTH," he told Liz.

After ten minutes of national and local news, the talk show host announced they we're going live to the White House and that President Ballard was entering the room.

"This morning China's ambassador came to the White House to hear directly from me several changes the United States is making in the way we do things in the Asian Pacific region.

"China's increasing aggressiveness is a growing concern for the security and sovereignty of all our allies and friends. The peace-loving nations in the region, as well as our allies around the world, need a clear understanding of the commitment the U.S. has made to achieve peace there, as well as our allies around the world.

To assure that this occurs, I'm calling today for a summit meeting to be held in Tokyo for our allies and friends next month, to adopt new military and economic agreements that will protect us all.

"The scope of these new agreements will include the development of new nuclear weapons programs and mutual defense alliances. The agreements that will be made at the summit will make it clear to the world, and especially our allies and friends, that an attack on one of us is an attack on all of us.

"The new agreements will also include new economic alliances and trade agreements, and the consideration of new trade embargoes on technology, semiconductors, and the equipment to make semiconductors, that China may wish to acquire. In addition to the four countries that make up the Quad, Japan, South Korea, India, and Australia, we are inviting our European allies to join us at the summit in Tokyo.

"We've had peace in the Pacific region for forty plus years and the United States is committed to keeping it that way.

"One last thing I should mention. The FBI recently conducted raids in ten U.S. cities that resulted in the arrest and detention of one hundred Chinese nationals who were in the country illegally. They are being detained and questioned. If they have committed crimes while being here, they will be tried in U.S. courts. If no crimes were committed, they will be deported to China and China can deal with them. When we know more about this, I will let you know.

"That's all for now. God bless the United States of America," President Ballard said amid the chaos of questions shouted at him from reporters.

"Wow," Liz said. "China will go ballistic with the news that an Asian NATO is in the works."

"They will, but it's less than what they deserve," Drake said, shaking his head. "They could be staring at radar screens with a hundred incoming ICBM missiles raining down on them, instead."

"Will he really put the Chinese commandos on trial?"

"That's up to China. China doesn't want the world to know it was willing to risk starting World War III. China wants to be seen as everyone's friend, a peacemaker in the eyes of the world, standing up to the hegemony of the U.S. and the West. A public trial of their commandos will show everyone what a lie that is."

"Colonel Walker deserves a medal," Liz said. "If he hadn't asked you to help him find out who killed his friend's son and rescue Madison Sanchez, we wouldn't have found out about any of this."

"I know and the president agrees," Drake said. "He's going to call and thank him personally. There won't be a medal, but he said his staff will find a way to support non-profit organizations working with victims of sex trafficking."

"He should give you a medal too."

"That's the last thing I'd want him to do," Drake said. "The other intelligence contractors will find out soon enough about the role we played in uncovering China's Taiwan deception. A medal would put a target on our backs and keep us from flying under the radar. I like things just the way they are."

When the iconic lodge came into view, Liz reached over and squeezed his leg. "Me too," she said with the biggest smile he'd seen in a while.

THE END

ACKNOWLEDGMENTS

The first person to read this, and every other book I've written, is my wife. Her unwavering support and ability to offer solutions and corrections that make each book better puts her at the top of my list for thanks and acknowledgement.

The second person to review the rough manuscript is my friend, Dan Q. I'm forever grateful for the time and effort he puts into editing and proofreading, and finding all the silly mistakes that need to be eliminated.

I also want to acknowledge and thank Mark Dawson and James Blatch from Fuse Books for adding me to their authors portfolio. I look forward to working with them on this addition to the Adam Drake Thriller series and many more as we go forward in this new venture.

The idea for this novel originated with the news earlier this year about the U.S. Border Patrol reporting on the number of Chinese nationals entering the U.S. illegally on out southern border.

https://www.foxnews.com/politics/border-patrol-apprehensions-chinese-nationals-southern-border-800-source.print.

In 2022, just under 2,000 Chinese nationals crossed the border illegally, but in the first months of 2023 the Border Patrol has already encountered 4,300 Chinese entering illegally.

https://www.foxnews.com/media/reporter-says-filmed-hundreds-military-age-chinese-men-heading-toward-us-migrant-groups.

Some members of the U.S. Congress are concerned that China is exploiting the border crisis to insert military operatives into the U.S. for nefarious purposes, like sabotage.

https://www.washingtontimes.com/news/2023/jun/14/chinese-may-be-inserting-military-operatives-throu/

Those concerns may or may not be valid, but the possibility that they are provides the basis for a good story.

Printed in Great Britain
by Amazon